"YOU'LL DROWN!"

... Cadet Jayme Miranda shouted. "That tunnel we came down—it's lower than this cave. It must be filled with water too!"

Hammon Titus swallowed, remembering how long the tunnel was. "We may not have oceans on Antaranan, but that doesn't mean we didn't have water. I'm a good swimmer."

"I'm not!" Bobbie Ray wailed, trying to shake the water from the fur on his hands.

"Then get up to the top ledge and stay out of the water," Titus ordered with more confidence than he felt. "And hang tight. I'll get us out of here." His fellow cadets stared back at him in mute skepticism.

They could at least try to look reassured, he thought bitterly as he dove into the icy water. . . .

⎯STAR TREK®⎯

THE BEST AND THE BRIGHTEST

SUSAN WRIGHT

POCKET BOOKS

New York   London   Toronto   Sydney   Tokyo   Singapore

An *Original* Publication of POCKET BOOKS

POCKET BOOKS, a division of Simon & Schuster Inc.
1230 Avenue of the Americas, New York, NY 10020

ISBN: 0-671-01549-4

First Pocket Books printing February 1998

10   9   8   7   6   5   4   3   2   1

Acknowledgments

I owe a great debt to John Ordover and Carol Greenburg, my editors at Pocket Books, and Paula Block, Director of Publishing at Paramount, for their insight and suggestions about the characters and development of this novel.

And a special thanks to Willie and Maria Gonzalez for the use of their extensive video library.

THE BEST AND
THE BRIGHTEST

Prologue

Summer, 2371

WHEN SHE HEARD THE NEWS, Jayme Miranda was in exocellular biology class, part of an intensive summer course at Starfleet Academy. At first the rumors seemed unlikely, an exaggeration of a severe battle. But even that was frightening enough to send her running to the comm to try to reach her great-aunt, Marley Miranda, an admiral at Starfleet Headquarters.

As Aunt Marley's image appeared on the screen, Jayme could have been looking at herself in forty years—all the Mirandas had the same straight, dark hair and strong-boned face. Jayme knew her family considered her to be the "excitable" one, so she didn't bother concealing her fear as her aunt confirmed that the *Enterprise* D had crashed on Veridian III. Even worse, a fatality had occurred during the battle with a Klingon bird-of-prey commanded by the Duras sisters. While they were talking, an official statement was released notifying the United Federation of Planets about the crash of Starfleet's flagship.

"Who was killed?" Jayme asked her aunt. "Was it . . . Ensign Moll Enor?"

"The name hasn't been released, pending notification of next of kin." Before Jayme could insist, her great-aunt added, "I don't know, Jayme."

"How long before you find out?" she asked, feeling frantic inside. "It's been hours since the crash."

"As soon as I hear, I'll call you," Marley assured her, looking concerned herself.

Jayme managed not to panic as her aunt signed off. Instead, she tried every trick she knew to get hold of Moll via the starship *Farragut* or one of the other starships assigned to the salvage and rescue of the *Enterprise* crew. But over one thousand crewmembers had been on board the Enterprise, and Starfleet was requesting that only family members contact Veridian III.

Later that evening, another cadet poked her head into Jayme's room, interrupting her efforts. Jayme glanced at the chrono, hardly able to believe that, this time yesterday, Moll and the *Enterprise* had been perfectly all right.

"Did you hear?" the cadet asked her.

Jayme was nodding, but the cadet added in a hushed voice, "They're saying that the crewmember who was killed was someone we know from the Academy."

Jayme couldn't even answer, choked with the same foreboding she'd had for weeks, ever since Moll had told her about Jadzia Dax. Dax, an old friend of Moll's from the Initiate Institute, had been forced to return to the Trill homeworld because of a serious symbiont malady. Jayme had been studying Trill physiology ever since she met Moll, fascinated by the joint humanoid and symbiont species, yet fearful of the many things that could go wrong with the delicate balance.

But this—Moll killed during a battle with Klingons! It was unbelievable. Why, barely four weeks ago they were vacationing in Rahm-Izad. Jayme kept trembling with suppressed agony and rage, afraid that it would be true, that Moll was . . .

Jayme got on the comm again, determined not to quit until she spoke to someone who could officially confirm that Moll Enor was alive.

Bobbie Ray Jefferson had been on an airboat trip for a few days with friends, cruising down the Canadian River, when he returned to his parents' environmental bubble-spread in the Texas panhandle. The bubble-spread overlooked the vivid blue waters of gorgeous Lake Meredith, reflecting the endless sky overhead. As he tried to find his parents among the crowd, he overheard guests talking about James T. Kirk, killed on Veridian III at the same time the *Enterprise* had crashed.

It was easy to pick out his mother, the only Rex among a group of humans seated near the fireplace. Her fine, golden brown fur was covered with a hooded cloak, and she towered head and shoulders above her friends as she gracefully held court.

"Darling," his mother called, gesturing him closer. This bubble was having a gentle snowstorm, but for once she didn't seem bothered by the way his dirty shorts and tank top clashed with the decor. "You know people on that starship, don't you?"

"Sure," he agreed, knowing his mother loved having a direct connection to things. "Three members of my first Quad-"

"That must be a record!" she exclaimed, looking at the others as she made her point. Her long fingernails were painted bronze, complementing the dark fur around her face. *"Three* members."

"Sure, Moll Enor, Nev Reoh, and Hammon Titus."

One of the guests, a young Kostolain who had been trying to catch his eye, asked, "Aren't you worried about your friends?"

"On the *Enterprise?*" Bobbie Ray countered, laughing at the idea. "What's to worry about?"

"But it crashed," she insisted, smiling now that she had his attention.

"It's still the *Enterprise,*" he reminded her. "It's built like a brick . . ." His mother's disapproving eyes made him think better of finishing the sentence. "Look, Mom," he continued, more decorously. "The only thing that'll happen is that Titus, my old roommate, will bore everyone sick with his stories. I would have been on the *Enterprise,* too, if I had gotten that field assignment—"

"I'm glad you didn't," his mother assured him, shuddering.

"They'll probably build another *Enterprise,*" Bobbie Ray told the Kostolain. "It'll be in commission by the time I graduate."

"I'm sure you'll serve on it someday," his mother blithely contradicted herself, completely missing the interplay going on between him and the Kostolain. "You always distinguish yourself, darling."

Bobbie Ray grinned to himself as he left the group, swiping some meat puffs on his way out. He and his mother might as well speak two different languages, but he couldn't get upset, knowing that he would never have gotten into Starfleet Academy without his parents' connections in high places. Even though his family had accepted the local customs and he had been born on Earth—in Texas, in fact—he still needed a high-ranking Starfleet officer to vouch for him, since the scattered Rex population had never joined the Federation.

Bobbie Ray knew he could have stayed and charmed the Kostolain a while longer, but in spite of his assurances, he wanted to find out exactly what had happened to the *Enterprise*. He knew it was dangerous sometimes being in Starfleet, but that was the trade-off you made for living life more intensely. He had already seen it and experienced it for himself during his field assignments. The people in Starfleet were getting more from every moment than anyone else in the galaxy, and he was glad to be part of that.

Starsa found out about the *Enterprise* while she and some fellow cadets were backpacking through the six inhabited planets of the Rigel system. They all heard the news shortly after disembarking from their transport, standing in the Stargazer Lobby of Starbase 34 with their gear piled haphazardly around them.

Starsa, like the others, quickly accessed the communiqués waiting for them at the starbase. Jayme hadn't sent a message, which was strange. Usually Starsa got all her inside information from Jayme, who would surely know the identity of the crewmember who had died on board the Enterprise.

Starsa couldn't stop thinking about Nev Reoh's last message (they arrived like clockwork every month, ever since he had graduated a year ago). He had mentioned he might transfer to a post at Starfleet Academy at the beginning of the school year. Starsa couldn't understand why the Bajoran wanted to leave the best ship in Starfleet, and she hadn't answered him. Now that she thought about it, she hadn't answered the past few communiques. Reoh was much better at sustaining their friendship than she was.

Without waiting to find out where her companions would be staying on Starbase 34, she ran to find a comm so she could send Reoh a message. Every nice thing the older cadet had ever done for her flooded back—helping with her science assignments, taking care of her when she had acclimation sickness, and explaining why Riker and his girlfriend got upset when she wandered into his room to watch them. She had thought they were just wrestling—how was she to know any different?

Reoh was the only one who understood she was simply curious, that she wasn't deliberately trying to be annoying. There were so many strange customs she didn't understand her first year, and without Reoh's hesitant suggestions—which she had usually laughed at, but basically tried to follow—she would have gotten in twice as much trouble.

The comm told her it would take five days for her message to reach the rescue ships, so it was routed to Earth to await the return of the *Enterprise* crewmembers.

Starsa checked her passage back to Earth, departing early the next morning. It would take nearly a week to return, but with some creative juggling, she still might make it before the rescue ships returned to Starfleet Headquarters.

Chapter One

First Year, 2368–69

JAYME TOOK THE STAIR-LIFT two steps at a time, but the antique monorail let out a melodious chime, announcing the closing of the doors. Using the guardrail as support, she propelled herself onto the platform as the monorail began to silently slide away from the Academy station.

It was nearly midnight, so there were no people on the platform and few were inside the monorail. Jayme ran alongside the train, nearing the edge of the platform, unable to stop and give up. She could see Elma sitting inside, her head held high and her back stiff, unable to relax and lean back even in the empty passenger compartment. Jayme could also see her own tricorder in Elma's hand.

She scrabbled to get hold of the monorail, but its smooth, modular design gave her no purchase. As it began to pick up speed, Jayme lunged desperately at the rear of the last car. One of her booted feet got purchase on the small brake box protruding right over the rail.

Her fingers strained to hang on to the groove of the rear window, and she realized she had made a very bad mistake. She was wearing the new waffle-cut style shoes instead of her regulation Starfleet-issue boots. As the monorail pulled out of the Academy station, heading into San Francisco and parts unknown, along with Elma and the tricorder, Jayme's foot slid off the brake box.

Jayme hit the rail with a solid *ooff!* and tried to grab on. The double rail was about a meter wide, and her arms could barely get around it. As her legs went over, she had nothing to grab hold of. She hung for a second by one elbow, and almost stuck her hand into the tempting grooves on the side of the rail. Anyone else would have, but Jayme's trained engineering reflexes made her jerk away from the highly charged conduit.

She had just enough time to congratulate herself on her own wisdom before she fell.

It flashed through her mind during the twelve-meter drop that it was her own fault if she got killed. Then she hit something solid, but not solid, sending a tingling energy shock wave through her body as her stomach seemed to keep on falling. She let herself go limp, knowing better than to resist a forcefield.

All she could see beneath her were the orange, gaping mouths of Ibernian tulips, freshly planted and protected from dimwits like her by a forcefield bubble. She slid off the side of the bubble, headfirst into the grass.

Rubbing her head, Jayme groaned at the rips in her cadet uniform. One sleeve was hanging by a few threads, looking exactly the way the pulled muscle in her shoulder felt. Next to her, the blue residue of ionization crackled over the flowers before the force-field became invisible again.

At least it was the dead of night, so there wasn't a crowd gathering around. Jayme knew she should feel lucky at her narrow escape—the cobblestone pathway was two paces away—but she was upset about Elma getting away. Where was Elma taking her tricorder? She knew her roommate had taken it before, but the temporary memory of the tricorder was always erased after Elma used it. So Jayme had been watching her carefully for several weeks to catch her in the act.

She pulled a small device from the roomy trouser pocket of her cadet uniform. With a few keystrokes, she activated the homing beacon she had recently planted inside the tricorder, and a map appeared on the tiny holoscreen. A green blip appeared, moving slowly across the grid as the centuries-old monorail system carried Elma east of the Presidio, into San Francisco. Jayme glanced around, looking for the Golden Gate Bridge to orient herself. The graceful span of the bridge was visible from almost everywhere on the Academy grounds.

"That was pretty impressive," a voice said right behind her.

The homing map flew into the air as Jayme startled. If it wasn't for the forcefield, she would have crushed the tulips a second time.

Her hands clutched at her chest, staring at the intruder, her heart beating faster than it had from the fall. "Who are you?"

A woman stepped forward, letting the light of the monorail tower fall on her smooth, dark skin. For a moment, from the strange shape of her head, Jayme thought it was an alien she'd never seen before—and she had seen more than most. Then she realized the woman was wearing an odd, bulbous hat made of some kind of plushy maroon material.

"I'm Guinan. And who are you?"

"Cadet Jayme Miranda," she replied, straightening her uniform. She ignored the hanging rags of her black sleeve as she tried to regain her dignity. "You're not Starfleet, are you?"

"Not exactly. I'm the bartender on the *Enterprise.*"

"The bartender?" Jayme repeated incredulously.

Guinan stooped and picked up the homing map, considering it. "You know, on Earth, electronic eavesdropping is illegal."

"It's my own tricorder," Jayme quickly defended herself. "My roommate took it."

One smooth brow lifted, slightly incredulous. "Your roommate stole your tricorder? Is that why you almost killed yourself?"

Jayme wasn't about to mention the extra gadgets it had taken months to jury-rig into that tricorder. "It's more than that. Elma's a member of my Quad, she's my roommate. We're responsible for each other."

Guinan's eyes narrowed slightly, as if considering the well-known Starfleet policy that made a unit out of the eight cadets living on each floor of the dormitory towers. The Quads were often a cadet's first taste of what it took to be a team. If a cadet got in bad enough trouble, the members of their Quad were questioned and if negligence was found, then they were disciplined as well.

Overhead, a monorail chimed as it pulled into the tower station. Voices emerged from the cars and a few cadets descended the stair-lift on the other side of the station, disappearing toward the Quads. The hum of the white monorail as it smoothly passed by overhead wasn't loud, but Guinan watched it with interest as if she had never seen anything like it before.

Jayme decided to take the offensive. "What are you doing here? I thought the *Enterprise* was in the Signat system for those trade negotiations."

"They are. I'm here to see a friend."

"Here at the Academy?" Jayme asked doubtfully, eyeing the bartender's outlandish costume again. If she had a few hours and a bonding tool, she might be able to make something interesting out of Guinan's tunic and that hat—but right now all you could see was the round oval of her face.

Guinan's pleasant expression never changed. "You may know him. His name is Wesley Crusher."

Jayme stopped herself from letting out a laugh of disbelief. *Wesley Crusher?* Who *didn't* know Crusher and the rest of the Nova Squadron, who had tried and failed to perform a Kolvoord Starburst?

"Yeah, he's in the class ahead of me," Jayme said diplomatically, leaving out the fact that the members of Nova Squadron were repeating a year.

"You don't sound very sympathetic," Guinan told her.

Stung, Jayme protested, "There's only so much you can sympathize, especially when people do stupid things. Besides, we're *all* getting punished because of Joshua Albert's death. The Academy has clamped down on everyone, like we can't be trusted because a few cadets made a mistake."

Guinan shrugged slightly, undisturbed by Jayme's outburst. "People make mistakes. It could have happened to anyone. It could happen to you."

"Excuse me, I know he's a friend of yours, but I wouldn't do anything like that."

11

Guinan smiled, glancing up at the gleaming monorail overhead. "You wouldn't?"

Jayme shifted, trying to ignore the bed of Ibernian tulips that seemed to be mocking her with their vibrant orange mouths. "That's different. I'm trying to help my roommate. I can't just turn her into Academy security."

"Have you tried talking to her?" Guinan asked.

"Of course! I try all the time, but she's . . . she's an odd person. Elma grew up on Holt, in the habitat domes."

Guinan nodded as if she knew Holt well. "You would value your privacy, too, if you lived with that many people under one roof."

"So you understand my problem!" Jayme exclaimed in relief. "She won't confide in me, and I'm afraid she's gotten into something over her head."

Guinan turned her head slightly, once more considering the homing beacon in her hand. Jayme couldn't see the map, but she heard the tone that signaled that the beacon was now stationary.

"Listen," Jayme said urgently, taking a step closer to Guinan. "What is Holt known for? It's mostly Bajoran resettlement camps, right? Well, why do you think that is?"

"Because Bajorans are the only ones desperate enough to put up with those conditions?" Guinan suggested.

"Well, that's true," Jayme conceded. "But it's also in the perfect strategic position to serve as a resistance base."

Guinan furrowed her brow. "So what are you saying?" she asked.

"I'm saying that I grew up here in San Francisco, and most of my mother's family is in Starfleet. My aunt Dani is on a patrol right now near the border of occupied Bajor. I know the Federation can't risk their peace with the Cardassians by helping the Bajorans get back their homeworld. And I'm afraid Elma is trying to help the Bajoran resistance. She might get something from my aunt's messages, or . . ." Jayme glanced away, as if suddenly more interested in the lights on the Golden Gate Bridge than the homing beacon in Guinan's hand. "There's lots of programs in my tricorder that could be used to . . . well, used to compromise Starfleet systems."

"I see." For a moment Jayme thought Guinan really understood, then the bartender added, "If you turn in your roommate, they'll find out that you've juiced up your tricorder."

"No!" Jayme quickly denied. "I've done nothing illegal, just . . . unorthodox. If I thought there was a real danger, I would tell security even if I got into trouble myself. See, I realize we're in this together. I'd just like to be able to confront her with everything." She looked longingly at the homing beacon. "But it would help if I knew where she was going. She could be in a bar right now, and I'm making a big deal over nothing."

Guinan slowly nodded. "You're very good, Jayme Miranda."

For some reason, Jayme didn't think that was intended as a compliment. But when Guinan handed back the homing device, she was too pleased to care.

As she zoomed and focused the map, Jayme absently told Guinan, "You know, Crusher's lucky to have you for a friend." Finally the correct section of the city clicked in and the readout showed the location—the radio observatory.

Guinan waited, clearly leaving it up to Jayme whether to tell her.

"She's at the Deng Observatory."

"That doesn't sound too dangerous," Guinan commented.

"No . . ." But Jayme wasn't so certain, and while she owed Guinan for not turning her in for that crazy leap onto the monorail, she wasn't about to tell this stranger everything. "Maybe I should talk to my Quadmates about this."

"That's probably a good idea." Guinan kept staring at Jayme until the cadet started to squirm, feeling as if she *had* told Guinan everything. "Maybe you should think about going into a different line of work, Jayme Miranda."

"Why do you say that?" Jayme asked, startled.

"You aren't happy."

"Not happy? But I love Starfleet! I've waited all my life to join Starfleet."

"If you say so," Guinan demurred with a smile.

Jayme hesitated, but Guinan didn't seem concerned about pressing her point. Uneasily, she said, "Thanks," as she left.

At the end of the walk, she glanced back. Guinan was waiting in the soft pool of light around the monorail tower. Her hands were patiently folded together under her tunic, and she was apparently ready to stay as long as it took for Crusher to show up. Jayme knew she was being irritable, but she thought Crusher must not properly appreciate his friend to make her wait like that when she'd come so far.

But Guinan was wrong about one thing—her situation was completely different from Crusher's. The Nova Squadron had been acting like kids, playing a dangerous game to show off in front of everyone. Just look what it got them. Nick Locarno, the leader of Nova Squadron, expelled from Starfleet, and the others skulking around like pariahs, living, breathing examples for the other cadets of what *not* to do.

But Jayme didn't need that lesson. She was doing this to help Elma, not to get glory or praise for her own efforts. No, she understood the Starfleet code, and she would keep on trying to help her roommate, even if Elma didn't want her help.

"Why couldn't you build another subverter—or whatever it is you call it!" Bobbie Ray complained for the dozenth time. "Then we could have walked in the front door like normal people."

Jayme hardly had any breath left, and rather than argue with Bobbie Ray, she concentrated on climbing the endless ladder to the top of the peaks that supported the Deng parabolic dish. She did spare the time to glare at the furry orange humanoid clinging to the exterior maintenance ladder, the last one in line.

Starsa, who was just below Jayme, shot back, "What are you complaining about? You don't seem to be having a hard time."

It was true—the large Rex was a natural athlete, specializing in security and hand-to-hand combat. But to hear Bobbie Ray talk, he would rather curl up on a couch in the sun and sleep all day.

Bobbie Ray's roommate, Hammon Titus, gave Jayme an edgy grin. "You could have warned us about this part when we were back in the Quad. Is there any other surprises you have planned for us?"

"I thought I told you," Jayme muttered, letting Starsa relay what she'd said to the others. Then she had to ignore their indignant denials.

Okay, so she hadn't told them about this part. But

how else did they think they were going to get inside the closed observatory? They knew the dish was anchored in a large natural depression in the mountains, with the receiving station deep underground.

They had a saying in Starfleet—you always remember your first Quad. Jayme just wished her first Quad was worth remembering. All the spark was in her fellow freshmen cadets, and her opinion of them was falling fast under this test. It was only two thousand feet up, for the Horta's sake.

As for the four older cadets in their Quad, the ones they were supposed to look up to and emulate, that was an even sorrier lot. Not that she expected to have much fun around T'Rees since he was a Vulcan, and she gave Elma allowances for being socially twisted by her upbringing on Holt, but she had expected more from Nev Reoh, a former Bajoran Vedek, and Moll Enor, a newly joined Trill. The exotic possibilities in such roommates were endless, but Moll Enor had hardly spoken four words since the semester had begun, while Nev Reoh readily admitted that he was a failure at everything he had tried. It was practically the first thing he said, and he tended to repeat it periodically. Reoh was different, even among the few Bajoran cadets—he was older than everyone else, and it didn't help that his prematurely receding hairline added even more years to his appearance. With so many somber people around, Jayme sometimes felt like she was living in a geriatric ward instead of a Quad.

Jayme heaved herself onto the perimeter walkway, shifting over to allow the others up behind her. Bobbie Ray took one look at the five thousand foot parabolic dish, with the opposite edge so far away that the regularly spaced lights disappeared in the darkness, and said, "I'm having second thoughts about this."

Titus crossed his arms. "Yeah, what makes you so sure Elma's helping the Bajoran resistance? She's got a class in radio astronomy this semester. Maybe she's doing lab work."

"After midnight?" Jayme countered. "And what about those Cardassian code files I found hidden in the back of her closet?" She hurried on before they could think to ask her what she was doing in the back of Elma's closet. "What else is she doing with code files if she isn't decoding intercepted material and sending it to the resistance?"

"But this antenna only receives," Titus protested. "It doesn't transmit."

"Ah, but it *does* transmit!" Jayme said triumphantly, pleased that she'd taken a few minutes to flip through some of Elma's technical manuals on the large radio telescope. "It has to send coordinates to an orbital satellite to focus the telescopic electronic camera. That beam could be aimed at a communications satellite, relaying information that the antenna has picked up. Or it could be used to tap into the orbital satellites, relaying the faster-than-light subspace radio communications from Federation starbases and starships throughout the Alpha Quadrant."

Bobbie Ray stood right on the edge of the dish, perfectly comfortable with the sheer drop. "I think we should quit while we're ahead."

"And what if she *is* a spy?" Starsa asked. "Do we just march into Superintendent Brand's office and tell her we were right here but didn't bother to go inside and see what Elma was doing?"

Jayme silently applauded Starsa's spirit. Her species experienced a late puberty, so she was basically a ten-year-old both physically and in the amount of impulsive daring she possessed. Unfortunately, the tall, slender girl was also suffering from severe acclimation sickness, so her slow metabolism had to be regulated and adjusted for Earth's pressure and gravity.

Jayme had almost rejected Starsa for this mission on physical grounds, but now she was glad she had brought her along. Especially when Starsa leaned over the edge, shuddering at the drop but laughing at the vertigo it caused. The others shifted uneasily, clearly reconsidering their protests in the face of her courage.

"Come on," Jayme ordered, taking advantage of their indecision. "We've got to climb out on the truss and take the antigrav lift down."

She gestured to the enormous cross-lines high overhead, anchored to three towers around the edge of the dish. The lines met in the center, supporting a ring that allowed the feed to move, steering the beam that was reflected from the dish anywhere within five degrees of the zenith.

"Up there?" Bobbie Ray protested, looking at the lines overhead, then down into the black hole in the very center of the dish. "It looks dangerous."

"The maintenance crew does it all the time," Jayme tossed off, heading toward the nearest tower.

"More climbing," Titus grumbled, but he followed her.

Starsa was kicking her heels over the edge. "Why is it so big? Our telescope at the Academy isn't nearly as big."

"That's because it's a light wave telescope," Jayme explained. "Radio waves go from a few millimeters to about thirty meters in wavelength. So the bigger the parabolic dish, the bigger waves it can catch."

"Oh, I knew that—" Starsa started to say, then she let out a piercing scream.

Jayme wasn't sure what happened, but Starsa was suddenly plummeting down the nearly vertical wall of the dish, screaming like she was being burned alive.

An orange blur shot down the white, curving wall as Bobbie Ray dived after her. While Starsa tumbled, bouncing against the reflective metal plates that lined the dish, Bobbie Ray took an aerodynamically correct position as he zipped down headfirst.

Jayme jammed her fist in her mouth as she hung over Titus, watching their descent. Bobbie Ray's greater bulk caused him to rush past Starsa. They receded to tiny dots as they neared the flattened curve at the bottom of the dish, but they were still going fast, straight toward the gaping black hole in the center.

Bobbie Ray splayed his arms and legs, turning into a dark gray *X* against the dish, spinning as he slowed. But Starsa was still tumbling out of control. Jayme didn't think Bobbie Ray would have time, but he got his feet under him and made an impossible leap sideways. Even his tremendous strength wasn't enough, but at the last second, he snagged Starsa by the hair, stopping her right at the edge of the hole.

Starsa's screams continued to echo out of the dish as Jayme frantically tapped her communicator, set for a special frequency just for this mission. "Is she hurt? Is she hurt!"

Titus had put on his spotting loop and was peering through the misty air. "He's got her! He's picking her up. Now he's shaking her—"

Starsa's screams abruptly stopped.

Bobbie Ray's lazy drawl came over their communicators. "She's fine."

"He grabbed my hair!" Starsa shrieked in the background as Bobbie Ray released her. "It's half pulled out! You big stupid *cat!*"

Jayme let out her breath, sitting down on the walkway with a jolt. "That was close!"

"Good thing she's *got* all that hair." Titus murmured, still watching them through the loop.

Jayme was still shaking her head, thinking—*Now what?* But she didn't want Titus to know how shaken she was.

Bobbie Ray was poking around at the edge of the hole, not bothering to respond to Starsa's complaints, which came clearly through the communicators. "Hey, there's a lift down here," Bobbie Ray said. "Why don't you slide down and join us?"

"What?!" Jayme exclaimed. "Do you think we're insane—"

"Just make sure you catch me!" Titus sang out. "Yee-*ha!*"

With that, he leaped over the side of the dish, laughing as he whizzed down feetfirst.

Jayme watched him quickly dwindle, falling nearly two thousand feet. But this time Bobbie Ray jogged over to position himself in Titus's path, leaving plenty of space between him and the hole. As the big Rex grabbed hold of the cadet, Titus's momentum carried them spinning the last few meters. Starsa tried to help by getting between them and the hole, but she nearly got knocked in.

They were all jabbering at once, so that Jayme couldn't tell what was happening down there. But everyone seemed to be all right. She didn't need a spotting loop to tell when all three faces expectantly turned up in her direction.

She almost called for them to wait for her while she took the truss-lift down like a normal human being. But it would take forever for her to climb all the way up the tower and walk to the middle of the truss. Their presence must have already been recorded by the deformation of the enormous dish, supported by sensitive antigrav nodes, and surely there was an alarm going off somewhere that the dish needed adjustment.

Jayme swung her legs over the side. For a moment she hung there, facing a near-vertical drop, her instincts crying *danger*. But a good officer knew how to roll with the punches.

"Ex astris, scientia!" Jayme cried out as she jumped off the edge.

The first part was the worst, when it felt like she was actually falling with hardly any contact between her and the wall. Then the drag of the slope caught her, redirecting her and making it feel like she was going even faster and out of control. Instinctively her hands tried to grab hold of the smooth surface and she flipped over on her stomach. All she could see was the sharp, white edge of the dish far overhead, cutting into the night sky.

Then something caught her ankle and jerked her in a big circle. Jayme cried out as her leg was practically pulled from her hip joint.

When she was convinced she was fully stopped, she checked to make sure the hole was safely far away. Then she finally rolled into a sitting position.

"Did you have to pull so hard?" she asked Bobbie Ray, digging into her pocket for the portable biogenerator that came in standard cadet first aid kits. Between the shoulder injury from the monorail and now this, she was beginning to realize why doctors were routinely assigned to away teams.

Bobbie Ray showed his teeth—his way of laughing. *"Kvetch, kvetch, kvetch.* Why doesn't anyone ever thank me?"

Starsa was rubbing her head, mussing her thick curly ponytail as she glared at the Rex. "Can I have that when you're done?" she asked Jayme.

Jayme handed it over and went to the access port. The tertiary mirror was positioned inside and down a few meters on its own steerable truss. A catwalk ran along the inner edge, with an antigrav lift right next to the cable that carried the amplified radio signal down into the receiving station.

"Well, we're halfway there," Jayme said, trying to think positively. "Let's get going."

Moll Enor woke from a deep sleep as the beeping got louder and more insistent. For a moment, the tonal quality reminded her of the wake-up chime at the Symbiosis Institute and she thought she was back on Trill, awaiting notification that a symbiont had been selected for her.

As she struggled to sit up, still mostly asleep, she realized she was in the Academy Quad. The beeping was the sensor on Starsa's pulmonary support unit and physiostimulator pack, warning that her activity was exceeding recommended limits. In the four weeks Moll Enor had known Starsa, the girl had exceeded her recommended physical limits thirty-one times. The beeping was so routine that Moll had become accustomed to it and ignored it, knowing that the relay would buzz uncomfortably on Starsa's implant, warning her to slow down.

But when she glanced at the time, she realized that T'Rees was still out, giving a workshop on extended meditation techniques. Usually Starsa's Vulcan roommate took it upon himself to monitor Starsa's habits and scold her when she was thoughtless.

Moll couldn't understand what could be causing a medical alert at this time of night, when Starsa was usually in bed asleep. She quickly got up, noticing that Nev Reoh was still sleeping soundly in his bed, his mouth open and his face pressed against a pillow, with the blanket twisted impossibly around his body. One bare foot jutted over the edge. He didn't even shift as the beeping escalated.

Moll Enor ran the few steps down the circular hallway and knocked on Starsa's door. She could hear the beeping more loudly, and she knocked more insistently. When there was no answer, she went inside. But both the beds were empty, and a quick check in the refresher reassured her that Starsa wasn't lying on the floor in distress.

With a sinking feeling, Moll checked the other two rooms in their Quad and found both empty. All four of the first-year cadets were probably together—they had seemed to bond fairly quickly. But Elma's absence surprised her. Elma was a year ahead of Moll, but until they were assigned to the same Quad, she had never seen the Holt woman. And Moll made it a point to notice everything. As the first host for the Enor symbiont, it was her duty to provide a solid foundation of experiences, as well as a wide-ranging understanding of the numerous alien races that inhabited the Alpha Quadrant.

But Elma was a nonexistent presence in the Quad, and Moll was at a loss as to why she would be gone so late. She had never even seen a friend of hers come to the Quad.

Returning to Starsa's room, Moll glanced around, but Starsa's pulmonary support unit and physiostim-ulator pack were not immediately identifiable among the wreckage on the girl's side of the partition. The room looked schizophrenic, with the Vulcan half painfully neat and bare while Starsa had almost covered her walls with pictures and holoscreens that ran loops of her favorite shows and family members performing odd customs. Moll had thought it was bad living with Nev Reoh, but at least the former Vedek maintained order on his side of their room. It was his verbal messiness that wore on her. He would ramble cheerfully for hours while she tried to concentrate on her studies, but he was so awkwardly eager to please that she never censored him, resolving that the experience must be good for her symbiont in *some* way.

Moll tapped the wall comm. "Computer, location of Cadet Starsa Taran."

"Cadet Taran is not on Academy grounds."

Moll could hardly think of the implications of that as the maddening beeping chose that moment to escalate to its highest level.

"What are you doing?" Nev Reoh suddenly asked behind her.

Moll Enor started, feeling guilty in spite of herself. "I'm looking for Starsa."

Reoh sleepily rubbed his face, glancing from the empty beds to Moll Enor. Starsa noted the way even his pajamas bunched in odd places, just like his computer-fitted cadet uniform somehow never seemed to hang right. He was wincing at the sound of the medical alarm.

"Did the first-year cadets say what they were doing tonight?" She had to raise her voice.

"I don't know." His mouth hung open as he thought about it. "I don't remember anything—"

The door whirred electronically and swung open. Moll Enor felt a leap of relief, but it was T'Rees, not Starsa. The Vulcan pulled back in surprise to see them.

"Hi," Nev Reoh said innocently.

T'Rees tightened his lips, vexed at his slight display of emotion. "What are you two doing in my room?" Moll Enor gestured, but he had already noted the sound of the physiostimulator pack. "Where is Starsa?"

"We don't know," Reoh said. "The others are gone, too."

T'Rees lifted one brow. "Everyone?"

"Yes."

"Did you report this?" T'Rees asked, turning to the comm.

Moll crossed her arms defensively. "We were just about to."

T'Rees pressed the emergency sequence. "Then we shall delay no longer."

At the Deng Observatory, the four cadets stood on the circular platform of the antigrav lift as it gently descended into the receiving station. Bobbie Ray and Starsa gazed over the side, but Jayme never wanted to see another drop like that.

From the maintenance tubes at the base of the well it wasn't far to reach the computer rooms. In the darkened, vaulted chambers, the radio signals were displayed on screens in colored patterns moving across the recording graphs. Numerous digital sequencers flashed the numbers of incoming data streams.

This was the part Jayme had been waiting for, sneaking up on Elma and catching her red-handed. Her tricorder was out, recording the activity in the room; it indicated there was a human female on the opposite side.

Jayme tried to stay in the lead, but her team had other ideas. They fanned out among the terminals, making much more noise than she had anticipated. *"Psst!"* she hissed at them, trying to get them to fall into position. But Titus didn't even glance her way, trying to take the lead as always, while Starsa was apparently mesmerized by the shifting abstract images on a large colorful display. Bobbie Ray had disappeared. Jayme forged on, clenching her teeth but determined to make it work out in spite of her team.

Suddenly the lights came on and Elma stepped onto an elevated platform. The cadets froze, absurdly caught in their stalking positions.

But Elma was clutching the rail, her knuckles white as her gaze shifted desperately from one to the other, as if *she* was one who was caught.

"What are you doing here?" Titus demanded, pointing an accusing finger up at Elma.

"I was working . . ."

Bobbie Ray hitched one leg over a console, leaning casually back against the monitor. "Most people work when the observatory is open."

"Yeah," Titus said, inching closer to her. "What are you doing that you have to sneak in here at night?"

Elma swallowed, unable to let go of the rail.

"You might as well tell us," Bobbie Ray advised her, examining a long, curved nail before chewing gently on it to smooth out a snag. "Or would you rather tell security?"

"Stop it!" Jayme ordered, shoving Titus out of the way so she could look up at Elma. "We're not here to make trouble for you. We want to help."

Before she could coax Elma into revealing the truth, they were rudely interrupted by the arrival of the observatory personnel. Doors banged open on all sides of the computer room, and at least ten technicians and scientists poured into the control room in various states of undress, rushing to the various monitors.

"What happened to the dish?" one of them blurted out, hanging onto the keyboard as he tried to make sense of the data. "There couldn't have been an earthquake—"

"Who are you?" another one demanded, torn between the distressing numbers on their equipment and the strangers in the control room. Exclamations rang out over lost data and destroyed projects.

Jayme's quadmates were inadvertently herded closer together by the frantic technicians. Then one older scientist pulled her robe tighter around herself, twisting up the side of her mouth as she realized what they were dealing with.

"Cadets!" she snarled, as if that one word said it all.

The cadets were at attention in a line in front of Superintendent Admiral Brand's desk. Jayme noted that the room was perfectly proportioned to allow all eight members of a Quad to stand shoulder to shoulder. The fact that this was probably a common occurrence didn't make her feel any better.

Admiral Brand sat with her back to the windows, where the dawn's first rays tinted the sky, casting her face into shadow. Only her silver-white hair caught the light, swept high off her forehead, while her hands were calmly folded on her desk.

"Then I saw the alarm from the subsidiary arrays," Elma was explaining. "So I knew something was occluding the focus. From the variance of the interference fringes, it had to be a deformation of the main dish. I'd seen something like it before when the plates were being cleaned, so I was afraid the staff was working the night shift. I hid until my Quadmates showed up."

Brand turned to the three other senior cadets. "Cadet First Class T'Rees, when was the first time you knew something was happening?"

"When I returned to my room and saw that Cadet Starsa Taran's medical relay was on alert," T'Rees replied, the epitome of attention. "I signaled the Academy medical unit immediately."

Jayme couldn't help rolling her eyes. Of course T'Rees had ratted on them.

Brand noticed and turned her attention to Jayme. "You were fortunate the observatory personnel handed you over to Academy security without pressing charges of trespassing. However, they may still claim compensatory damages for the loss of data and injury to the parabolic dish."

"That was my fault," Starsa freely admitted. "I slipped off the walkway and slid down the side. Cadet Jefferson jumped over to save me." She gave the tall Rex a surprisingly sweet smile.

28

Bobbie Ray gave her a deadpan look, obviously remembering her indignant wailing.

Admiral Brand wasn't distracted. "That doesn't explain why you were attempting to break into the observatory in the first place."

The other three cadets looked at Jayme, deferring responsibility to her. Jayme haltingly explained the sequence of events, from the first few nights when Elma had taken her tricorder, to her realization that she was going into the Deng Observatory after it was closed. She left out the part about falling off the monorail, figuring it would only confuse things.

Brand turned back to Elma. "Why did you take Cadet Miranda's tricorder?"

"Because it has a security override I could use to get inside the observatory." Elma kept her head down, her voice so low it was hard to hear her. "I had to. I couldn't work during the regular lab hours. All those cadets talking and moving around . . . I can't concentrate, so I've been doing my summaries when everyone's gone."

"Oh, we thought you were a Bajoran resistance fighter," Starsa said artlessly.

"*What* did you think?" Admiral Brand asked, her voice strained with incredulity.

"Jayme—I mean," Starsa quickly corrected herself, "Cadet Miranda said Elma was tapping communiqués with the telescope and relaying them to the resistance fighters."

Jayme wanted to kick Starsa, but it was too late. "Uh, you know, because she's from Holt . . . and I thought, it seemed to make sense at the time, why she was being so secretive . . ."

Elma actually raised her head, blinking rapidly as if

she couldn't believe what she was hearing. All of Jayme's fantasy scenarios crumpled under Elma's blank, uncomprehending stare.

T'Rees sniffed in disdain. "You should have informed the senior cadets in your Quad."

"Well, since you bring it up, I tried!" Jayme shot back. "Remember when I came into your room last week? But you wouldn't even listen when I told you it was about Elma. You said she had seniority since she was a last-year cadet, and that I had to work my problems out with her!"

"That's enough," Brand ordered. The cadets immediately stiffened, facing the window again. "I believe this incident reflects a failure of your entire Quad. You are responsible for each other, and I hope that before the end of the year you will have learned that." She paused, letting her words sink in. "A formal reprimand will be placed in each of your academic records, and you are all hereby placed on probation for sixty days."

Jayme flushed at the sentence. Her family was going to have a fit when they heard she was already in serious trouble after barely arriving at the Academy.

But the worst was yet to come as Brand walked around her desk to stand directly in front of Jayme. "Cadet Miranda, I expected more from you. Henceforth, you will refrain from letting your . . . fancies interfere with your duty to Starfleet. If you do detect a spy in our midst, we would all be better served if you alert your commanding officer."

"Yes, sir!" Jayme agreed. "It won't happen again."

"No, it won't," Elma suddenly agreed. The cadet broke ranks, stepping forward. "Superintendent Brand, I would like to resign my commission to the Academy."

"No!" Jayme blurted out.

Brand waved a hand at Jayme, silencing her. "What is your reason?"

"I'm not suited to Starfleet. I can't stand being around people who don't act right—" Elma stopped herself. "I mean, act like we do on Holt. I belong there, and I've been delaying the inevitable by sneaking around, trying to avoid everyone."

Brand considered her for a moment, then her expression softened as she gently clasped Elma's shoulder. "I've been impressed with your persistence, and I had hoped you would become accustomed to the different culture."

Elma stiffly shook her head, unable to speak.

Brand nodded. "Very well, remain here, cadet. The rest of you are dismissed. You will be notified if the Deng Observatory pursues compensation."

The others practically ran out of the superintendent's office, but Jayme dragged her feet. She would have protested again, but Brand silently shook her head and motioned to the door. Jayme's last look at Elma caught the older cadet staring down at her fingers, twisting them together painfully, unable to return Brand's reassuring smile.

All day Jayme kept thinking about the way Elma always twined her fingers together, pulling and bending them as if to distract herself from some outer torment. Why hadn't she been able to see what was happening?

When Jayme returned to the Quad from her classes, Elma's half of the room was empty. The cabinets were cracked open and the desk under the other square window had been cleared off.

Jayme sat down on the bare mattress, feeling like

she should be shot. "What have I done?" she moaned out loud. "This is awful! What can I do?"

The door slowly swung open and Nev Reoh stuck his head cautiously around. "Uh . . . is there something wrong?"

With tears starting to form in her eyes, Jayme wordlessly held out her arms to the empty room.

"She's gone?"

Even in her sorrow, Jayme was exasperated. "What do you think? I'm surprised they didn't expel me, too."

"But Elma quit. She didn't get expelled."

"I'm talking about Locarno!" Jayme buried her head in her hands, thinking of the last self-styled hero who had hit the Academy. Who was she to think she could save the universe, much less one frightened woman from Holt?

"Nick Locarno?" Nev Reoh's brow creased in confusion, making him look even older. "You mean the leader of Nova Squadron?"

"Who else?" Jayme sighed, letting her hands fall into her lap. "I don't expect you to understand, but I . . . I haven't been doing as well in my classes as everyone seems to expect. I thought this was a way I could prove myself. . . ."

"But you're getting *B*'s, Jayme! That's not failure. Believe me, I know what it means to fail—"

"I know, I know. You were such a terrible Vedek; you've told everyone that."

Abashed, Reoh bent his head. "I admire what Elma did. It's hard to make a big change. To give up everything you've planned on. I bet that's why she didn't say good-bye to us."

"Because she was ashamed," Jayme agreed.

Surprisingly, Reoh shook his head. "No, because we

didn't matter anymore. She knew this part of her life was over. So she could walk away."

"That's pretty heartless," Jayme protested. "She's been here almost four years. She was practically ready to graduate."

Nev Reoh shrugged. "You can only struggle for so long. If something's not working, then you have to try something else." He glanced shyly up at her. "You know, *I* was in the Bajoran resistance."

"You!" Jayme exclaimed.

Nev Reoh nodded, unhurt by her obvious shock.

"You were?" she asked, unable to stop herself from looking harder at his wrinkled Bajoran nose. "Really?"

"I was very young and wanted to help like everyone else. But I don't like to fight. I can't even hold a disrupter-rifle, much less point it at anyone," he confessed. "So I thought that meant I should be a Vedek. Nonviolent resistance, but you know the rest . . . that wasn't right for me, either. I'm better suited to geological studies."

Jayme stared at his honest, open face. "I didn't know you fought Cardassians."

Even when Reoh grinned, he looked vaguely worried. "Everything works out the way it's supposed to, Jayme. Even Nick Locarno got what he wanted."

"You don't mean he *wanted* to be expelled."

"No, not exactly. But he wanted everyone to remember him. So he tried to take a shortcut, and now no one will ever forget him."

"Yeah, you'd think he was still around, as much as everyone whispers his name when something goes wrong," Jayme agreed ruefully.

"That's good, because that means Joshua Albert didn't die for nothing. Everything's tightened up, shipshape. It should be. Too many people were killed fighting the Borg last year. We're the only ones who can take their place. Even if we aren't perfect."

"Right," Jayme agreed, straightening her shoulders. Maybe she wasn't as good at engineering as she should be, but she could only keep trying. Besides, *she* never claimed she was as brilliant as her mother or her older sister. "I guess you're saying I'll have to do it the hard way, right?"

"I never found any other way," Nev Reoh earnestly assured her.

Chapter Two

TITUS COULD FEEL THE SWEAT on his palms making his grip on the *antara* slip as he swung it around again, trying to hamstring Bobbie Ray. The big orange Rex took advantage of his hesitation and began pummeling his *antara*, trying to break through the back stave. Titus went down on one knee, very much aware that they were fighting without the protective face shield and arm guards usually worn during *antara* competitions. But this match was for real.

Bobbie Ray's face bent over him, his long teeth bared in a grin as he kept pressing his advantage. His heavy breathing was the only sound.

"You know you snore at night," Titus told him between blows, managing to summon up a defiant grin of his own. "Maybe you should get that checked—"

"Grrgh!" Bobbie Ray rumbled as his *antara* flashed down, then jerked up—a move Titus didn't know the

35

Rex was aware of. A move that had no proper defense when an opponent was down.

The long, jagged blade seemed to slow as it came toward his face. The point buried under his chin and ripped through his head, coming out the top. Blood spurted everywhere, darkening the white padded floor and walls, while a universal groan of disgust rose from the cadets who were watching.

As Titus's body crumpled, Bobbie Ray took up position over him, bowing slightly to the scattered applause. Victoriously, he raised one foot to place it on his prostrate opponent.

Titus's image flickered and disappeared. "Don't you dare put your dirty paw on me!" Titus exclaimed as he dropped the handles of the hologame.

Bobbie Ray's image also disappeared as the Rex stood up, stretching. He had an unbearably smug look on his face. "Something wrong, roomie? It was a fair match."

"No, it wasn't!" Titus muttered, handing over the holocontrols.

"Excuse me?" Bobbie Ray drawled. "You picked the weapons. Though I don't know how your people accomplish anything with a toy like an *antara.*"

Titus smothered his anger in the face of the laughter from the other cadets who had crowded into their room to watch the match.

"That's a great hologame," Jayme told Bobbie Ray. "Did your parents gave it to you during the midyear break?"

"Yeah, they got it from a environmental designer they work with." Bobbie Ray carefully put the holocontrols in a foam contoured box. "It's a prototype that won't be on the market until the end of this year."

Starsa was sitting cross-legged on Titus's bed. "Is there any kind of game you *don't* have?"

"I doubt it." Bobbie Ray was looking unbearably conceited again. Their friends started to drift out of the room, saying good-bye.

Jayme sidled up to Titus. "You aren't exactly the poster boy for good losers."

"It's *his* game," Titus retorted. "How can anyone beat him at it?"

Jayme shrugged, grinning. "You were the one who challenged him to an *antara* match."

Titus turned away. "I'm not used to those controls."

"Hey, everyone, look!" Starsa called out, "Comm, sound on."

The small screen over the door routinely ran the Federation news service, along with information that was pertinent to the Academy, like announcements from professors or the superintendent herself. This time it was breaking news from the San Francisco local media station. The announcer had a fashionably shaved head with a blue forehead-cockade, and she seemed unusually shaken.

"We take you live to the site," she was saying as the sound came up. The image switched to a view of workers wearing the orange uniforms of the city maintenance department climbing out of an underground tunnel.

"Starsa, who cares—" Titus started to say.

"Look at that!" Jayme exclaimed as the image switched again.

It was a head, like the severed head of a mannequin lying in the dirt. As the camera swung around to view the face, it revealed the blank, golden stare of Lieutenant Commander Data.

The announcer was saying, "Work crews excavating beneath the city of San Francisco today discovered artifacts suggesting an extraterrestrial presence on Earth sometime during the late nineteenth century. Among the artifacts discovered is an object identified as the head of Lieutenant Commander Data of Starfleet. According to isotope readings, it has decayed from having been buried for some 500 years."

"That's impossible!" Starsa blurted out, and was shushed by the others.

"Starfleet Command reports that their flagship, the *Enterprise*-D, has been recalled to Earth to investigate this anomaly." The blue cockade bobbed impressively. "Now we take you to the tunnels near the Presidio, home of Starfleet Academy, to view the remains."

"Remains!" Starsa exclaimed again.

"Will you *please* shut up?" Bobbie Ray asked with exaggerated politeness, shouldering some of the remaining cadets aside to get a better view.

Titus sat down at his desk, staring out the window at the Golden Gate Bridge. He was just as pleased to have their minds so quickly diverted from the *antara* match. He listened with only half an ear as the announcer described how the workers had discovered the severed head while installing additional seismic regulators in subterranean caverns to control earth movements that were typical along the San Andreas fault.

"Subterranean caverns," Titus repeated under his breath, realizing what that implied. Impatiently, he waited for the broadcast to end and the last of the cadets to depart to spread the bizarre news.

Finally only Bobbie Ray and Jayme were left, and Titus knew Jayme would probably linger in their room all evening unless he asked her to leave. He had noticed she didn't like spending much time in her half-empty room, ever since Elma had resigned from the Academy. Jayme had more than once voiced her hope that a new cadet would fill the space after the half-year break, but her room was still empty.

"I have an idea," Titus told them both. "That is, if you want to have some real fun instead of holo-fakery."

Bobbie Ray curled one lip at the intended slight. "What's your bright idea this time?"

"You've never had a real thrill until you've descended a hundred meter fissure into an underground cavern."

"You want to go down to the caves?" Bobbie Ray asked in disbelief. "Are you crazy? You know how many security teams they must have posted?"

"We can't disturb the excavation site," Jayme agreed. "It could interfere with the *Enterprise*'s investigation."

Titus raised his eyes to the heavens. "I'm not stupid. We can explore the caverns without going near the Presidio." He directly challenged Bobbie Ray. "Unless, that is, you're too scared."

Bobbie Ray hesitated, then shrugged, willing to go along with anything, as usual. Jayme briefly considered it before shaking her head. "You don't know these caverns. They're dangerous; that's why they were sealed off ages ago."

"We're not worried," Titus assured her. "It's better to have three people on an underground exploratory team, but we'll go duo without you if we have to."

"Even if I did agree to go, you'd never find a way to get inside."

"Just leave that to me," Titus told them, feeling

39

much better now. "I'll get us below ground. Or I'm not an Antaranan."

Titus had grown up in the human colony of Antaranan, more in the caves than on the surface, so he figured there was nobody better to find their way through these puny San Franciscan caverns than himself. His mother was a biospeleologist, and had often taken him into the unexplored caverns and passageways that riddled the crust of Antaranan, far beyond the familiar chambers used by the colony to grow the essential fungal-meats and fragile vegetable matter away from the harmful solar rays.

It wasn't difficult to access the maintenance records of the seismic regulators under San Francisco, as well as the original surveys of the caverns performed hundreds of years ago. Most of the main access ports were in the heart of the city—the financial district, in Union Square, even the ancient yards of the Southern Pacific Railroad.

When he showed Jayme the map, she shook her head at all of the access ports he suggested. As she liked to tell the other cadets, she knew the city inside out.

"This is where we should go down," she insisted, pointing to a small auxiliary porthole near the Cable Car Barn Museum.

Bobbie Ray squinted at the print over that area. "Chinatown?"

"I was looking for a more out-of-the-way place," Titus protested. "That's one of the most crowded areas in the city."

"Exactly!" Jayme exclaimed. "Everyone's too busy and there's too much going on for anyone to pay much attention to a few people going down the access port."

"Sounds reasonable," Bobbie Ray agreed. "Maybe we should get some orange coveralls. After all the media attention with the arrival of the *Enterprise*-D, no one will think it's unusual for workers to access old tunnels."

"Fine," Titus said, resuming control of the expedition. "Then you'll be ready to go on the next free day?"

"Sure; should we tell Starsa?" Jayme asked.

"The last thing we need is her medical alert going off," Titus protested. "This isn't some joyride we're going on. It's serious. Both of you should make sure you really want to do this."

Jayme nodded. "If you go, then I should go, too. I checked, and it *is* safer with three people."

Bobbie Ray yawned, reclining back on the cushions of his bed. "I think you're blowing this whole thing out of proportion. We saw those caves. Looks like an afternoon stroll to me."

"Just you wait and see." Titus tried to sound ominous, but Bobbie Ray ruined it by laughing.

Irritated, Titus left as the laughter continued to ring out behind him. He decided to take the transporter to the workout arena to blow off some steam. He couldn't wait to get that big Rex down on *his* turf. Then they would see how tough he was.

By the time their next free day came along, the *Enterprise*-D had finished its preliminary investigation on Earth. The analysis of the artifacts found at the dig site suggested they originated from the planet Devidia II in the Marrab sector.

It was barely dawn when Titus woke to the news that the *Enterprise*-D was breaking orbit and was en route to Devidia II to investigate. He quickly called the others to get them moving. They needed to get past the upper tunnels and into new territory before the caverns were filled with secondary Starfleet investigators.

Bobbie Ray was like a limp rag, never eager to get up early, and being provocative undoubtedly because he knew how impatient Titus was to get down to the caves. "Yeah, yeah, just a few more minutes," the Rex repeated, rolling over lazily.

Titus prodded him again, fresh from his own shower and ready to go. When Jayme poked her head around the door, also up and eager, Titus finally warned, "I'll tell everyone you wimped out and we had to go without you."

That did the trick, and within minutes the three cadets had transported into Chinatown. Jayme had taken the entire Quad on a tour of the city soon after the academic year began, so Titus had already gotten a glimpse of the riot of color and noise and smells offered by the historic district. The streets were narrow canyons—very different from other Earth cities he'd seen so far, with their open green parks and towering spires. They had to watch their step along the sidewalks to avoid the squatting Asians who were tending their ion-grills, roasting a variety of real and exotic animal products right on the street.

Bobbie Ray kept stopping to toss credits at the vendors, picking up skewers of unidentifiable meat, while Jayme kept running into the makeshift booths to rifle through colored scarves and costumes. Titus was too busy trying to get his bearings with the map on his padd, but somehow in the past few hundred years, the street locations and names had inexplicably shifted.

"We'll never find it!" he finally exclaimed, standing in the center of a five-way intersection that shouldn't have existed.

Bobbie Ray stuck a large fried insect in his mouth and briskly began crunching. The guy had a bottomless pit where his stomach should be.

"Close your mouth!" Jayme snapped, obviously disgusted by the sight of legs and feelers being randomly mashed around in the Rex's mouth.

"Want one?" Bobbie Ray asked, offering her a plasteen container that was piled with the desiccated bodies of Terran grasshoppers.

"You know," Jayme told him with a wicked glint in her eye, "you shouldn't wear that color. Orange on orange makes you look like a big Zarcadian squash."

"Will both of you pay attention?" Titus demanded. "We're going to have to pick another access port. We'll never find the one in here."

"Oh, give me that!" Jayme snatched the padd from his hand, muttering under her breath about "tourists."

With a few flicks of the screen, she overlaid a current map and zoomed in on their targeted access port.

"Here it is," she said. "Right behind the Ho Ching Acupuncture and Telekinetic Healing Clinic."

"Oh, what a relief," Titus said sarcastically, taking back his padd.

"What would you do without us?" Bobbie Ray commented, grinning around the spindly legs of the grasshoppers.

* * *

Jayme was right—no one paid any attention to three orange-clad workers opening the access port in the alleyway. Kids were running past, people were hanging clothes out overhead, and antigrav carts trundled by on both sides laden with warehouse goods or fresh produce.

Closing the access portal overhead, they stood in a rounded dirt-floored chamber similar to the one shown on the media broadcasts where Data's head was found. Titus felt a sinking feeling, wondering if all the caverns had been reconditioned by the work-forces over the years.

"This way," he ordered, keeping his worries to himself. At the rear of the chamber was a long ladder, leading down. Here the walls were rougher and the black pit was too deep to be illuminated by their handlights. Titus began to feel a little better. "Down we go!"

"Wait," Jayme said, unslinging her pack. "We have to put these on."

She held out the white jet-boots issued by Starfleet.

Titus took one look and groaned. "We don't need those!"

"I'm not going down without safety gear," Jayme insisted. "And I'm not going to let you two go, either. This is supposed to be fun, not life-threatening." She glanced down into the shaft. "And those rungs look slimy."

Bobbie Ray checked the two pairs she set out for them. "You brought my size!"

Jayme slipped her white boots on and tightened the straps. With a little puff of dust, she activated the jets and lifted a few inches off the ground. "Good for thirty hours use."

Bobbie Ray buckled his boots on and was soon

lifting himself up to the ceiling. "Maybe we should skip the ladder and go down this way."

"Maybe you want to give up now and go back to the Quad!" Titus retorted. "What's the use of exploring if you might as well be in a holodeck?"

Both of them hovered silently, staring down at him. After a few moments, Titus flung up his hands. "Have it your way, then! But we only use the boots in an emergency or I'm quitting right now."

Jayme sank back down to the ground. "That's why I brought them. For emergencies."

Titus waited until Bobbie Ray also slowly floated down before jerking on his jet-boots and tightening them in place. *"I* think if you can't manage to hang on to a ladder, then you get what you deserve."

Bobbie Ray laughed. "Then you go first, fearless leader."

Titus had the satisfaction of hearing the Rex's laughter abruptly end as they started down the ladder. For most humanoids, any sort of vertical drop offered a test of nerves. Especially when you couldn't see the bottom.

The light at the opening at the top dwindled as they descended. He skipped several side tunnels that went in the direction of the Presidio and Starfleet Academy, choosing to go as deep as he could. The fracture widened at the bottom, becoming more rugged and raw. They climbed through a steeply inclined crack, into an underground canyon that stretched as far across as the Academy Assembly Hall. A stream had eroded the bottom into a gorge, and they had to edge along the wall, brushing their hands against the slippery, calcified coating on the rocks. Titus could imagine the tremendous force of earthquakes breaking open the crust around the San Andreas Fault, leaving behind this network of caverns and crushed rock.

They passed cave flowers slowly extruding from holes in the rock, growing from the base and curling back like squeezed toothpaste. Titus checked one of the largest, nearly twenty-five centimeters across, and found that the delicate formation was pure gypsum. There were also shields or palettes forming from water seepage through cracks. The ridges of calcite were deposited on both sides, growing radially into parallel plates or disks, separated only by a thin opening through which drops of water continued to fall. Jayme stopped behind two large circular shields, her light outlining her body through the translucent calcite.

Titus was more than pleased with their awe and wonder at the underground world. But he wasn't satisfied yet. Bobbie Ray refused to acknowledge the effort it took to climb down so far, and he even scaled the wall bare-handed to get the tip of a crystal-clear stalactite for Jayme. Her glance at Titus clearly said who she thought was winning this little contest of skills.

Titus took them up a high talus mound and into the next cavern, where flowstone coated the cave fill, narrowing the volume of the void. This cavern was filled with fallen ceiling blocks and most of the stalagmites had been broken off near the base by earth tremors. Additional seepage gave them an unusually fat, short appearance.

They retreated back to the shaft. Though the ladder left off, the fractured hole continued down. Titus uncoiled the rope he had brought and hooked it onto his belt. The other two followed him without a word of complaint.

A couple of dozen meters down the shaft narrowed, too small for them to go any further, but another fracture led east, fairly horizontal, following the path of the caverns far above them. Water coated the walls and floor, and here Bobbie Ray had even more of an advantage with his surefooted agility. Titus and Jayme kept slipping, and once Titus would have fallen badly except for Bobbie Ray's obliging hand.

After clambering carefully some distance through the tunnel, Titus noticed a fissure overhead only because he was looking for it. With the help of Bobbie Ray's height and reach, they muscled their way up the fissure into another large cavern, in line with the other two they had already explored.

"It was cut off from the last cavern by the talus mound," Titus explained nonchalantly as first Jayme, then Bobbie Ray, emerged through the jog in the fissure that led into this small cavern. They were slightly elevated above the floor.

Titus was pleased that he had guessed correctly. Jumping down, he felt the loose rock shift and slip under his feet. Jayme actually went down on her hands and knees, unable to keep her balance, while Bobbie Ray hung on to the stone lip they had just jumped over, staring up open mouthed at the dramatic low-hanging ceiling that dripped continually. The fat drops sparkled like rainbow stars under their handlights.

Titus knelt and picked up some of the rocky debris on the floor. "Hey, these are cave pearls."

"Real pearls?" Jayme asked, picking up a handful of the shiny white spheres. "They're huge!"

"It's calcified gravel and bits of stuff," Titus clarified. "You don't find them very often, usually only in unexplored caves. I wonder if we're the first ones to find this place."

"That was a tricky entrance," Bobbie Ray agreed. "I would have never seen it."

Titus finally had his moment of satisfaction. He felt as if he had been trying to catch up to his roommate since they both arrived at the Academy. Except that Bobbie Ray had all the advantages of a childhood on Earth, supported by wealthy parents, while Titus felt like some kind of country bumpkin, unable to tell a sonic haircutter from a steak knife.

"Look up here!" Jayme called, halfway up the gentle slope of the talus incline. "I think the ceiling fell in back here."

"It looks like the roof sank until it ran into the ground," Bobbie Ray agreed, swatting at the elusive, fat drops that continually bombed them from above.

They climbed the shifting slope to the point where the ground and ceiling met. The rounded debris constantly moved under their hands and knees. Titus examined some of the bits, and was surprised to see elongated pieces as well as the more traditional "pearls."

"Why aren't there any stalactites in this cavern?" Jayme asked, standing in the last possible space at the upper end. A dense curtain of drops speckled the air in front of them.

"This cavern is lower than the others. If there's too much water, there's no time for the sediment to form between each drop," Titus explained. "That's what makes the cave pearls—the sediment forms as they're polished and agitated by the water."

"I think they're beautiful," Jayme said, gathering a few in her hand.

Titus squatted down next to her in a relatively drip-free zone. He aimed his tricorder at one of the elongated pearls. "This is bone! Human bone!"

Bobbie Ray immediately dropped his pearls, absently rubbing his hands on his coveralls as he looked at the tricorder readings. "You're right. They're ancient!"

Jayme was also hanging over his arm, trying to see. "Give me a second," he ordered, keying in the commands. "Somewhere between twelve and fifteen thousand years old!"

"That's when humans first moved onto this continent," Jayme breathed, gently cupping her pearls in her palms. "They must have used these caves as shelter or storage. Maybe even burial. This is amazing!"

Titus barely had a second to absorb their find before Bobbie Ray muttered, "Uh-oh! I think we've got trouble."

The Rex was staring back at the hole they had climbed up. Water was welling up and pouring over the low lip that held back the piles of cave pearls. It made a rushing sound as it disappeared into the cave pearls piled on the floor.

"Oh no!" Titus exclaimed, running back down to their only entrance to the cavern. Now it was full of water. Even worse, water continued to pour over the stone lip and began to rise among the cave pearls. Soon, it had flooded the shallow basin and was rising higher, filling the cave.

"What's happening?" Bobbie Ray cried in true panic. "How are we going to get out?"

Jayme dipped her fingers in the water, sticking

them in her mouth. "Salty. That's what I was afraid of. The tide must be rising."

They both turned to look at Titus, mutely demanding that he do something. He knew he probably looked as panicked as Bobbie Ray. "The tide?"

"Yes, the tide's coming in," Jayme repeated, frantically scrambling through the cave pearls to the wall, searching up it with her handlight. "I don't see a high-water mark anywhere. Could it . . . is it possible . . ."

"You mean this whole cave gets filled with water?" Bobbie Ray asked in a high voice.

Titus could only shake his head. "I don't know! We don't have oceans on Antaranan!"

"What!" Jayme shrieked. "You brought us in here and you didn't know what you were doing?"

Bobbie Ray leaned over the hole, digging at the rising water with his hands. When he came up soaked, his fur sticking out in clumps and clinging to his surprisingly skinny neck, Titus had no urge to laugh. The fear in the Rex's eyes was too real.

"I'm going in," Titus said, suddenly feeling much calmer, knowing that he had to take control. He got them into this mess.

"You'll drown!" Jayme cried out. "That tunnel we came down—it's lower than this cave. It must be filled with water, too!"

Titus swallowed, remembering how long the tunnel was. "We may not have oceans on Antaranan, but that doesn't mean we didn't have water. I'm a good swimmer."

"I'm not!" Bobbie Ray wailed, trying to shake the water from the fur on his hands. He was shivering and wet through.

"Get up to the top," Titus ordered. "I'll have you beamed out of here in no time."

The other two cadets reluctantly retreated as he flung gear from his pouch—water flask, extra rope—leaving only the necessities, with just enough room to spare so he could wedge his jet-boots in.

Standing hip-deep in the hole, wincing from the biting cold water, he glanced back up at the cadets. "Hang tight!"

They didn't look reassured.

Taking a deep breath, he ducked under the water. Immediately he knew it wouldn't work. The surge of water welling up carried him back to the surface.

As he broke into the air again, he was saying, "All right! It's all right! I've got an idea."

He quickly removed the jet-boots and strapped them on. Water was nearing his waist now. He didn't care if it killed him, he wasn't going to give up this time.

Diving down headfirst, he got around the jag in the fissure and then turned on the boots. The jets churned the water and almost drove him into the rock wall, but he eased off the power and used his hands to guide him down to the tunnel. Underwater, even with the handlight, he could hardly see, so he groped his way down, feeling the scrape of rocks against his coveralls as the boots propelled him through the water.

He knew he had reached the tunnel by the strong surge of the current pushing him in the direction he wanted to go. But he was running out of oxygen. His jaw clenched as he gunned the boots, squinting his eyes against the pressure of the water as he shot through the murky light cast by the glow of the jets.

Everything was getting dark and hazy, and his chest seemed ready to burst. Titus wasn't sure he was going to make it to the vertical shaft.

* * *

Jayme felt sorry for Bobbie Ray, huddled next to her at the top of the talus slope. "Maybe it won't reach this far," she offered.

Bobbie Ray was wiping at his fur with the fleshy palm of one hand, smoothing and smashing it, pressing all the water out. Then he would twitch and shake, making the damp hair stand out again. Then he would pick another patch and begin the whole process over again. It seemed like more a nervous reaction than an effort to dry himself.

"Do you think he drowned yet?" Bobbie Ray asked, unable to meet her eyes.

"Umm," she murmured, "by now, he either drowned or got out alive."

"Are you going to try it?" Bobbie Ray asked.

Jayme wasn't aware that her calculating glances at the hole had been that obvious. "I'll try it before I drown in here."

Bobbie Ray went back to stroking his fur, concentrating on every swipe.

"I'll help you," she assured him.

"That won't do any good. I could barely pass the Starfleet swimming requirements. And you don't know how hard that was for me."

Jayme silently patted his knee. She wasn't sure she could make it, but every bit of her mind and body was focused on that hole, ready to dive through the water and turn on her jet-boots just as Titus had done. Even if it killed her. Because that was better than sitting here until the water rose up around her chin.

"I just wish I knew if he made it," she murmured.

"Wait a few more minutes. Maybe he's at a public transporter terminal right now. There was one right outside the access port."

They both stared at the hole.

* * *

The shaft was full of water, too. Titus desperately revved the boots, aiming straight up, his hand clenched on the control so tightly that even if he drowned he knew he would surface.

When he thought he was passing out, he broke into air. A shower of water rose with him, and his surge in speed left him gasping and laughing and, when he finally could, crying out in relief. Arrowing up, he raised both arms, trying to pick up more speed, thinking about Jayme and Bobbie Ray back in that death trap.

He was going so fast that the opening approached before realized it. Braking, he hit the ceiling and bounced down, managing to twist in midair so he would land on the floor of the access entrance.

Still panting and gasping, almost hysterical with his near miss, he rolled over in the dirt, trying to wipe away the muddy dust that settled on his face and eyes. When he could finally see, Starsa, Moll Enor, and Nev Reoh were several meters away, standing in the access room and staring at him.

"What happened to you?" Moll Enor demanded.

"What are you doing here?" Titus said at the same time.

Starsa raised one hand slightly, blinking in amazement at his dramatic appearance. "I listened outside your door the other night, and I heard you planning to come down to the caves without me—"

"You what!" Titus interrupted.

"I followed you," Starsa admitted, "but then the hole started filling with water, and you didn't come out."

"We beamed over when she called us because we were afraid you were in trouble," Moll Enor added.

"Jayme and Bobbie Ray!" Titus forgot about Starsa's gross invasion of privacy—just one of many. "They're trapped in a cavern. We've got to beam them out fast—"

"I already tried that!" Starsa interrupted. "You went below the network of seismic regulators. The active energy field is interfering with the sensor locks on the transporter."

"That's why we brought the sonic cutter," Reoh agreed as Titus clutched at his hair.

"Where?" Titus demanded. He grabbed the cylindrical unit, practically ripping it from Reoh's back. Leaving the others to follow as best they could, he turned his jet-boots on and jumped into the shaft, hardly breaking his fall toward the rising water.

Jayme and Bobbie Ray were treading water, barely six feet over the original opening into the cave. "It's easy," Jayme told him. "Just dive and when your boots are pointed up, hit the jets."

Bobbie Ray nodded glumly, more concerned with keeping his chin out of the water than judging the angle of the hole. Jayme reached up, but she couldn't touch the low-hanging ceiling.

"We're running out of time. You have to try it," she told him.

The Rex took a few deep breaths, then a few more, hyperventilating to get enough oxygen in his system. With a thumbs up, he splashed awkwardly under the water. Jayme peered through the brackish water, ready to cheer as he dove through the hole. But even before his hindquarters went through, he was pushing back out and paddling frantically up for air.

He grabbed onto her, almost pulling her under as he

sprayed her with water. "Let go!" she shouted, trying to pry his fingers off her. She gulped air just before going under. Then her instincts kicked in and she was more concerned with getting away from him than helping.

"I'm sorry!" was the first thing she heard. "I'm sorry!"

Jayme tried to catch her breath, treading water out of his tremendous reach. She knew Titus had brought then down here because he wanted to get one over on Bobbie Ray. She had agreed to come along because, secretly, she also wanted to see the dashing know-it-all brought down a few notches. It seemed like all the girls in the Academy—except for her and Starsa— thought Bobbie Ray was the hottest thing in a uniform. She couldn't get over the fact that all her friends were drooling over that smug, self-satisfied grin. Now his whiskers hung almost straight down, dragged by the water at his chin. If only Titus could see him now.

But they hadn't counted on this.

The water was rising. She could almost touch the ceiling. But she couldn't desert Bobbie Ray. "Now what do I do?" she moaned.

"Right there," Titus ordered, positioning himself at the top of the talus slope.

Nev Reoh nearly knocked over the sonic cutter as he and Starsa hung on to stabilize it. Titus swore under his breath at the Bajoran. He had tried, but the cutter was too powerful for him to stabilize it himself. And it took too long for the others to climb down and join him.

Water poured into the first cavern and coursed through the crevice just below the ledge they had to use to get to the next cavern. Titus practically ran to the rear of the second cave, working on the assumption that the top of the talus slope was the narrowest point of the barrier leading into the next cavern.

Moll Enor adjusted her safety glasses. "Are you sure about this?"

Titus took hold of the handles of the sonic cutter, snapping to Reoh, "Get it locked, will you! We're running out of time."

With more brute force than was usually necessary, Titus aimed the cutter at the rubble near the ceiling of the cave. Dust and bits of rock were flung back and caught in the stasis field, hanging in mid-air until he shut off the cutter for a moment to see his progress.

Reoh clambered up peering under his arm. "How far?"

"You think I know?" he demanded, taking hold of the cutter once more.

With another everlasting flurry of stones and the straining whine of the cutter, Titus kept the beam pointed at the rocks long after he should have paused and checked his progress. "Come on!" he muttered through gritted teeth. "Give!"

"Wait!" Moll Enor yelled through the rumble of cut rock. "I see—"

Titus was suddenly pulled forward as the sonic cutter broke through the rock. Leaving the beam on short intensity, he swiped around at the rock to widen the gap.

As soon as the cutter was deactivated, Moll Enor ducked through the hole ahead of him. "Bobbie Ray! Jayme! You okay?"

Titus pushed her through and with one pass of his handlight, he knew. "It's not the right one."

Moll Enor splashed down into the water. "Jayme!

56

Bobbie Ray!" Her dark skin made it difficult to see her in the dim light.

Nev Reoh poked his head through. "Are you sure they aren't there?"

"Pass that cutter in," Titus ordered. He had been afraid they weren't in the next cavern—it was even lower than this one. "It's the next cave."

As he set up the sonic cutter, he didn't add the words that rang through his head—*I hope it's the next one.*

"The water is rising in here," Moll Enor murmured behind him.

"Yeah, and every cave is lower than the next one," Titus explained.

"Why are you going through this part?" Reoh asked, even as he helped.

"The ceiling's collapsed in the next cave. We've got to aim lower or we'll just bore through rock over the top of it."

"Oh." Reoh looked frightened, standing knee-deep in water. Starsa clutched him, practically pulling him off balance to keep herself from falling into the water. Reoh steadied her and aimed the tricorder at the wall. "I don't read any lifesigns. Do you think they're okay?"

"I don't know," Titus said as he opened up the power on the cutter again.

"You better try it," Bobbie Ray told her, gasping in the depleted oxygen. Their faces were bobbing near the ceiling now. "Before we run out of air."

"We would have already suffocated if there weren't air seeping in," she countered.

"The point is," Bobbie Ray reminded her, "you can't breathe underwater."

"What about you?" she asked.

"I'll take my chances."

Numbly she looked at him, those big golden eyes, the orange fur plastered to his face. "I can't leave you here!"

"You have to try to get out."

Desperately she glanced down at the hole, nearly ten feet below them now. "I don't know if I can make it."

"You have to try," he insisted.

"I'll try only if you follow me."

For a moment Bobbie Ray seemed about to refuse, then he suddenly nodded. "Sure. Maybe I can make it if I follow you."

Jayme narrowed her eyes. "You serious?"

"Sure, why not? Die here, die down there—what's the difference?"

She hardly believed him, but in their current situation, what choice did she have? "You better follow me," she ordered. "Or *I'll* kill you."

Bobbie Ray actually smiled at that. "Yes, sir!"

"Okay, breathe deep." They both took deep, cleansing breaths, five or six each. "Ready? Then here we go—"

Jayme ducked underwater, but she heard the rumble and saw a bright light glinting through the water. When she broke surface, Bobbie Ray hadn't even submerged. Instead, he was pointing to the side wall near the ceiling. A hole was opening up, and they were drawn along with the water pouring out of the cavern.

"Hello?" a frightened voice called.

"That's Moll Enor!" Jayme cried out. "We're here! Enor!"

They started swimming toward the hole and were easily sucked through with the water. Sitting on the rocks, hip-deep in water, looking up at Moll Enor, Nev Reoh, Starsa, and Titus, all she could say was, "What took you so long?"

"Hey," Titus said defensively. "I told you I'd take care of everything."

"Well, at least you're working together now," Superintendent Brand told the Quad as they stood in a row in her office. "That's some progress."

Bobbie Ray and Starsa looked pleased with themselves. Even Reoh relaxed. But Jayme, Titus, and Moll knew better.

"You would be good cadets if only you could work toward something constructive," Brand added. "Since T'Rees is on field assignment, he won't receive the formal reprimand that will be placed on each of your records."

Titus was glad to hear he wouldn't have to explain this to their Vulcan quadmate. He thanked whatever gods there were that T'Rees was temporarily on field assignment at Starbase 175.

Brand's severe tone eased somewhat. "Because you conscientiously notified the authorities about the cavern you discovered containing the calcified human bones, I have decided *not* to place you on probation."

Titus finally began to breathe easier. They had just barely gotten off probation from their first Quad reprimand, and it felt like he'd been waiting forever for the next tryouts to join the Parrises Squares League.

Titus shifted. "Excuse me, Admiral?"

"Yes, Cadet?"

"I checked before we went down, but there are no rules against entering the access tunnels."

Brand raised one brow. "No, but there are rules

against doing something that can get yourself killed. You *do* admit you nearly got yourselves killed?"

He swallowed. "Yes, sir."

Brand turned to Moll Enor and Nev Reoh. "And you *do* admit that taking a sonic cutter down there was dangerous? The maintenance workers have to shore up that region. You could have destabilized the entire fault zone."

"Yes, sir!" they both answered immediately.

Brand considered them seriously for a few moments. "I won't ask what possessed you to venture into the caverns in the first place, however it was a smart move to have a backup team ready." Titus couldn't look at the smirk on Starsa's face. "But I warn you that another Quad reprimand will require that you re-do this academic year—the same class, same Quad next year."

"Oh, no!" Starsa exclaimed, then quickly put her hand over her mouth.

"Oh, yes," Brand assured her. "In Starfleet, we either win together or fail as a group. Here at the Academy, when a group regularly fails together, then we find that it serves in the long run to give them additional time to work things out." She actually smiled. "It saves wear and tear on your fellow officers later on down the line."

All of the cadets looked a little queasy at the prospect of repeating their hard work. For the first-year cadets had the hardest time. Rarely were field assignments given to unproven freshmen. They would be stuck at the Academy, stuck in their Quad, for another year. While everyone else they knew would venture into the galaxy, serving temporary duty on starships and starbases from here to the borders of the Romulan, Klingon, and Cardassian territories.

The others glanced at Titus more than they had in the beginning. He suddenly knew how Jayme must have felt the last time they stood in Brand's office— like all the silent blame for their punishment was being heaped on *her* head.

"Wc'll do better," Titus assured Admiral Brand, taking it on himself to speak for all of them.

She fixed her all-seeing gaze on him. "Make sure that you do."

Chapter Three

"BE SURE TO TELL ME what it's really like," Moll Enor insisted to Bobbie Ray. "Describe exactly what happens into a tricorder and send me a copy."

Bobbie Ray rolled away, pulling a pillow over his face. "Come on, you've seen the holos like everyone else."

"That's not the same as being there." Moll Enor crossed her arms, realizing it was impossible to make the spoiled Rex understand what a unique opportunity he had. By next month, Bobbie Ray and his parents would be visiting the Bajoran sector, where a stable wormhole had recently been discovered. Moll was absolutely certain that the view from the newly designated Starbase, DS9—watching the wormhole open to another part of the galaxy, millions of light-years crossed in an instant—would be vastly different than merely looking at a holo-image.

"You're so lucky your parents are taking you,"

Jayme told him enviously. "The *Endeavor* will be leaving the Cardassian border and probably won't get anywhere close to the Bajoran sector this summer. But my aunt is hoping we do get into Klingon territory while I'm visiting."

"I wanted to go with friends," Bobbie Ray said from under the protective shadow of the pillow. "But Mother keeps talking about 'losing me' and how we have to spend more time together."

"I'll take your place," Nev Reoh offered. But his tentative joke had too much yearning in it to amuse anyone.

Moll bit her lip, ducking her head. It was Reoh who should go to Bajor now that the Cardassian occupation had ended—not Bobbie Ray but Reoh, the former Vedek who had never set foot on his own homeworld. From his tone, she could tell he hadn't been able to arrange passage during the upcoming summer break. Yet he had been all smiles lately, too pleased with the liberation of his people from the Cardassian occupation to talk about his own thwarted desire. Moll liked him even better for that.

Titus stood up, his hands on his hips. "Are we here to finish our Quad project or gossip about our summer vacations?"

"We've only got to test it again and we're through," Moll Enor reminded him.

"Then we're through for the year!" Starsa exclaimed, clapping her hands. "No more classes for two months!"

"Then let's do it," Jayme agreed, rocking forward on her knees to examine their proton chain-maker one last time. "Where's the sample?"

Even Bobbie Ray rolled over and watched their

preparations. A limen stalk was placed in the receptacle where the target laser fell on a crosshair.

Moll moved closer to watch Jayme and Starsa, their resident engineers, work over the chain-maker. Moll's contribution had been the data on proton structure and characteristics. One of her specialties was astrophysics, and she had suggested using protons, the chief constituent of primary cosmic rays. Titus and Jayme had wanted to use an antiproton chain, figuring it would be more dramatic, but the others voted down the idea because of the large containment field that would be necessary to hold the chain-maker and its fuel.

"Kind of simple, if you ask me," Jayme grumbled, not for the first time.

"It's brilliant!" Starsa contradicted, laughing. "It's a variation on an old idea. Instead of a molecular beam, we're narrowing the focus to protons. That means it can be used for ultrafine incisions."

Titus held up another limen stalk, jabbing it at his neck as if the errant vegetable was attacking him. "The dreaded limen stalk! That'll teach 'em!"

Everyone laughed, but Nev Reoh tentatively said, "If we can indicate that genes can be cut in living tissue without damage, that would be a genuine contribution."

Titus patted him on the back. "Sure, you just keep thinking that. All I want to do is ace our Quad project and report to the moonbase for shuttle-supply duty."

The cadets went back to talking about their plans for summer vacation as Jayme ran through the preliminary sequence, heating the gas and mixing the vapors. Even T'Rees confided that he planned to go back home to Vulcan before beginning his last year at the Academy.

No one had asked Moll what she was doing, and naturally, she volunteered nothing. It was a little-known fact of Trill physiology that some needed to return to the pool periodically after being joined with a symbiont. The first two years of a host's joined life was usually spent in or near the Institute, adjusting to the memories and new sensations. Since Moll was a first host, she didn't have the memories—except of the pool and some sort of common mental bond that all the symbionts shared before joining. But she did have the strange sensations, feeling different than she used to be, yet not anything in particular.

Maybe she didn't *need* to go back to the pool, but in a very real way, it was the most familiar thing she had left. More familiar than her parents and her family, left so long ago and not by her choosing.

Suddenly Moll Enor realized Jayme was looking right at her, that strange fascination in her eyes. She was pointing to the lever that would release the proton beam. "Do you want to open it? It was your idea to use protons."

The others nodded, mostly not caring one way or the other. Moll stiffly went over to the chain-maker, shying away from the questioning smile in Jayme's eyes, wondering as always why the younger woman always seemed to be watching her. Not for the first time, Moll thought that maybe she should confess she wasn't as interesting as Jayme obviously thought. That contrary to the popular stories about Trill, there was no one inside her body except for her. No extra lives, no superior wisdom, no exciting stories to tell. But now it would only be another few days and their Quad would scatter to the four corners of the galaxy, to return to Starfleet next year to a new Quad and new roommates.

"It's been a memorable year," Moll Enor told them all as she flipped the lever.

Since she was closest, she was the first to see the fine trail of smoke that rose at the contact of the beam with the limen stalk. She was turning in question to Jayme when the beam exploded.

Jayme hit the floor next to the bed, flung there by the percussion wave. Moll Enor landed next to her, but she didn't open her eyes. At first, all Jayme could see was the smoke and destruction in the room. Starsa's gasps sounded painful, and Titus was swearing in Antaranan, a pungent language for a frontier colony.

"Moll," Jayme called softly, coughing, then tried again. Before she could get really worried, Moll opened her eyes and blinked up in confusion. "Are you okay?"

"I bumped my head, I think," she said, sitting up and avoiding Jayme's supporting hand.

Vaguely disappointed, Jayme went to help the others. Starsa's arm and back had been burned right through the uniform. Echoing down the hall, from somewhere in her room, her medical monitor began to beep.

Jayme ran for her biogenerator in the drawer next to her bed. T'Rees had more experience with Starsa's various injuries, so Jayme gave him the generator and went to Titus, who was still sitting on the floor, looking dazed.

"What happened?" he asked.

"I don't know." She knelt down to examine the long cut on his cheek caused by some of the flying wreckage. "Protons are one of the most stable subatomic particles you can work with. Maybe the velocity selector was creating two discrete beams and they got crossed somehow."

Starsa was pale beneath T'Rees's arm. "That would have blown up the Quad."

Bobbie Ray was sitting bolt upright, staring at the blackened wall and the melted table where the chainmaker had once sat. "It *did* blow up the Quad!"

"I meant the entire building," Starsa retorted. "That was nothing as far as proton explosions go."

"Oh, *really?*" Bobbie Ray asked. "Why didn't you mention this little fact about proton explosions *before* we started this project? We should have stuck with my idea."

"Your idea was illogical," T'Rees told Bobbie Ray. "We were required to complete a Quad project, not a sports competition."

"Now we don't *have* a Quad project," Titus reminded everyone. "Now we are in very deep trouble."

Nev Reoh ran into Jayme's room, having fetched another biogenerator. She snatched it from his hand.

"Hold still," Jayme ordered Titus, making him turn back to her so she could aim the biogenerator at the cut. "You're lucky it didn't get your eye."

"Yeah, sure," Titus agreed sourly. "Then we'd be in sick bay right now, reporting the failure of our Quad project instead of waiting another twelve hours for the review board to convene."

"What happens if we don't hand a project in tomorrow?" Starsa asked through gritted teeth.

Jayme finished swiping the biogenerator over Titus's cheek and jaw, taking away the last reddening. "Then we get a Quad reprimand."

"But if we get another reprimand—" Starsa started.

"We have to repeat the year!" Titus finished for her.

Moll pushed herself up unsteadily, making her way to the remains of the chain-maker. Nev Reoh joined her, staring down anxiously. "Maybe there's some way we can salvage it," the Bajoran suggested.

"Salvage?!" Bobbie Ray exclaimed, gesturing to the remains. "There's nothing left of it! Eight months work down the drain."

Moll took Jayme's tricorder, silently gesturing for Jayme's permission. She nodded as Moll began a systematic sweep of the destroyed device. Meanwhile, Jayme told Starsa, "Stop squirming, you're making T'Rees miss huge spots."

She turned her biogenerator on Starsa, relieving T'Rees who stood and surveyed the ruin with an almost satisfied expression. "I would like to remind everyone that I am on record as objecting to this choice of Quad project."

Titus turned on T'Rees. "You're just calm because you know you won't have to repeat this year like the rest of us."

Stiffly, T'Rees replied, "I am calm because I am a Vulcan."

"Yeah, well, I'd like to see how a Vulcan takes it when an entire year's work gets blown out the window!"

"There is no need to raise your voice," T'Rees said mildly.

"That's easy for you to say!" Titus yelled.

Quietly, Moll turned to Jayme. "I'm reading minute traces of copper ions in the lead chamber. Are they supposed to be there?"

Jayme went to look at the tricorder. "It could be from the barrel of the slot. I think it had some copper in the superstructure." Moll was doing a subatomic survey of the chain-maker. "Why bother?" she asked. "It didn't work."

"Now what are we going to do?" Bobbie Ray wailed. "I don't want to take quantum physics again!"

T'Rees placed his biogenerator back in the pouch. "We report the failure of our project to the review board."

"No, we've got to come up with something else," Starsa insisted.

"Something we can do in one night that will look like it took the entire year to make?" Titus asked. "I don't think so."

The sounds coming up the lift tube were familiar to the Quad. *"Hsst!"* Bobbie Ray called out, his sensitive hearing the first to pick up on their visitors. "It's the medical team."

"Quick," Titus ordered Starsa. "Get back to your room. You go with her, T'Rees. Tell them you just had a little accident—nothing important."

T'Rees stayed right where he was. "I am incapable of lying."

"Jayme, you go then," Titus said in exasperation.

Starsa slipped out of the room with Jayme right behind her. She turned to say, "Better clean up in here in case they come in."

Titus gave her an affirmative signal and Jayme left, thinking everything was at least partially under control. But the medical team took an unusually long time examining the burns, which both girls admitted came from Starsa's contact with a malfunctioning proton device. They were worried about the traces of radiation they found in her skin caused by the beta decay. They had to explain that the breakdown was supposed to take place inside the lead-chamber, during the spontaneous transformation of the neutrons in the nucleus of the sulfur atom that would release the protons. Jayme thought it was fascinating the way the medics traced the exact amplitude of the beta decay, comparing the magnetic polarization of the nucleus against the spin vector of the electrons.

The medics checked Jayme, too, and when there were no traces of beta decay in her skin cells, they asked to see the accident site. Jayme was impressed by their through investigation of the room. But the others had already removed the slagged table, and the blackened wall was covered by a colorful bedspread that usually adorned Bobbie Ray's bed. Jayme wondered why she hadn't thought of putting up some sort of decoration in this half of the room. Maybe then she wouldn't have been haunted for so many months by the departure of Elma. That's why she had offered the space for their Quad project, to give the others a good reason to come over and keep her company.

"You're clean," the medic finally told Titus. To Jayme, she said, "Good work on that cut. Nice edges for an amateur." As she murmured her surprised thanks, the medic added, "You know we have to report this."

Bobbie Ray flung himself down on the bed again. "Report everything! It doesn't matter. The review board will know soon enough."

"Take that up with the Superintendent," the medic said with a shrug. She gave Starsa a reassuring pat. "Just get some rest and you'll feel better. You're already 80 percent acclimated, so next year should be much easier on you."

"Thanks," Starsa said as the medic left. "Great, I'll be raring to go and we'll all be stuck here again. We'll never get off-world assignments if we have to stay first-year cadets. It's humiliating!"

Jayme glanced around. "Where's Moll? With T'Rees?"

Rom shrugged. "She cleaned up the debris and packed a few pieces in that bag of hers. Then she left."

"You let her go?" At Titus and Bobbie Ray's nod, Jayme exploded, "How could you? She got hit on the head! Something could be wrong with her."

"She's fine!" Bobbie Ray said defensively. "She was poking around in that mess, muttering about acid catalysts and oxidation. I figured it was some kind of astrophysics thing."

"Do you see any stars in here?" Jayme demanded. "She could have been delusional. And none of you even noticed."

"Hey, she can take care of herself," Titus protested. "Come to think of it, I've never seen *anyone* take better care of themselves. We better start worrying about what we're going to show that review board tomorrow."

"Today," Starsa corrected, chewing on her thumbnail.

Titus glanced at the chrono. "Great, today. The day we all get put back a year."

Jayme was shifting back and forth uneasily. "I think we should look for Moll Enor. Something could be wrong with her. It doesn't sound like she was thinking rationally."

"Maybe you should start looking for an explanation for all this," Bobbie Ray pointed out. "It was your idea."

"*My* idea?" Jayme repeated incredulously. "I wanted to use an antiproton chain. Didn't I, Titus?"

"We both did."

Starsa rubbed her eyes sleepily. "I thought using a proton chain would be safer. I guess I was wrong."

No one could chastise Starsa when she looked so strung-out. Reoh was quick to assure her, "We all worked on the project. Who knows why it failed? You can't blame yourself."

Starsa still looked worried, an unusual sight. "Maybe we could get B'Elanna to look at it. She's just down two floors."

"You mean *Torres?*" Bobbie Ray asked incredulously. "Great! Do you want to make things worse?"

"Torres is a great engineer," Starsa insisted. "Better than any of us."

Jayme silently agreed, having watched, mouth hanging open along with the rest of the first-year engineering students, as Torres argued with Professor Chapman over material stress levels and Starfleet safety protocols.

"It's no use, even Torres couldn't fix this," Jayme told Starsa. "You should go to bed before you fall down." Jayme helped her quadmate back to her room and into bed, leaving Titus and Bobbie Ray to mull over the mess they were in, with Nev Reoh hovering in the background offering useless suggestions with infinite hope, as always.

Jayme didn't go back to her room after Starsa had lain down. First she made sure T'Rees would keep one eye on his roommate, then she went down to the transporter room to check the logs. There was no record in the short-term memory of Moll Enor beaming out of the Quad tower. She checked the gardens around the Quad, asking other cadets if they had seen Moll, until she realized that she had been busy with Starsa and the medics for over an hour during the beta treatment. She rushed back to the transporter and found a record of Moll's transport in the long-term log. The Trill had gone to the Academy Database.

When Jayme reached the Database, the cadet staffing the entrance confirmed that Moll Enor had arrived a couple of hours ago, acting focused and preoccupied, as usual. Jayme felt a little better, but she searched through the mostly empty rooms of the Database, too worried to give up and go back to the Quad, but not so upset that she wanted to make the situation worse by notifying security.

Jayme placed a message on the network, but Moll didn't respond. She checked the transporter logs of the Academy Database when she was certain Moll was no longer there, but there was no record of the Trill beaming out. She wandered along the cobblestone walkways between the Quads for a while longer before she finally gave up.

As she slipped back into their Quad, trying not to wake everyone, Titus, Bobbie Ray, and Nev Reoh were waiting in her room.

"Well?" Nev Reoh asked eagerly. "What did you find out?"

"I couldn't find her," Jayme admitted. "She went to the Database and then disappeared."

"What?" Bobbie Ray exclaimed. "You've been looking for Moll all this time? What about our Quad project?"

"What about it?" Jayme countered. "It blew up."

"But *why?*" Titus insisted, stepping closer. "We have to tell them something—"

"How am I supposed to know why it blew up? That would take weeks of reductive analysis!"

Bobbie Ray shrugged helplessly, turning away.

"Well, I guess that's it. Might as well get a few hours rest before the review board."

"You're going to sleep again?" Titus demanded.

"I'll stay up," Nev Reoh offered.

"For what?" Jayme asked. "There's nothing we can do now. Even if I did figure out what went wrong—that the velociter malfunctioned or the gas streams were mixed at too high a temperature—what does that give us? Nothing! We'll have to take the bits and pieces in to show the review board that we tried. Then our careers are in their hands."

When Titus rolled out of bed the next morning, having never really gone to sleep, Bobbie Ray was briskly snoring on the other side of the room. That guy could fall asleep anywhere, anytime.

"Get up!" Titus ordered, roughly prodding the large mound beneath the blankets. "Doesn't anything ever get to you?"

"You do," Bobbie Ray assured him, raising his head and peering through sleep-heavy eyes. "I'm rooming with Starsa or Jayme next year."

"How can you lie there and act so blasé about being left back?"

Bobbie Ray sat up and stretched, seeming to isolate every muscle in his body through the most incredible contortions Titus had ever seen. Of course, after eight months of watching the Rex do exactly the same maneuvers, he could have mimicked every one. That is, if he cared to look like that.

Finally Bobbie Ray grinned down at him, still blinking sleepily. "It's only a year. I bet I ace mechanical engineering next time around."

Titus just stared at him. "How stupid of me. What a fantastic reason for the six of us to repeat an *entire* year—so you can get a better grade. I feel so much better, now."

Titus left his roomie laughing behind him, but it wasn't much better when he ran into T'Rees in the hall.

"We have twenty-four minutes before we must report to the review board," the Vulcan told him. "We should not compound matters by being late."

"Hey, you're talking to the wrong guy," Titus defended himself. "I'm here, I'm ready to face the plunge."

T'Rees cocked one brow. "What 'plunge' are you referring to?"

"Never mind," Titus told him. "I'll get the others."

When he went into Jayme's room, she was stuffing the pieces of their proton chain-maker into a carryall. "This looks carbonized," she told him, holding up one piece of metal with a blackened edge.

"Is that all you discovered?" Titus asked.

Jayme shrugged. "If I had a week and a lab, we could probably put some of the pieces together and figure out what went wrong. Do you want to tell that to the review board? That we need another week?"

Titus grimaced as he shook his head. "Very poor planning. But we put it through all those tests a couple of weeks ago, and nothing happened then."

"Maybe something went wrong when we were working the bugs out, those last calibrations of the velociter, maybe. Or one of the structural components failed." At Titus's glare, she added, "It happens! It happens all the time. That's what engineers are for—fixing malfunctions."

"Well, it's time to face the review board," Titus told her, realizing that he had to ease off. The others didn't know how difficult it was for his family to have him away from Antaranan. Or how important it was that he succeeded, so he could send back the supplies and equipment they needed to bring life to the barren soil of the colony.

Everyone was in the hall except for Moll Enor. Jayme was instantly panicked. "Where is she? Did she come back last night? We have to call the medics—"

"Calm down," Titus told her, grabbing hold of Nev Reoh's wrist to show everyone that he held a disc in his hand.

"Moll sent me a message," Reoh told them, finally able to speak when the rest of them shut up. "She'll meet us at the review board."

"Then shall we proceed?" T'Rees suggested, ignoring Jayme's relief.

"Proceed away," Titus told him with a sigh. At least T'Rees wouldn't be held back a year along with them. Titus had been angry after their spelunking disaster that Moll, Reoh, and Starsa had gotten a Quad reprimand when all they had done was save Bobbie Ray and Jayme. T'Rees hadn't done a thing *and* he didn't get punished.

Titus had petitioned Admiral Brand to review the matter, thinking it wasn't fair, but she had denied his request to remove the Quad reprimand from the academic records of Moll Enor, Nev Reoh, and Starsa Taran. Not for the first time, Titus was grateful T'Rees hadn't been involved. Even having to repeat the year wouldn't be so bad without that Vulcan in their Quad.

Moll was starting to think her quadmates wouldn't arrive by the time the review board convened. But they tramped in together at the last minute, looking as glum as any set of cadets she'd ever seen.

Only Jayme seemed happy to see her, anxiously asking, "Are you all right? Where were you last night? I looked all over the Database."

"Oh," Moll said softly, wanting to hit herself when she realized what she had done. She had run off alone again instead of working with the group like they were supposed to. No wonder they were all looking at her like she was a freak.

Before Moll could tell them what she had discovered, Admiral Leyton's aid was standing at the door of the conference room. "Quad #64C. Are you ready to present your project?"

"Yes, sir," T'Rees said for them.

They filed in and stood at attention in front of the review board: Superintendent Brand, Admiral Leyton, and Professor Chapman, since they had submitted their preliminary designs and requested an engineering specialist on their board.

"Quad #64C, at ease." There was a hint of warm humor in Brand's voice. "How nice to see you all together under more auspicious circumstances."

The other cadets shuffled and murmured, while Jayme held up the carryall in her hand. "Umm . . . we had a little trouble with our Quad project—"

T'Rees interrupted, acting as their spokesman as they had agreed, "Quad #64C attempted to create a proton chain-maker. I believe you have the specs we submitted."

"We have gone over your proposal," Admiral Brand agreed. "An intriguing idea."

Jayme shook the bag, letting the sound of broken components tinkle out. Chapman and Leyton began to look concerned.

Moll realized she would have to present her material first in order to get the most impact out of it. The others could add whatever they had discovered afterward. It wasn't the right way to do it, but her mistaken approach made it necessary.

"That is the waste material," Moll said, pointing toward Jayme, who obligingly held the bulging bag a little higher. *"These* are the components that tell us what happened."

Moll set the cracked spin velociter and part of the lead-chamber with the gas indicators down on the table in front of the review board.

"You have the proposal containing the original intent of our Quad project," Moll reminded the review board. "However, we discovered a new process, whereby a controlled, deflagrating explosion can be chemically created using a pure proton chain."

Bobbie Ray's mouth was hanging open, a sure sign he knew nothing whatsoever about their Quad project. But then again, last year, one of Moll's quadmates had questioned their project as if he was part of the review board—and they had still managed to pass.

Professor Chapman had his chin cupped in his hand, and Moll wasn't familiar enough with him to know if that was a good sign or bad. But Brand was looking interested.

"Usually molecular chains are used in detection chambers," Moll explained, "for studying the deflection and dispersal properties of various molecules. With our proton chain, we were able to do the same thing on a subatomic level."

"But what about the uncertainty principle—" Starsa started to say, but was nudged into silence on both sides by Titus and Jayme.

Professor Chapman glanced at Starsa. "I agree with Cadet Starsa Taran—what about the uncertainty principle? It is impossible to specify or determine simultaneously both the position and momentum of a particle."

"That's nullified by the deflagration, the explosion, which freezes a microsecond in the sample mass." Moll gestured to the pieces in front of them. "Unfortunately, we weren't expecting to create the potassium nitrate that caused the explosion, but four things came together in our experiment: the potassium hydroxide in the base gas with protons effused from sulfur atoms, along with the nitric acid in the lemin stalk that was catalyzed by the carbon of the cut edge."

In the pause, Nev Reoh added helpfully, "There are unusually high levels of nitrogen in lemin stalks."

Jayme started rummaging in the bag. "I have a piece of the carbonized metal where the proton-chain made contact. If you want to see it."

Professor Chapman held out his hand. "Yes, please."

Moll Enor waited until Jayme had handed over the bit of metal. "If the same combination could be used in strictly controlled levels of chemicals under a stasis field, then a detection chamber could be created that offers a new window into the nature of subatomic particles."

The members of the review board were nodding, fairly impressed. Even Professor Chapman spoke as if to a colleague. "Brendenson has been working on something similar on Maxum V, but it's a highly theoretical and innovative approach."

"It's way out of our field," Moll Enor agreed. "We discovered this purely by accident. And, now, if my quadmates would like to add anything."

As a group, the other cadets pulled back slightly,

shaking their heads, trying to deflect the attention of the review board.

T'Rees must have realized the flustered picture they made, because he smoothly interjected, "Thank you, Cadet Enor, I believe you have adequately summed up our project."

"That was beautiful," Jayme agreed fervently.

"I must agree," Brand said, smiling as she stood up and came around the review table. "I think there's a certain irony in the fact that your Quad project failed, and yet you generated useful and insightful information from that failure."

"Yes," Professor Chapman agreed. "I recommend you send your research to Maxum V. It's a fine thing for cadets at the Academy to be able to contribute to cutting-edge science."

Brand shook Moll Enor's hand, since she was the closest. "I'm glad to see your Quad has learned to triumph in the face of adversity. Your Quad project has passed."

"Congratulations," Admiral Leyton said, and for the first time there was a slight easing of his normally stern expression. "May your next year at Starfleet Academy be as successful."

Moll Enor smiled along with the rest, shaking hands next with the Admiral, then the professor. But she couldn't help hoping that next year she would do better than she had this year.

The next day, Jayme still hadn't gotten over the miracle Moll Enor had accomplished with a tricorder and one night's work. The rest of the Quad had jumped on Moll the moment they were outside, with everyone asking questions at once. Moll had explained that her eidetic memory had allowed her to instantly make associations and connections across the engineering disciplines. Jayme confirmed that it would have taken her a week of computer analysis to reach the same facts, and even then, she might not have seen the new use for the proton-chain that Moll had discovered.

It was beyond genius, and Jayme even defended Moll when she meekly agreed with T'Rees's chastisement of her for not including the rest of the Quad in the analysis. Jayme would have loved being involved in the research, but she knew they would have slowed Moll down by questioning her and following false leads.

Jayme kept sighing with envy at Moll's accomplishment—and the Trill wasn't even interested in engineering!—while she packed her transport containers for the break. She couldn't decide what should stay in storage over the break and what she should take with her. Since it was her vacation, she included all of her body paints and every one of her tights, figuring she might find use for everything while she was observing the Starfleet crew of the *Endeavor*.

Starsa suddenly called through the halls, "Everyone, you have to see this!" She poked her head around Jayme's door. "Have you seen it yet? The class standings were released."

Jayme took the padd from Starsa and quickly ran through the first class as Starsa chattered, "We're all in the top half. I barely made it! But it's the second-year cadets you have to see."

Jayme scrolled past the names until Starsa impatiently pressed the key that took them to the top. "There," she said, as if it were her own name listed at the head of the sophomore class. "Moll Enor is first!"

"Moll . . ." Jayme breathed, feeling a rush of pride

at having known it all along, having seen the brilliance of the Trill before anyone else. "I should have expected it."

"Really?" Starsa asked, giving her a curious smile. "I knew she studied a lot, but I didn't think she was that brainy."

"Look what she did with our Quad project," Jayme reminded her.

"Moll saved our butts," Starsa cheerfully admitted. "Look, everyone," she told the cadets coming down the hall. "Moll Enor is first in her class!"

The others had just heard as well, and soon there were more cadets in their Quad than Jayme had ever seen, all looking for Moll to celebrate her success. The Trill came into the Quad in the midst of it, and the gracious, humble way she accepted everyone's congratulations impressed Jayme like nothing else had.

She was struck silent by the sheer number of Moll's friends. It seemed like everyone at the Academy was here, with more coming in, a steady stream of cadets shaking Moll's hand and patting her on the back. Her dark face was flushed to the spots as she ducked her head slightly, abashed by all the attention.

Jayme felt all choked up, and as Moll passed by, she reached out to grasp her hands, trying to convey her feeling through more than words. "I bet you get all kinds of assignment offers now. You can go anywhere for the break." At the leap of surprise and realization in Moll's eyes, at her sudden yearning, Jayme added, "Even to the wormhole."

Moll Enor was quickly guarded again, in spite of her pleasure. "How did you know I wanted to see the wormhole?"

"I heard what you said to Bobbie Ray," Jayme said sheepishly. "I could tell how much it means to you."

"Maybe I will go to Bajor," Moll agreed with a rare smile, as others moved in to shake her hand and pull her along, all of them wanting to touch her, as if she were a talisman of good luck.

Jayme was jostled to one side, watching Moll's dark, glossy hair clinging close to her head as she moved gracefully among the crowd. Suddenly a year's effort to push away her feelings collapsed in ruins. She had always been fascinated by Moll Enor, and lately, it seemed as if everything the Trill did was designed to enchant in the most subtle and perfect ways. Jayme's admiration for her had grown with every moment, snowballing since their Quad project review. Now, watching her proudest moment, Jayme realized she was helplessly, hopelessly in love with Moll.

Chapter Four

Second Year, 2369-70

"THIS LOOKS LIKE SHUNT," Nev Reoh said, blinking at the low, brown hills that ran to the horizon under a blinding white sun.

"What's that?" Bobbie Ray asked.

"Shunt is the Bajoran resettlement camp where I grew up!"

As a last-year cadet, Nev Reoh had waited as long as he could before taking the required survival test. His two teammates, Bobbie Ray and Starsa, were second-year cadets, and had chosen to take the test as soon as they could. He knew the only reason they had agreed to have him on their team was because there was a certain sense of obligation that came from being in their first Quad together.

There were lots of other cadets who would have liked to team with Starsa and Bobbie Ray. They were both athletes—Bobbie Ray because of his admirable physique and Starsa in spite of hers. It had taken

Starsa nearly a year to acclimate, but now she seemed to be making up for lost time.

Reoh had watched her the entire summer, and she hadn't seemed to mind being stuck on Earth for her vacation break. From his workstation assisting at the Academy Database, he could see a bunch of cadets who grav-boarded on the concourse. Of all the crazy cadets who were left on the campus, it was Starsa who made him swallow in fear. The way she hung off the front edge, riding that fine line between the fastest speed the human body could achieve and out-of-control tumbling, made him dig his fingers into his own thighs until blue bruises rose to the surface.

Reoh hadn't dared to ask Bobbie Ray and Starsa if he could join their team. It had been their decision to include him. When he had first found out, he gave thanks to the Prophets, in spite of his crises of faith. At least he had a chance to survive, let alone pass the test.

Reoh had prepared for the test by taking extra survival courses every semester. Now, they were standing on a ridge overlooking a barren, rocky desert of sharp cliffs and flat-topped plateaus very much like the only place he really did know. "Shunt!" he repeated, shaking his head.

"You say that like it's bad," Bobbie Ray pointed out. He was looking very uncomfortable in his rubber suit. "Where's all the water? Down in the cracks?"

"If this is like Shunt, we'll have trouble finding enough water to stay alive."

Bobbie Ray undid the neck buckle of his waterproof suit. "Everyone said there would be water. The last eight times the survival missions took place in a marsh, a bog, two swamps, and four rain jungles."

Reoh shrugged, just as boggled as Bobbie Ray was over this unusual twist.

Bobbie Ray let out a frustrated growl as he peeled the rubber suit off his fur. He had been so smugly satisfied as the cadet ship had beamed them down to the surface, so certain that he wouldn't have to suffer four days of wet fur, that his disgruntlement at finding themselves high and dry was ironic, to say the least.

"Where's Starsa?" Reoh asked, glancing around.

Bobbie Ray tossed the rubber aside. "I didn't see anything until you came over that ridge."

"I was put down a few meters inside that ravine," Reoh said.

Bobbie Ray judged the angles and decided, "I bet she's over there. If not, we'll be on higher ground and able to see better."

"What if we don't find her?" Reoh asked.

"We'll find her." Bobbie Ray started toward the rise about a hundred meters away from them. "You've got room for that, don't you?"

"Uh, sure." Nev Reoh paused long enough to gather up the rubber suit and stuff it in his bag before hurrying after the Rex.

From their vantage point on top of the slight rise, Reoh could see that, like Shunt, this plateau desert was a step-by-step series of fairly flat-topped units separated from each other by cliffs and broken, steep-sided slopes. One glance revealed it to be a vast and lonely land, with no signs of life other than a few brown, scraggly plants on the edges of the plateaus or down in the narrow canyons.

Bobbie Ray planted his feet firmly, looking around for Starsa and bellowing her name—"Starsa!!" They could hear his voice echo against the flat-sided canyons for what seemed like miles. In an aside to Reoh, he added, "This is the ugliest place I've ever seen."

Reoh swallowed. "I sort of like the colors." The layers of rock exposed by the canyons were brilliantly varied in hues of purple, red-orange, yellow, gray, and creamy beige. Maybe that explained his innate desire to study geology—rocks, he knew. "It could be a color chart lesson in planet-building."

Bobbie Ray gave him a look. "It's useless land. All chopped up."

Reoh gave up trying to explain exogeology to the Rex. "Where's Starsa?"

"How should I know?" Bobbie Ray retorted, looking annoyed.

"What will we do if we can't find her?"

"We'll find her."

"How?" Reoh asked.

"Stop asking me so many questions!" Bobbie Ray kept gazing around, as if hoping Starsa would pop up from one of the canyons.

Nev Reoh obediently kept his mouth shut. The only thing that made him feel better was knowing that his vital signs and location were being closely monitored by the cadet ship. The four dozen cadets participating in the survival test had placed the temporary orbital satellites in the stratosphere of the planet themselves. If anything serious went wrong with a cadet, a transporter would pluck them from the surface before serious injury could occur. There were a number of stories at the Academy, like the one of a cadet losing her grip at the top of a Cipres tree and falling thirty meters before dematerializing in front of the shocked eyes of her survival team. Of course, that cadet had failed the test, but all Reoh cared about was that she had lived to tell about it.

Reoh opened his mouth but remembered in time that Bobbie Ray didn't like questions. He quietly followed the orange Rex as they tried to triangulate their arrival positions. Ideally, a survival team rejoined shortly after transporting to their test site, and then rejoined with as many other cadet teams as possible while managing to stay alive.

By nightfall, Nev Reoh and Bobbie Ray hadn't found a single cadet—including Starsa.

Reoh ventured to ask, "We'll fail if we don't find her, won't we?"

"Yes," Bobbie Ray said shortly, as irritable as if Reoh had personally caused Starsa's disappearance.

They settled in for the night under an overhang of sandstone, where the shale at the base of the cliff had been cut away by the wind. There was a nice pile of sand that had been deposited by the last rush of water that had run through the canyon—but from the lack of growth, Reoh estimated that had been seasons ago.

"I hope Starsa is all right," Reoh worried as they smoothed the sand into a place to sleep.

"She's fine. She's just down in one of these pits, like us," Bobbie Ray grumbled. They hadn't been able to build a fire because of the lack of suitable vegetation. But the absence of any sort of print or trail in the sand had led them to believe it would be safe to sleep on the ground. Actually, they had no choice. It was either here or up on one of the plateaus, exposed to the rising wind. At least in the canyon they had a semblance of shelter.

Bobbie Ray yawned, obviously feeling better now that they weren't tramping uselessly all over the place. "Besides, as long as we find another team, then we can still get a qualified-pass."

"But Starsa's part of our team," Reoh protested. "We *have* to find her."

Bobbie Ray shrugged, no longer assuring Reoh that they would find her. Reoh didn't say anything, but he didn't like it that Bobbie Ray was giving up on her. He worried about Starsa almost as much as he envied her innocence of sexual tensions and her lack of fear or self-doubt. She lived completely in the moment, unrestrained, yet unaware of her own freedom. But that made her vulnerable in ways the other cadets couldn't imagine.

Reoh slept uneasily that night, and at one point he felt Bobbie Ray get up and squirm into his rubber suit for warmth and protection against the wind. Without any cloud cover, the heat was released from the atmosphere and the rock walls lost their warmth almost as soon as the sun went down.

Soon after, Bobbie Ray passed out so solidly that even when Reoh moved in closer, trying to get out of the wind behind the bulk of the Rex's body, Bobbie Ray didn't stir. He kept thinking about Starsa, out there all alone.

The next day they spent circling the area where they had beamed down. They stayed on top of the plateaus except when they had to descend into the canyons to cross to another section. In the morning, Bobbie Ray once again seemed confident they would soon find Starsa. But as it turned out, the plateaus were deceptively hilly, hiding variations and crevices in the land until they were nearly upon them.

Nev Reoh felt completely at home in the arid place. Most of the scant vegetation grew in the eroded crevices leading off the plateaus—a few pygmy trees similar to Austrid conifers. The central portions of the high lands were barren hills formed from ancient layers of volcanic ash that had turned to clay. It was likely that plants couldn't get a hold in the clay because it swelled in the brief wet periods and shrank when dry.

Half the morning was gone when they came upon cadets Puller, Reeves, and Ijen. Nev Reoh's worst fear was finally confirmed when he saw Puller's contorted, misery-filled face. Reoh had suspected something was wrong because of Starsa's disappearance, but Bobbie Ray hadn't listened to him.

Now, none of the cadets could ignore Puller's anguished breathing and sweaty skin. The other team was halfway down a cliff, in an inpromtu camp on a narrow ledge. Nev Reoh couldn't stop staring at the shreds of Puller's uniform hanging down one side, echoing the torn flesh underneath. He wheezed from ribs broken in the fall, through his chest was now bound with a support bandage from the medkit.

Reeves and Ijen looked almost as bad as Puller, having tended their pain-racked teammate all night on their exposed perch.

"Why hasn't the cadet ship picked him up?" Bobbie Ray demanded, his voice rising in fear. They were all looking up into the shimmering pearl grey sky.

"Didn't you call?" Nev Reoh asked, nearly panicked at Puller's streaky white pallor. He was already digging into his pocket to grab his own alarm-summons. Bobbie Ray tried to stop him, but Reoh activated it anyway, not caring if they failed their own test. He wanted Puller off these rocks and in sick bay *now*.

They waited, expecting a medical team to appear or to hear a summons on their comm badges, keyed to the cadet ship overhead. But nothing happened, and there was no sound but the wind whistling around the rocks.

Ijen sat with her head in her hands, obviously too weary to get her hopes up that a different alarm-summons would work. "Something's happened to the cadet ship," she said dully.

"What could happen to the cadet ship?" Reoh blurted out.

Reeves obligingly began to supply possibilities. "It was attacked, it crashed, the crew died of food poisoning, the life-support system failed . . ."

"What are you saying?" Bobbie Ray demanded. "That we're on our own down here?"

Ijen slowly raised her head. "Yes."

Bobbie Ray didn't believe it. Starfleet wouldn't desert a bunch of their own cadets. There would be so many people protesting in the Federation Assembly that the Academy would never recover from the scandal. Even with the evidence right in front of his eyes, he couldn't believe they would all slowly die on this waste-planet.

"Maybe there's something magnetic going on," Bobbie Ray told them. "Something in the ionosphere. You hear about it all the time."

Nev Reoh was nodding in support, still anxiously looking to the sky as if to expect the cadet ship to suddenly appear overhead.

But Reeves shook his head. "You helped deploy the satellites. This planet has a very weak magnetic field because it's no longer tectonically active."

"Well, it's got to be *something*," Bobbie Ray insisted. "Excited electrons in the stratosphere, or solar flares. We just have to wait for it to subside and they'll come get us."

Now both Reeves and Ijen were looking at him, their expressions dull from lack of sleep. "If we don't get more water soon," Reeves said, "we'll be dead before that happens. We've explored as far as we dare to go alone, and we can't leave Puller—"

"We'll find water," Bobbie Ray told them, glad to have a firm objective in mind.

Reoh hesitated. "Uh, that might not be so easy."

"We'll find water," Bobbie Ray repeated, looking straight at the former Vedek, willing him to shut up.

"Uh, sure," the other cadet agreed, cowed into submission.

It was difficult climbing down the rest of the way into the canyon, even for Bobbie Ray. He couldn't understand why the other cadets had tried to descend at that point—it was obviously unstable. Perhaps the cadet ship was waiting to see how the other two handled the situation they'd gotten themselves into. But Bobbie Ray somehow doubted that. Puller was in real pain; no one in Starfleet could be that callous.

Bobbie Ray led Reoh down into the canyon, heading in the direction that Ijen and Reeves said appeared to lead toward a larger canyon. He and Reoh would be needing water soon, too. They had been looking for water all morning, in fact, and Bobbie Ray was becoming adept at recognizing the types of terrain that seemed like they should contain water, but in fact, didn't.

"Sometimes you find seeps back in these overhangs," Reoh said for perhaps the dozenth time.

Bobbie Ray folded his arms, waiting while Reoh crawled forward on his stomach under the sandstone ledge, feeling around cautiously with one hand. The only life-forms they had discovered were long, ovoid insects with too many short legs that burrowed into the sand. He shuddered, thinking of where they had slept the night before, but at least he'd had the protection of the waterproof—he knew it would come in handy!

There was also a round-bellied rock-dweller that had extra-long legs and lived in the dark places in the cracks. The Bajoran soon emerged, shaking his hand as if he'd encountered something scurrying inside. Bobbie Ray couldn't help twitching his own hands, as if invisible insects were crawling across his fur.

"No water," Reoh reported glumly.

Bobbie Ray started to say, "I could have told you—" when the sound of rocks falling further up the canyon made him stop.

"Starsa!" Reoh exclaimed to Bobbie Ray. He called out, "Star-sa! We're over here! Starrr-sa!"

Bobbie Ray led the way down the canyon, heading further away from the sick-camp, as he was beginning to think of it. They went much further than it had sounded, calling out all the way, but they didn't see or hear anything else. Not for the first time, Bobbie Ray regretted that their comm badges were only linked to the cadet ship rather than the other cadets.

"Look at this," Reoh suddenly said.

Bobbie Ray joined him at the base of a loose pile of sedimentary rock. A few had rolled beyond the pile, and nearby there was some sort of mark on the hard-packed, rocky soil. Four parallel grooves dug deeply into the ground.

"What is it?" Reoh asked.

Bobbie Ray glanced around, unsheathing his knife. "I don't know."

"It doesn't seem natural," Reoh said hesitantly.

Bobbie Ray stuck the point of his knife into the groove and it sank nearly three inches. "Looks dangerous, whatever it is."

"Try scratching the surface," Reoh suggested.

Bobbie Ray jabbed at the dirt; he had to dig a few passes to make his ragged groove as deep. When he stood up, he kept his knife out—the only weapon the cadets had been allowed to bring on this test.

"It looks dangerous," he repeated. "I figured this was too easy."

"Easy? You call this easy? Puller's chest is shattered, we can't find Starsa, and all of us are going to die if we don't find water soon." Nev Reoh stared at him. *"Easy?"*

Bobbie Ray let him blather on, mainly keeping an eye on the surrounding cliffs. He led them out of the narrow chasm as soon as he could, certain that their best tactical situation would be to climb up on the plateaus.

Luckily, when they reached the top, they were on a long and winding plateau that was interconnected with several other large islands in the midst of the canyonlands. Nev Reoh pointed excitedly to a fluff of green vegetation at the bottom of one of the deepest canyons. "There has to be water down there."

The sun was at its height, and the day grew hotter as they slowly made their way down into the canyon. But they were rewarded at the bottom, where there was a small seep in the wall. It trickled through a thick, green mat of algae before disappearing into the damp sand at the base of the cliff.

Bobbie Ray shoved his way through tall grass and tiny-leafed bushes that grew protectively around the seep. Filling all five canteens took some time, as Reoh patiently held each nozzle up to the trickle. Bobbie

Ray scouted the area, never going much further than a few hundred meters before Reoh's worried call drew him back.

Bobbie Ray was certain he heard footsteps, and twice he turned to see the movement of a shadow. But on this planet they'd seen nothing capable of moving or casting a shadow—not a cloud, not a plant, not any animal.

As Reoh was capping the last canteen, Bobbie Ray stood over him, keeping an eye out for his stalker. He was certain he was being stalked. If Titus had come on the survival test, he could have assumed it was him, because that would be typical of the cadet. But Titus and Jayme had passed Academy-approved survival tests the summer before their first year.

"I'm finished," Nev Reoh announced, moving stiffly from having crouched so long next to the seep.

Bobbie Ray ignored Reoh's request to rest, and he rushed the older cadet back to the spot where they had descended into the canyon.

Nev Reoh tried to pull away. "If we follow this canyon, we should meet up with the one below the sick-camp."

"No, we need to get higher," Bobbie Ray insisted. "We're easy targets down here."

"It will take extra time to climb to the top," Nev Reoh said patiently. "Can't we follow the canyon a little ways to where the walls aren't so high?"

Bobbie Ray wasn't looking forward to scaling the cliffs either, but he wasn't in the mood for arguments. "I'm not leaving our ropes here."

"Why not? We'll have to come back again to get more water. We've got three more days left of the survival test." Before Bobbie Ray could veto his suggestion, the Bajoran added, "And if we can find a way through the bottom of the canyon, we can carry Puller here. That way we won't have to keep taking the water to him."

The threat of having to plod back and forth every day between the sick-camp and the seep was enough to make Bobbie Ray agree. But as they made their way down the canyons, he kept a wary eye out for the stalker.

Nev Reoh kept pointing to rock outcroppings and shimmering heat distortions, asking Bobbie Ray what they were. The Rex mostly ignored the Bajoran, focusing outward, refusing to believe that, like Reoh, his own paranoia was making him see and hear things.

The first warning came almost subliminally, a subtle whine carried with the wind. Then a distant wail that rose and sustained, raising the hackles on his neck.

Reoh's eyes grew round as Bobbie Ray tensed, instinctively bracing himself for an attack as the wail ended in a shriek.

"What was that—" Reoh started to ask.

"Hsst!" Bobbie Ray cut him off with one firm swipe of a paw just millimeters from his face. Nev Reoh looked as if he swallowed his own tongue, but he was quiet.

Bobbie Ray paced around the other cadet in a tight circle, looking upward as another wail began to rise, echoing back and forth against the canyon walls. His tail kept twitching and his fur told him there was something moving nearby, but they saw nothing.

After that, it was easy to convince Reoh that they should take to higher ground. The nearby wall was fortunately broken down at the confluence of the two canyons. Bobbie Ray could have scrambled up in minutes, but he had to go slowly and practically drag Reoh to the top of the plateau. They kept the canyon close by so they could see into the bottom—both to make sure there was nothing moving down there, and to see if it was possible to transport Puller to the seep.

They reached the edge of the plateau directly across from the sick-camp just before sunset. Signaling to the others that their mission had been successful, they started down into the ravine. Near the bottom, as Ijen was descending to help them carry the canteens, she suddenly screamed and put her hand over her mouth.

Silhouetted on the plateau above them, against the ruddy sky, was a massive, hulking form, pacing from side to side as only a hungry animal would. A low wail began to rise again, sending a shiver response down Bobbie Ray's back. They couldn't see what it was, but it slowly rose on its hind legs, lifting its arms as if in attack position.

"It's huge," Nev Reoh whispered in fright.

As the wail rose to that distinctive, soul-shrinking shriek, Bobbie Ray could only agree. "Maybe that's why we haven't found Starsa."

"Don't say that!" Nev Reoh quickly denied. Ijen joined them in the bottom, panting in fear as she stared up at the plateau where they had been not long before.

All three cadets scrambled up the opposite wall as fast as they could to the sick-camp. They weren't sure if the silhouette could reach them before they made it to their ledge, and they didn't know how many companions it might have.

"What else could have happened to her?" Bobbie Ray asked Reoh on their way up. "She's either lying at the bottom of one of these canyons, like Puller, or . . ." he drawled, nodding toward the disappearing silhouette. "We better make sure the same thing doesn't happen to *us.*"

They reached the camp, where Reeves was using a scope to see across the ridge. As the last light was fading from the sky, Bobbie Ray seized the scope from Reeves, focusing on the lurking silhouette. It took a moment for the image to clearly resolve, and then he couldn't believe his eyes.

"It looks like *him,*" Reeves said ominously, pulling away from Bobbie Ray.

"Like who?" Nev Reoh asked, not understanding.

Bobbie Ray lowered the scope, feeling dazed. "It's another Rex."

Starsa couldn't go very far with the stasis restraint locked around her ankle, keeping her within a couple of meters of the Rex. He never paid much attention to her, seemingly content with having her nearby as they hiked over the rough desert and started climbing down into one of the ever-present canyons.

She had tried talking to this Rex, as well as the other Rex who regularly appeared and disappeared as they descended to the bottom. But without universal translators, they couldn't understand her. She could understand a few words of what they were saying, but the problem was, they didn't speak very much. Mostly they seemed to communicate through body movements and subtle posturing that she couldn't begin to understand.

She had been captured remarkably easily, giving herself up before she realized the Rex had hostile intent. Her first night had been spent alone, curled up between several boulders on the edge of the largest plateau, wondering where Bobbie Ray Jefferson and Nev Reoh could have possibly disappeared to.

When she woke in the morning, the Rex was leaning over her, and at first she had smiled in greeting, saying, "Bobbie Ray! I'm so glad you found me."

But it wasn't Bobbie Ray, and the Rex had clamped one sharp-clawed hand around her ankle, locking on the stasis restraint before she knew what was happening.

Once they reached the bottom of the canyon, the Rex took her to a space shuttle that was stashed out of sight in the bottom of the canyon. He locked the stasis restraint to one of the bunks while he and his partner went exploring. Starsa could hear the wails and cries of the other Rex over the comm and with the words her universal translator could understand, it sounded as if the other Rex shuttles had drawn off the Starfleet cadet ship. She wasn't sure if they had attacked the ship, but from the viciousness of their language, she wouldn't have been surprised.

One thing she knew, these Rex weren't anything like Bobbie Ray. They looked alike—tall, broad-shouldered, with blondish-orange fur. But these Rex wore their hair longer, teased up in decorative tufts. Their teeth also seemed bigger, and their claws were much longer, sharpened to a microfine point.

At first they went out and explored the terrain together, and she could see them through the view portal at the front end of the shuttle, curved and offering a nearly 300-degree view around the sides of the shuttle. The Rex ventured out in ever-widening circles, starting off and returning to home base, as if extremely cautious about leaving her there.

Starsa was mesmerized by the view, but it was also incredibly disorienting. After several hours, she actually had to turn around, it had given her such an ungodly headache. By then the Rex had begun to split up and disappear for longer periods of time.

Starsa absurdly wished one of them would stay. She hated being alone. Her one night on the rocks had been the longest amount of time she had ever been completely by herself.

On Oppalassa, her homeworld, no one was ever alone. She came from one of the most crowded environments in the galaxy, averaging almost 100,000 people per square mile on the islands that were scattered through the shallow seas. But her people had been living under those conditions for seven centuries. She missed having her extended family just beyond the walls around her, but the Academy Quads were so similar that her heart, as well as her body, had soon gotten over her first fierce bout of homesickness.

But now she was forced to stay alone in the darkened shuttle, shackled to the bunk. She couldn't reach her bag with her gear to try to short out the stasis, and she couldn't get anywhere near the control panels of the shuttle. The interior of the shuttle was so confusing that, even if she did get loose, she wasn't sure she would be able to fly the ship. And that was saying a lot. Prior to this experience, Starsa would have said she could pilot anything that was capable of becoming airborne. But this ship was different. The dark gray bulkheads bulged outward, and there seemed to be control units and readout screens on the walls and ceiling as well as the floor.

All Starsa could do was wait, biting her nails at her inactivity, wondering if the Rex would ever return for her. She drank the last of the water from her canteen and her stomach was trying to twist out of her body in its demands for food. She wished she had eaten more last night before the Rex took away her bag, but she remembered Nev Reoh's caution just before they beamed down that they would have to conserve their supplies.

Then she started to wonder if something had happened to the Rex. Maybe she was stranded. She knew better than to panic, certain that the cadet ship would not be kept long from the planet. Someone would arrive to save them—she just needed to hold on. But her fear of being by herself, of hearing nothing but her own heartbeat, was beginning to drive her crazy. She tried singing to herself, but she had a terrible sense of rhythm and her attempts offended her own ears.

Long after it had gotten dark, both Rex returned about the same time. Starsa could see them through the front portal as they approached and softly bumped heads in greeting, a quick rub before twisting away. When the door opened, she could hear their slow, chirruping noises. Mainly it sounded like queries, questioning each other about what they'd seen, what to do about it. They both grew agitated, their tails abruptly slashing back and forth as one or the other would snarl or reach out with a sharp swipe.

They kept mentioning "Rex." That was one word familiar to Starsa because Bobbie Ray often dropped his native name into conversations. Women seemed to love the rumbling murmur, and Starsa had sometimes teased Bobbie Ray by mocking him with the sound in front of another one of his girlfriends.

Now, Starsa thought she would try it out for real. "Rum-murrow-ah," she murmured in a low voice, trying to catch that precise rise at the end that gave the Rex name such a lilting, enchanting flair.

The two Rex stopped short, looking at Starsa with almost comical surprise. She laughed out loud, unable to stop herself. Then they looked annoyed.

"No, I'm sorry," she tried to tell them. But she couldn't help giggling again at their affronted expressions. They looked exactly like Bobbie Ray that time she put double-stick tape on his sleep cushions.

The slightly smaller Rex let out a short, sharp note, very high, while the other gave a plaintive, high-to-low tone, much lower-pitched. Starsa's translator beeped and gave a literal interpretation, "Indignation! Protest!"

"All right," Starsa told them, raising both her hands. "I said I'm sorry."

Grudgingly, the Rex gave her a twisted piece of some kind of dried flesh that she had to gnaw on. They also gave her water, which she was properly grateful for. She banged the dried meat against her bunk a few times before dunking it in the remains of the water to soften it. She hoped they would get the message, but the Rex were concentrating on their shuttle controls.

Soon after that, a thrumming sound began to vibrate the bulkheads. Then she understood why her bunk was padded both below her and along the curved bulkhead. As the ship lifted off the ground, she felt a subtle pull toward the hull. She realized the gravity generators were situated so the hull was "down" from every direction. The Rex moved easily around the interior, using the controls on all four of the curved walls, resting casually on the small bare platforms and protruding benches.

Suddenly, the engineering puzzle became clear and Starsa understood how the Rex could pilot their strange craft. They leaped from one control to the other, defying the gravity to twist and turn in the air, landing exactly where they intended. It was so effortless that it looked like a beautiful dance.

The shuttle lifted out of the canyon, rotating as it cleared the top of the plateau. Starsa felt her stomach heave against the lazy turn, jostling the food and water she had eaten too fast. At first she swallowed, maintaining control, but when the ship seemed to fall sideways out from under her—while her eyes told her they were flying straight up—she let out an unattractive burp.

Both Rex swiveled their heads around to gape at her. Starsa held onto her stomach, her eyes bulging expressively as she hung on.

The Rex showed by every stiff motion that they knew what was going on. Their ears were twitching rapidly back and forth as they gently slowed the motion of the shuttle, giving Starsa's body time to adjust.

They seemed annoyed at having to move at a crawl, but Starsa thought that it served them right after leaving her alone all day. Defiantly, she took another bite of her meat stick. Maybe if she disgusted them enough, they would toss her back where they found her.

As the shuttle began to descend, she thought her idiotic plan might actually be working. But the wicked glare in the Rex's eye as he leaped toward her told her otherwise. Then he touched a hypospray to her neck and she dived into blackness, her hand still clenched around the half-gnawed meat stick.

At first Starsa thought she was dreaming, then from the brightness against her eyelids, she realized that time must have passed. She could hardly move at first, and had trouble convincing herself that she had been knocked out all night. It felt like only a second, and she was very groggy, as if she had spent the night walking around and around the shuttle. But according to the deep crease in her arm from the half-eaten meat stick, she had been lying there like a log for hours.

Neither of the Rex were in the shuttle, and moving to the furthest reach of the stasis restraint, she still couldn't see them outside. The shuttle was resting in a different canyon now, aimed toward a sort of oasis along one wall. It was the first truly green vegetation she'd seen on this planet, but then, she hadn't had a chance to see much.

Her canteen was nearby, so she drank some water to clear her head, then finished off her meal from the night before. When she had drunk as much as she could, she considered what to do with her only tool. Tightening the cap, she took aim and hurled it at the main control panel. The canteen bounced against the plassteel, but there was a reassuring crunching sound from one panel.

Unable to reach her canteen for another throw, Starsa spent her time dismantling the supports of her bunk. It was like a compulsive action, peeling the cushions off the base and wall, shredding them as she did. But if she stopped, words and images swirled around in her head as if trying to fill the void. She almost longed to be knocked out again. She had never woken up alone before, and it was deeply unnerving. The silence spoke too loudly, telling her that she wasn't there if no one was able to validate her existence. Life was interconnected—she was nothing, yet she couldn't be nothing, and she had to do something, anything to prove she was alive. At least the destroyed bunk was a testament to her will.

She noticed immediately when one of the Rex came down the rocky wash at the bottom of the canyon. He dropped down to one knee and perked his ears at some sound. Her only warning was a slight sideways flattening of his ears as the other Rex leaped out from behind a pile of jagged boulders that had fallen from the wall. Starsa thought they were fighting, but the bigger Rex rose up on his toes, dodging back before darting in to give the smaller one a few solid bats on the side of the head.

The smaller Rex bared his teeth, then, with a huge leap, he crossed the gap between them, grabbing onto the big Rex like a wrestler. They tumbled over the sand and rocks until the smaller one suddenly darted off. The big Rex let him go, shaking out his fur before opening the door to the shuttle. The chirping he was making sounded like he was laughing.

Then he saw the pile of bunk shreds scattered throughout the shuttle. Starsa looked around with him as if she had never seen it before, either. Actually, she hadn't realized how much damage she had done, and it looked even worse than it was.

The Rex made high-pitched, sustained noises aimed in her direction. He never stopped scolding her as he gathered up some of the shreds, dismayed by the extent of her work. Starsa had to cover her ears at the incessant, infuriating sounds, and she almost didn't realize how much the translator was catching.

"Pestering little female! Useless! Get rid of it," he muttered, giving her a murderous glance.

The other Rex appeared in the doorway, his ears up and alert. Their argument over what to do with her came through loud and clear. After listening to their plaintive whines, she realized how Bobbie Ray came by his fastidiousness.

Starsa didn't care—at least she wasn't alone anymore. Even better, while one of the Rex removed her restraint from the bed to his own ankle, Starsa managed to grab the tiny tool kit that was hooked to the flap of her bag. The two Rex were squabbling so hard that they didn't notice as she slipped the palm-sized kit into her pocket.

Before she could congratulate herself, she was jerked along with the Rex as they left the shuttle. She hated having to run to keep right by his side as she stumbled over rocks that he treated like smooth pavement. Climbing while restrained was even tougher. It took a great deal of time, but she managed to get up the side of the cliff, slipping more than once in what would have been a deadly fall. Every time, the stasis restraint caught her ankle and held her dangling until the other Rex could lift her up so she could grab hold of the rocks again. She felt like a toy bobbing on a string, and she began to wonder why they were bothering with her at all.

She found out when they staked her to the top of the plateau. She had a clear view of the oasis down below. The two Rex climbed back down, nearly to the floor of the canyon.

She thought they were leaving her there, exposing her to die. Her initial flush of indignation seemed absurd in the light of attempted murder, but she was comforted by her kit resting snugly against her ribs. All she needed was a little time with her tools, and she would be free of the restraint.

But the Rex stayed in sight, and she didn't want to risk them catching her before she could trip the locking mechanism. As she fidgeted, she saw what they were watching for.

Several cadets came around the bend of the wash,

distinctive in their gray coveralls. Even from a height of several hundred meters, Starsa easily recognized Bobbie Ray. They were tightly grouped, and a dark-haired cadet was being carried. She could recognize Reoh by the way he walked, a hurried rush forward, a pause to check on the hurt cadet, calling forward to the lead cadet who walked in front with a bare knife. Starsa thought she recognized Reeves, one of the guys she grav-boarded with.

She waved to get their attention, but they saw her almost at the same time. "Starsa!" Nev Reoh shouted, running forward as if a cliff didn't rise between them.

"Watch out!" Starsa frantically gestured downward, trying to get them to see the Rex. "Bobby Ray! Bobby Ray! Down there!"

They couldn't hear her because of the wind whistling through the narrow canyon. She could tell because they carefully set down the hurt cadet, while Bobbie Ray loped up the side canyon, heading toward the lowest part of the wall to help her.

She kept shouting, but it was no use. She could feel the wind snatch the words from her throat until it was raw. Her panic only made Bobbie Ray hurry faster, watching her, trying to figure out what her problem was. Nev Reoh was not far behind, calling up some kind of encouragement.

Bobbie Ray was quite close to the Rex when they emerged from the shadows of the rocks. One was on each side of him, moving in slowly.

The other two cadets below jostled in panic, dragging the injured cadet in the opposite direction. Bobbie Ray backed down the slope as fast as he could, catching up to Reoh, who was also trying to get away from the big Rex as they slowly closed the distance between them.

Starsa shielded her eyes against the blazing sunlight that glared off the polished white rocks at the top of the mesa. The Rex had used her as bait to lure the cadets in, making it easy to ambush them. Starsa leaned over the edge, straining against the restraint, trying to see as her teammates disappeared into the bottom of the canyon. They had used her as bait!

Grimly determined to make her escape, she pulled her kit from her coverall. Give her three minutes, and she would be free.

Bobbie Ray ran past Nev Reoh as they reached the canyon floor. It was like one of his childhood nightmares, being chased by a wild animal. Ijen and Reeves had dragged Puller into the niche that contained the water seep. They were standing among the pygmy trees, holding their knives out.

"I'll draw them off!" Bobbie Ray called out, hoping the Rex wouldn't stay and make mincemeat out of them.

He needn't have worried. Glancing back, he saw that the Rex loped past the other cadets as if they didn't exist. He also noticed that Reoh was right behind him, moving remarkably fast for a guy who couldn't seem to walk without stumbling over his own feet. Bobbie Ray picked up speed, wishing Reoh had veered off to help Ijen and Reeves.

"No! Stop!" Reoh called out. But he was running as hard as he could, too, with the Rex right behind him.

Bobbie Ray wasn't sure what Reoh was yelling about until he rounded a curve and came to a dead end in the canyon. He began scrambling up the steep sandstone side, honeycombed by weather. Some of the holes were a couple of feet across, others were a few meters or larger.

Nev Reoh fell further behind as Bobbie Ray reached a large hole. His whiskers quivered, sensing the eddies of the wind hitting the rear wall. The cliff grew steeper so he quickly made a tactical decision to make his stand here.

Nev Reoh was panting as he neared the lip of the shallow cave. Bobbie Ray reached down and grabbed his hand, hauling him inside.

They could hear the low-pitched growling, a curious, sustained noise. The two Rex were just below, making that sound from the back of their throats. Their tails rhythmically lashed back and forth as they crouched and glared at Bobbie Ray.

His own ears were flattened against his head in a way he'd rarely felt before. He let out a half-hearted squawk in response, a clear signal of his panic.

"What do we do?" Nev Reoh asked.

"How should I know?" Bobbie Ray countered.

"They're *your* people."

"Humans are my people," the Rex contradicted.

The two Rex climbed into their shallow cave, poised on the lip as if assessing the cadets.

"Maybe you should try to copy them," Nev Reoh suggested helpfully. "Use your tail."

"What do you mean—use it?"

"Swish it back and forth like they're doing."

Bobbie Ray glanced doubtfully back at his tail, then gave it a few experimental twitches, moving forward as he did. "That doesn't feel right, somehow—"

Before he could finish his sentence, the two Rex rushed the cadets, snarling and spitting, their tails furiously lashing back and forth. Bobbie Ray and Nev Reoh scrambled deeper into their cave, brandishing their knives more out of fear than bravado.

Snarling, the two Rex faced them until it was clear

they could no longer back up and that they weren't about to advance. Then the Rex slowly began to retreat, making odd chirping noises as if they were laughing, as if they were leaving simply to prolong the hunt. Bobbie Ray could tell by their upright ears that they knew they could attack the two cadets at that very moment and rip them into shreds with their four-inch claws.

"I didn't know they could grow that long," Bobbie Ray said in a hushed voice after the two Rex had withdrawn back down into the canyon.

Nev Reoh eyed the inch-long rounded nubs that were instinctively splayed from the tip of each of Bobbie Ray's fingers. "Maybe you should sharpen them up a little."

"Yeah, like your tail suggestion was such a great idea!" Bobbie Ray snarled. "When I want your advice, I'll ask for it."

Reoh backed up, holding up his hands. "I know you're better suited to handle this than me."

Wearily, Bobbie Ray sat down and leaned his forehead against the wall of their niche. "Problem is, I don't know what to do!"

Starsa grabbed Ijen's pack after descending the cliff to the seep. When she saw the direction they had run, she used the ropes that had been left hanging by the seep to climb to the top of the plateau.

Tracking the cadets through a side canyon, she saw the Rex pacing in the bottom. They were focused on a hole in the cliff wall, waiting for the cadets to come out of hiding.

Starsa ran around the deep cut in the plateau, to the edge just above Bobbie Ray and Reoh. She tied one end of the rope around several boulders. Crouching down to stay out of the range of the Rex's keen eyesight, she neared the edge to judge the right spot to lower the rope.

The bigger Rex abruptly stopped in his tracks, raising his head slightly and drawing back his upper lip. She could see his tongue flicking the roof of his half-open mouth. The Rex seemed to be almost in a trancelike state for a few moments, holding its breath and staring straight ahead. Then it abruptly shook its head and looked directly at her.

Starsa wasn't about to get into a staring match with the Rex. She never won with Bobbie Ray, always ending up blinking first or turning away from his huge, unwavering gold eyes.

She dropped the rope. "Bobbie Ray! Nev Reoh! Grab the rope!"

Bobbie Ray leaned out of the hole in the wall, giving her a wide-eyed stare. "Hurry!" she shouted at him.

As Bobbie Ray began to claw his way up the cliff, leaving deep grooves in the wall from his hind claws, the other two Rex retreated to a place where they could get up the cliff. Starsa chewed on her lip, watching their fast progress.

"They want *you!*" she told Bobbie Ray.

"How reassuring," he retorted, nervously watching as the Rex bounded gracefully up the steep slope.

"Help me!" Nev Reoh wailed from below, dangling from the rope like he'd run out of strength.

With Bobbie Ray's assistance, Starsa pulled Nev Reoh up at least a body length, looping the rope around the boulders to give them leverage. They gave another mighty heave, bringing the Bajoran near the lip of the plateau.

"Uh-oh!" Bobbie Ray exclaimed, as the Rex reached the plateau and headed for them.

"You're talking to them wrong," Starsa panted.

"They haven't given me a chance to talk to them," Bobbie Ray protested.

"They talk with their bodies, not their mouths! Go meet them," Starsa told him, hanging on to the rope with all her might. "Reoh, you'll have to climb up the last bit!"

Hesitantly, Bobbie Ray moved forward to meet them.

"Not like that!" Starsa exclaimed. "Make yourself look bigger! Fluff everything out—"

"I'm going to get killed," Bobbie Ray muttered.

"Think of it as stylized combat. I doubt they really want to hurt us—or they would have killed me. They're confused because you're not responding right." She grunted, holding onto the rope. "Reoh, get your Bajoran butt up here! A three-year-old could climb faster than you!"

Bobbie Ray faced the two large Rex as they cautiously approached, no longer growling as they had when he had run. He realized he was on the balls of his feet, and his shoulders instinctively squared to make as himself appear as big as possible.

They began to circle, and he kept his face toward them, backpedaling slightly to keep them from surrounding him. The smaller Rex fell back, letting the larger one move in.

All Bobbie Ray could see were the enormous incisors of the Rex and each one of those four-inch claws. The hair on his spine crawled, as if sensing the way those jaws would clamp on the back of his neck to deliver the killing bite.

"Make the first move," Starsa hissed from behind him.

Bobbie Ray gave her a quick glare. Why hadn't his parents ever taught him about Rex? Surely they knew that, going into Starfleet, he was bound to encounter his own kind. If he got out of this, he was going to have a long talk with his mother.

"Go on!" Starsa urged. "Be tough. Put your ears back, like when you're challenging someone to a fight."

"You're interfering with my concentration," Bobbie Ray snapped.

The Rex stopped, seemingly confused, looking from him to Starsa. Bobbie Ray realized she was right, and he began advancing slowly, weaving from side to side, taking care to rotate his ears so the backs faced frontward, in what Starsa said was his "growly" look.

It seemed to work, because the other Rex immediately flattened his ears, not just turning them back but making them almost disappear. Bobbie Ray tried out a low growl or two, but was less than pleased when a spine-chilling wail seemed to rise from nowhere.

"What's that?" Nev Reoh asked, peeking over the edge of the plateau.

"I think it's coming from him," Bobbie Ray said out of the corner of his mouth. This time he was careful not to break his stance. Knowing he could never compete with that unearthly sound, Bobbie Ray made a big show of moving forward a few inches, his legs absurdly stiff.

"That's good," Starsa called out encouragement. "I think you're scaring him."

"Is that a good idea?" Bobbie Ray murmured,

advancing, then pausing, giving the Rex plenty of time to call it quits.

As the Rex came very near, his head seemed to twist as if focusing in on Bobbie Ray from a different angle. He took a slow step forward and twisted his head the other way, and Bobbie Ray started to get the feeling that he was a sitting duck. A rather realistic growling whine rose from the back of his throat, rumbling out and rising in power as adrenaline-laced panic sang through his nerves.

They both slowed, moving in tiny increments, balanced only by each other's shifting. The Rex was screaming directly at him, frozen, and Bobbie Ray felt the same compulsion to glare at his rival, to move even slower, as if not to admit fear.

Suddenly his adversary lunged toward him, and Bobbie Ray shied back, trying to get room to maneuver. The Rex came in over his back to get his teeth on Bobbie Ray's neck. The cadet kicked out his leg, swiping support from under the Rex, causing both of them to tumble away from each other.

Bobbie Ray was quickly back on his feet, twitching his fur, trying to feel if he had been slashed by those deadly claws. But the Rex hadn't connected. Bobbie Ray silently blessed every hand-to-hand defense instructor he'd ever had.

The Rex seemed even more wary this time, but he stared hard at him before coming in again, taking a defensive posture. When Bobbie Ray immediately countered his stance, the Rex didn't move in as close this time. After a few frozen moments, wailing and rumbling loud enough to make Starsa cover her ears, the Rex finally began to ease back.

Bobbie Ray felt himself relax with every centimeter the Rex slowly retreated. It was so gradual that he wasn't sure it was over until both the Rex faded away, turning and disappearing down into the canyon.

"You did it!" Starsa exclaimed, clapping her hands. She jumped on Bobbie Ray, wrapping her arms around his neck.

He was practically rigid, still in his alert-stance, feeling strangely exhilarated and unwilling to break his pose. "Let go," he ordered under his breath.

Laughing, Starsa jumped down and did a little dance. "We did it! We did it!"

"They might come back any second," Nev Reoh said, edging up to them. Bobbie Ray noticed he stayed well out of arm's reach.

"No, they won't," both Bobbie Ray and Starsa said at the same time. She grinned, and he finally felt his whiskers move in response, lying smoothly against his face as his teeth showed in a smile.

They didn't even make it back to the seep to rejoin Ijen, Puller, and Reeves before the cadet ship signaled them to await transport. As the stark landscape faded from view, Bobbie Ray knew it would be forever burned into his memory, along with the victory he'd had facing down the Rex.

"There were no fatalities among the cadets," the survival instructor informed them on reaching the ship. "Everyone has automatically passed their survival test, whether they regrouped or not."

Bobbie Ray had completely forgotten about the Academy, and it seemed very far away with the battlelust still thrumming through his blood.

"When we realized it was a ruse," the instructor added, "we fought our way back though the Rex shuttles that were holding us off. We believe they were drawn here because of *your* lifesigns, Cadet Jefferson. We could tell there was a confrontation going on down there. What happened?"

Bobbie Ray shrugged one shoulder. "It was some sort of mock battle. As soon as I engaged them, they withdrew."

He knew that didn't explain everything, but he also knew there was no way to talk about what had happened. It was more subtle and more powerful than anything he had ever felt before. He was used to always being the strongest, the fastest, the most agile, but when his own kind had challenged him, he felt as bumbling and awkward as Nev Reoh. He had gone into security because it came naturally and was easy for him, but after seeing the Rex *laughing* at him while he was stuck in that hole, he realized how much he had let his natural abilities slide.

Now he couldn't wait to get back to the Academy and try some of those intimidation techniques used by the Rex. Just wait until his instructors saw what he could do!

Chapter Five

MOLL ENOR WAS RETURNING from the back of the science pod, balso tonic in hand, when she overheard Cadet Campbell saying to Cadet Wu, "I do not know the cadet well enough to say."

"Yeah, that's my point," Wu agreed with a wry grin. "You'd think after a month of living on the science station together—"

He broke off abruptly as Moll Enor appeared around the central power assembly. Cadet Wu was leaning forward curiously, intent on gossiping with the taciturn Campbell. Cadet Campbell was concentrating on his console, frowning slightly, but even he started in surprise at Moll's appearance.

That's when Moll realized they were talking about *her*. She flushed hotly, avoiding their eyes, thankful that they probably wouldn't notice the way her spots suddenly stood out. Ever since she had won top honors in her class, all the cadets knew who she was.

They constantly watched her and talked about her. She was the freak again, exactly as she had been on the Trill homeworld, where having a photographic memory was extremely rare.

"Excuse me, sir," Moll said to Cadet Mantegna, the designated commander on this tagging and tracking mission within the ring nebula. "Do you have the latest readings on the levels of interior microwave radiation?"

Mantegna sighed at her interruption, not bothering to look up. "It will have to wait a few minutes, Cadet Enor. I'm in the middle of the infrared sensor sweep right now." Mantegna flicked Moll a glance as she hesitated. "Is that all?"

"Yes, sir," Moll said, backing away.

She made it back to her station, where she was running a computer program of the numerous mathematical equations that plotted the movements of the asteroids as they spun and tumbled in the turbulence of the ring nebula, moving in a roughly helixical orbit. There was only a three-second delay from the sensor pickups to mathematical translation, so she was basically seeing a real-time flow of data, gathered for an in-depth analysis by the astrophysics lab. For Moll, the work had been routine the second day, and except when she was in command of their science pod, she had spent the better part of four weeks staring with glazed eyes at the screen, hypnotized by the chaotic pattern that appeared and disappeared within the data.

The Federation astrophysics lab, poised outside the Trifid ring nebula, was considered a prime field assignment. Though it was relatively small, it was close to Sol system, so teams of cadets were rotated in. The cadets used the science pod, the *Sagittarius,* to do the grunt work of collecting data in the neverending surveys of the debris. Based on the data, some scientists theorized that the protosolar system was destroyed when a subspace compression collided with the Trifid star, causing it to go supernova and eject most of its mass.

Whereas most nebula expand away from their source, diffusing high-energy particles and cosmic rays, the compression phenomenon caused the Trifid ring nebula to rotate in on itself, forming a churning toroid around a strong gravity well. It was almost as awe-inspiring as the Bajoran wormhole, which she had gone to see during the summer break while on field assignment on the *Oberth*-class science ship, the *Copernicus*.

Because of her first-place standing in her class, Moll Enor had also been able to choose to come to the Trifid ring nebula. From the science station, Moll liked to watch the toroid bands of color caused by the centrifugal action of the gases. The bands were separated into turquoise blue darkening to purple in the center, surrounded by a wide band of yellow, and thinner bands of red and green on the outer edge.

The colors were so brilliant that the first time she entered the gas cloud, she expected it to appear opaque inside. Instead, the interior shimmered with luminous discharges arcing between the tumbling asteroids, creating a delicate tracery of fine molecular chains, endlessly twisting and tangling together.

Her station signaled when data was received from Mantegna's internal synchrotron scan. Electrons moving at nearly the speed of light inevitably leaked into the *Sagittarius* as they spiraled about the magnetic field of the nebula. The other cadets were getting negligent with the Starfleet protocol of manually confirming the automatic scans, but it was necessary, since synchrotron radiation often distorted scanner readings.

Moll hadn't told them that Trill who were joined with the vermiform symbiont were particularly sensitive to annular phase transitions. Some joined Trill weren't able to use the transporter system. She didn't have that problem, but she didn't want to find out the hard way that the Enor symbiont was senssitive to higher levels of synchrotron radiation.

Mantegna muttered something as he abruptly began running a systems diagnostic check.

"What's wrong?" Wu asked.

Mantegna stood up to activate the power boost. "I'm trying to find out. The comm link won't open."

"Maybe something's wrong with the phase buffers on the emitters," Wukee suggested. "Or the ones on the relay. Remember last week—"

"If you would give me a moment," Mantegna interrupted, "I'll tell you where the malfunction is. . . ." Campbell turned along with Moll as Mantegna thoughtfully murmured, "Hmm . . ." over the data.

"Well? Are you going to tell us?" Wukee asked insistently.

Mantegna reseated himself at the navigation console. "The problem is in the communications relay." He scanned for the nearest relay buoy.

Since Moll received the same telemetry report on the asteroids, she knew the nearest relay was in the tertiary phase layer of the nebula—what appeared to be the thick yellow ring from the exterior. Inside, there was no difference in the twinkling brightness of layers upon layers of discharge filaments that constantly appeared and disappeared between the asteroids. But cadet research teams were only supposed to catalog and tag asteroids in the outer red and green bands, because the turbulence of the magnetic field increased exponentially toward the gravity well.

Mantegna asked Moll, "When will the next science team come through this section?"

They all knew that was the sort of question she could answer. Having once seen their assignment rotations, she would remember everyone's schedule. Suddenly, Moll felt as if the science pod was too crowded for four people and her eidetic memory.

"Not until next quarter," she said, tight-lipped. "They just came through this section."

Satisfied, Mantegna turned back to the helm to plot their course to the nearest relay buoy. He input the new coordinates to take the science pod in. "We're going into the tertiary zone."

"I'll reroute the comm to another relay buoy and notify the station," Moll agreed.

But Wukee sounded concerned as he asked, "Aren't we supposed to stay out of there?"

Mantegna raised his brows. "Communication systems have priority! Remember the regulations manual they gave us? What if a science pod got caught in a burst current and couldn't get a signal out because the relay was malfunctioning?"

Moll said reasonably, "Then they would divert their comm-link to another relay, as I just did."

Mantegna didn't deign to reply. He was too pleased by the break in their routine. Truth to tell, they all were. Moll felt a rush of anticipation at doing something new—an eager dread of not knowing, wanting to know, but uncertain without information to fall back on.

So Moll was more wary than the others, and was

the first to notice that something odd was happening. There were more asteroids in the tertiary phase, and they were moving differently. The science pod closed in, but Moll was still unable to see the buoy.

"Shields at maximum," Mantegna announced.

The pod slowed, letting their forcefield nudge away the jostling asteroids. Moll instinctively hunched down as a mountain-sized planetoid grazed overhead, shuddering as it impacted with another large asteroid, crushing a smaller boulder in between with a spray of energy sparks. Debris arched toward them, and the kinetic particles rocked the pod despite its stabalizers.

"Merdu!" Wu exclaimed, as they all shielded their eyes from the burst of light.

"Boost power to rear shields," Mantegna called out, barely keeping his voice from cracking.

Even Campbell was sneaking wide-eyed glances at the screen as he tried to adjust the deflectors to ward off asteroids.

"The buoy must have been destroyed!" Wukee gasped out. "We should go back—"

"No," Moll denied. "I've still got the subspace signal on telemetry."

Incredulously, Wu asked, *"How* could it survive—"

"There!" Moll exclaimed, pointing at the screen. "There's a break in the asteroids. . . ."

The deflectors of their pod were buffeted as they finally broke into the calm sphere at the heart of the spiraling asteroids. The communications buoy was spinning on its axis in the very center, with what appeared to be an asteroid stuck to it. They were whipping around so fast that the two blurred together.

As they moved in closer, Moll warned, "Don't get caught in the vortex."

"We're in the magnetic calm between the two

solenoids," Mantegna dismissed. "It looks like we've got a live one here."

Campbell crouched over his console as if snatching the data off as it appeared. "Radius approximately ten meters."

Wukee was shaking his head over the science console. "The spin is disrupting our sensors. I can't get a lock on it."

The other cadets kept glancing at Moll, even Mantegna, though he affected an air of calm. Self-consciously, Moll said, "We should notify the station immediately."

"We have another problem," Campbell spoke up. "This entire vortex is moving through the tertiary phase, spiraling toward the inner phases."

Moll read the vector analysis with a quick glance. "He's right. And we're picking up speed."

Mantegna checked navigational sensors. "We're in a primary jet stream."

"I've done my sensor sweeps, let's get out of here," Wu suggested. Mantegna raised one brow at Wukee, a silent reminder that *he* was the one in charge. His hands slowed as he deliberately reversed the coordinates to return them from where they came.

Moll accessed the sensor logs, scanning the data, while Mantegna announced, "One quarter impulse power."

"Wait!" Moll called out, running a computer analysis to confirm her findings. "I'm reading a subspace beacon on the tag emitter. It's very faint, but it's there. Number 09Alpha-99B4."

Wukee whistled. "Why such a high number?"

Mantegna started to check the tag inventory, but Moll already knew what it was. The ultimate find.

"It's a piece of planetary crust," she told the others.

"One of the original science teams found it in the inner band, but they had to jettison it when a charge arced between them. They tagged it and went back with a hyper forcefield, but it was gone."

"A rogue asteroid," Wu said admiringly.

"It's more than that," Moll insisted. "They found evidence of panspermia embedded in the matter. They've been looking for this asteroid for the past *eleven* decades."

The other cadets were staring at her, unused to an outburst from her.

Moll took a deep breath. "Don't you see how *important* this is? We can't allow the asteroid to be sucked into the gravity well!"

"Then what did you do?" the voice asked, seemingly echoing around the empty white room. Moll felt isolated, sitting on a chair in the very center, with no edges in the arched ceiling or curved walls to focus on.

She explained to the unseen voice, "Our team tried to stop the spin with a focused particle beam. We hoped that would break the magnetic field; then we could grapple the asteroid and take it back to the science station."

There was a pause, and Moll Enor couldn't help the jump in her heartbeat. She was in deep trouble, called to a hearing before the Symbiosis Commission. Her testimony would be used to help the Commission decide if she had deliberately endangered the Enor symbiont by her actions.

It was the highest crime under the Commission's jurisdiction, and the most severe sentence for a joined Trill was to be ordered into protective custody. If the host didn't comply with the ruling, they could even be put to death so the symbiont could be passed to a competent host. Much of the screening performed by the Symbiosis Comission was done to eliminate Initiates with psychological instabilities to prevent that from happening.

Moll knew she wasn't at that level yet, but her unseen judges beyond the curved wall could order her to leave Starfleet and return permanently to the Trill homeworld. And there was nothing for her here, nothing but the pool. Though it was her preferred retreat, a lifetime of the same experiences, compounded by her eidetic memory, would surely lead to madness.

The soothing monotone voice asked, "What was the risk level of this procedure?"

"We had never done it before, so we knew it could fail," Moll admitted.

"Did it fail?" the interrogator asked.

"Yes." Moll cleared her throat as she remembered the magnetic arc that surged between the pod and the metal-rich asteroid. An electronic fire had whipped through the *Sagittarius,* fusing power relays in every system of the science pod.

A holo-image of Wu suddenly appeared near Moll. She knew her fellow cadet was at the Academy on Earth, in an empty room, his image relayed via comm-link to Trill. He was smiling nervously, as the voice asked, "Starfleet Cadet Buck Wu, why did you agree to attempt the dangerous procedure that Cadet Moll Enor suggested?"

"Why?" Wu repeated, shifting his eyes upward, apparently addressing the ceiling for lack of a person to focus on. Moll could sympathize, facing the same thing herself. But the Investigators of the Symbiosis

Commission believed a more honest testimony was given this way, uncolored by a witness's reaction to the Commissioners.

"Yes, why did you do as Cadet Moll Enor suggested? Was she in command of your mission?"

"No, Mantegna was."

"Starfleet Cadet Mantegna is on record that he was against the attempt," the interrogator intoned, noting the sequence number of the testimony for the Commission members to access.

Wukee opened his mouth to reply, but he was replaced in a burst of static by Campbell. Campbell looked as if he was at attention, stiff and self-conscious.

"Starfleet Cadet Ho Campbell," the voice announced. "You were also a member of the research team on the *Sagittarius* science pod."

"Yes, sir!" Campbell snapped to attention. "I believe Cadet Moll conducted herself with bravery befitting a Starfleet officer, sir!"

The voice didn't respond to Campbell's declaration. "Was it part of your duties to retrieve asteroids?"

"Duty?" Campbell asked, shifting slightly, his voice lowering. "No, we tag asteroids with subspace beacons. It's the science teams who retrieve them."

"So the attempt to retrieve the asteroid was outside the normal bounds of your duties as you understood them, is that correct?"

"Yes."

Campbell's proud, pained face turned into static as his holo-image was replaced by one of Mantegna. He was settling the sleeve of his shirt, tugging lightly on the cuff, feigning nonchalance at the interrogation.

"Starfleet Cadet Yllian Mantegna," the voice announced. "Commander of the *Sagittarius* research mission. Why did you attempt to destroy the magnetic field with a focused particle beam, the procedure suggested by Cadet Moll Enor?"

"She said it would work. I trusted her judgment." He continued to examine his shirt. "She's supposed to be brilliant, isn't she?"

"Do you believe Cadet Moll Enor misrepresented the risk?" the interrogator asked.

Grudgingly, Mantegna admitted, "No. But she said she could do it."

Moll winced at his condescension. But she had seen him panic when their main power array was blown apart by the feedback from the particle beam. As emergency life support came on line with the distinctive ruddy lights, he had let out a frightened squeak like he was two years old. Mantegna knew she would never forget—and succeeding generations of hosts would never forget—the way he had nearly levitated out of his seat when the hatch to the lifeboat automatically cycled open. He was the first one inside the lifeboat, even though he had to push Wukee aside at the hatch to get in.

Smoothly the voice asked, "Did you order Cadet Moll Enor to remain behind in the science pod?"

Mantegna sat forward, his eyes narrowing. "No, Cadet Enor volunteered—insisted, actually. She said someone had to stay with the asteroid to try to stop the spin. I told her she'd never get the pod's systems powered up before it crossed into the inner phases, but she thought she could."

Moll crossed her arms protectively over her stomach and the symbiont. The way she remembered it,

Mantegna didn't say three words when she had explained that she would stay with the asteroid until they returned with a rescue team. He had cycled the hatch closed so fast they almost didn't hear her advice on how to best use the lifeboat thrusters to get out of the vortex. How could she describe her feelings as the vacuum broke between the pod and the lifeboat, when she desperately wanted to call after them to wait for her? It had been her idea to stay, but she felt abandoned.

"Did you agree with Moll Enor's analysis?"

"No. That's why I ordered the evacuation," Mantegna replied.

"At that time, did you believe the asteroid was worth the risk of staying behind?" the interrogator pressed.

"No, I did not."

"Did you believe Cadet Moll Enor was endangering her life?"

"No. She could have left in the other lifeboat at any time."

"Do you believe Moll Enor made the correct decision to stay with the asteroid?"

Moll held her breath, hoping Mantegna's arrogance would finally help her out. If he believed that what she had done involved no danger and was basically of little importance, the Commission might believe that, too.

But Mantegna stunned her by admitting, "I have to say, she did it. She stopped the spin and slowed the vortex, giving the rescue team time to reach both her and the asteroid before they entered the inner phases. She deserves the Starfleet commendation she was awarded."

Moll could have groaned at his unexpected accolades. Just when she least needed it, Mantegna finally gave her his approval. The problem was, she wasn't in trouble with Starfleet! It was the Trill who had her on trial.

Next, the investigators for the Symbiosis Commission played the internal log from the science pod, thoughtfully provided by Starfleet. Moll had to force herself to sit still as those desperate hours unfolded again. She couldn't watch her own face, knowing the doubts that drove her, with the fear that she had made a terrible mistake staying in the science pod. The lifepod was even less shielded than the *Sagittarius,* and while it may have saved her life, the symbiont would have been harmed—and the Commission had those facts right in front of them.

As the log played out, the interrogator counted the rising radiation rate within the pod, well over the acceptable tolerance levels for the symbiont. Then there was the final burst of activity as she finally created a link and filtered enough energy through her tricorder to create an arc between the pod and the relay buoy, shorting out the magnetic vortex. The asteroids spun away, finally released to rejoin the chaotic helix motion, while the buoy and the panspermia asteroid slowed, spinning around each other as they were jostled from the jet stream.

In the recording, Moll bowed her head to her arms. There was silence as the image continued, then the interrogator cut in, saying, "A rescue team arrived within the hour. Cadet Moll Enor was treated on board the rescue ship for fifth degree radiation burns."

Moll couldn't watch the holo-image. Nothing could

convey the gut-wrenching pain of synchrotron radiation exposure. Or her dread that she had made a mistake that would cost her everything.

"Were you aware you were endangering your symbiont?"

"Yes," Moll admitted, raising her chin. "But I believed it was an acceptable risk."

"Why do you consider your actions acceptable?"

"Because saving the asteroid with the panspermia fossil was of paramount importance."

"Importance to whom?" the voice inquired.

Moll tightened her lips. "To everyone! There's nothing more important than evidence of a fundamental connection between all humanoid life-forms. Especially now, when we have to work together to fight the Borg!"

Her voice rang out, but with no faces to judge reactions, she couldn't know if they understood. "Don't you see, this panspermia fossil supports Galen's discovery that humanoid species in our galaxy have a common genetic heritage. We were "seeded" in the primordial oceans of many worlds. It's proof of a biological imperative that we should work together."

"What is your primary concern, your duty to Starfleet or the safety of your symbiont?"

Moll shook her head, unable to answer either way. "All I know is that I have to stay true to myself."

The cross-questioning continued for another hour, until the merciless voice relented and dismissed the Symbiosis Commission until the next day, when additional witnesses would be called. Moll had seen the list of Starfleet officials, exobiologists, and even more Trill psychologists and medical specialists.

Everything she had ever done or thought would be questioned.

Already, under the expert grilling she felt as if she was being pounded while trying to maintain that she had done the only thing her conscience would allow her to do. But they had found out plenty about her, things she had tried to hide for years—her frustration at being a first host, her longing to be something other than herself, to belong to something.

She was finally taken away by two white-robed Symbiosis Commission officials. It was humiliating, the way they treated her as if she couldn't be trusted.

Moll's remarkable memory had already been the subject of one hundred and thirty-seven academic papers on Trill, but she knew there would be a flurry of new opinions produced by this hearing. She could imagine the resulting titles—"Systemic Reaction to Perfect Memory," "Instability as a Consequence of Eidetism," and "Tertiary Overload in Joined Trill."

Not for the first time, Moll was seriously doubting her own competence to be a host for Enor. She had always known the only reason she had succeeded thus far was *due* to her eidetic memory. Saving that panspermia fossil was the first thing she'd ever done that *wasn't* based on the capacity of her memory. As Jayme's constant, supportive communiques pointed out, it had taken sheer courage to stay in the science pod when she knew she might be killing her symbiont. Yet her pride at her accomplishment was rapidly dwindling. Perhaps she *should* only focus on mental pursuits rather than try to be more than she was by joining Starfleet.

But that was all Jadzia's fault.

"Your room," one of the officials informed her. "Will you wish to leave tonight?"

"I doubt it," she replied wearily.

"Very well, we will return tomorrow morning to escort you to the hearing room."

Moll leaned against the door as it closed behind her, wondering if she had the motivation to eat before falling into bed.

"Nice to see you again, Moll!"

A chair turned, making Moll start in surprise. "Jadzia! What are you doing here?"

Jadzia Dax seemed composed, seated with her legs crossed and a sly grin on her face. Moll had never seen her in the trim black Starfleet uniform with the blue shoulder placards, but it looked right on her.

"I'm surprised you didn't call me yourself," Jadzia scolded. "What are friends for?"

Moll summoned a weak answering smile. "So friends are supposed to prove each other's mental stability? I never heard that one."

Jadzia stood up to approach Moll. "Congratulations, by the way, on your commendation. You'll make lieutenant faster than I did. But then you always did everything faster than me."

Jadzia gave Moll a welcoming hug, but Moll could hardly respond. "You went through Starfleet before I did," she reminded her friend.

Jadzia waved a hand. "That's because the Initiate Institute wouldn't accept me until I had accomplished something important."

The Institute had accepted both of them the same year, but Jadzia was four years older than Moll, having already completed her Academy training. But in everything else, Moll was the most-favored Initiate at the Institute. She was clearly destined for a symbiont, while everyone else had to keep on their toes, competing with each other for the rare privilege. Moll had gotten the Enor symbiont a year before Jadzia was joined with Dax, during the period that Jadzia had been expelled from the Institute for reasons nobody knew.

"What's wrong?" Jadzia asked.

Moll gave her a look. "I'm on trial for my life, remember?"

"Oh, that will blow over. The Commission is constantly poking their noses into our business." Jadzia picked up an Oppalassa lucky charm that Starsa had given Moll last year. "Look what happened with me. They re-accepted me as an Initiate after kicking me out, and I still don't know what that was all about. If the Commission didn't do all these hearings and make big announcements, people would start to think they were unnecessary."

Moll laughed, but there was a bitter edge to it. "Maybe they're right about me. They say I have a profound ambiguity toward my symbiont."

"Who doesn't?" Jadzia smiled playfully. "Come on, don't take it so seriously."

"I can't help it."

"I knew you'd be this way. But I have something that's sure to help," Jadzia assured her.

"What is it?"

"Do you want to go in there tomorrow and prove you're competent to host that symbiont?"

"Of course I do!"

"Then come with me." Jadzia gestured to the door.

"I'm not supposed to leave my quarters."

"Correction: You're not supposed to leave the Institute." Jadzia held up a finger, warning her. "You're going to have to stop second-guessing everything and trust me on this one. All right?"

Moll let her pull her to her feet. "Last time you told

me to trust you, I ended up in Timerhoo without a return ticket."

"What are you complaining about? You had a great story to tell when you got back."

Dax practically had to drag Moll to the holosuite she had reserved. She didn't want to tell Moll how difficult it had been to get away from DS9, or how important this trial was. Moll already knew that. What she needed right now was to relax, so she could show the Commission she was in complete control.

Dax ordered, "Close your eyes."

"I'm not allowed to run a simulation of the hearing," Moll reminded her.

Dax made a face. "You'll have to answer all those questions tomorrow, why bother to do it tonight? No, this is much better. Three hours from now, you'll be ready to take over the Symbiosis Commission single-handed."

As usual, Moll drew her brows together, as if unsure whether to trust Dax or not. Like a flash, it brought back all their years together at the Institute. Jadzia hadn't been able to resist making friends with the shy, reserved genius. Everyone else had treated her like an untouchable icon, while Jadzia took perverse pleasure in treating Moll exactly like a younger sister—counseling her, bullying her, and basically treating her like a real Trill.

Now, with the added perspective of the memories of her Dax symbiont, she realized Moll had never understood why she had been so friendly through their years at the Institute. Mostly, Jadzia had felt sorry for the girl who had been shuttled from one intellectual think tank to another University demonstration from a very tender age, never really having a childhood.

"Go on," Dax urged. "Close your eyes."

Moll closed her eyes, and she didn't peek even when Dax put her hand over her face to make sure. "Turn this way," Dax ordered. "Begin simulation Dax 9J. Okay, now you can look!"

They were on a meadow overlooking the baths of Cydonia. A nearby waterfall tumbled over the rocks to fill the upper pool, spilling down the curved walls that spread like petals over the gentle slope. Steam rose from some of the warmer pools as naked figures moved through the white mist, sliding into the water and gliding away among the ripples.

"You think *this* is going to help me?" Moll demanded.

"Well, it can't hurt," Dax assured her.

Moll let out an exasperated sound, turning back to the door. "Why did I trust you? I should have known you came here to make fun of me."

Dax caught her arm, stopping her from leaving. "I've never made fun of you, Moll! I only teased you a little because you never seemed like you were enjoying yourself."

"Thanks for your help," Moll said dryly. "I don't think *now* is the time to enjoy myself."

A male Risan approached, wearing only a smile and a towel over one arm. "Would you like a massage?"

Moll turned away in disgust.

"Stop being so uptight," Dax recommended. "If you tell the Commission you're happy with the way you're living your life, they aren't going to force you to do anything. Forget all the witnesses. What matters is how you present yourself."

135

"That's easy for you to say!" Moll suddenly snapped. "You got what you wanted. You got the memories, the experiences. I wanted that, too, but instead all I got was *this!*" She gestured to herself. "Nothing changed when I was joined. Except I feel like I'm being watched every second, knowing that the next hosts will remember everything I say, everything I do. I'm just a starting point, a blank slate, as if nothing I've ever done is enough to cause a wave in that smooth pool where Enor sits inside of me, watching every moment."

"But you're the first—"

"Don't tell me what an honor it is! I believed all that, and I didn't even try to say no when they told me I would get Enor. I didn't even try to refuse," she repeated bitterly.

Moll left the holosuite as Jadzia sadly watched her old friend leave. She never realized how disappointed Moll had been over joining with Enor. But then again, she had sent at least a dozen messages to Moll after hearing she had been accepted to Starfleet Academy, but Moll had always replied with only a few brief lines, resisting even a shadow of their former intimacy.

Another Risan, this one androgynous, approached Dax with a towel over one arm. "Would you like a massage?"

"Yes, thank you." As they began walking toward the cabana, Dax said, "Maybe you can give me some advice. What do you do when a friend won't let you help them?"

Moll knew she appeared extremely defensive, but she had to cross her arms to hold on to herself, to keep from shaking. She held her head high as the voice intoned, "Are there any final statements from the witnesses?"

So many of the Starfleet officers, as well as her cadet teammates, had already testified to her courage and skill. But Moll knew that wouldn't satisfy the Commission. Jadzia had done her best to prove that an allegiance to Starfleet was not detrimental to the well-being of the symbiont, pointing out the examples of Curzon Dax and herself. But the questioning had shifted to Moll's psychological ambiguity over her symbiont, and no one could help her there.

"We have a request from Lieutenant Jadzia Dax," the voice announced. "You wish to make a final statement?"

Dax's image flickered on. She stood up to face the unseen Commissioners. "Yes, I have something to say. Your investigators have been very thorough in digging through Moll's psychological motivations. And you've explored the issue of exactly how important the panspermia fossil is to the Trill. But you've forgotten the most important thing."

Moll sat forward, wondering what Jadzia could possibly be talking about. She was incapable of forgetting *anything*.

"Moll is the first host for Enor. Her life will be the moral and ethical foundation for every succeeding host. For those of you who are joined, you know what I'm talking about." Moll never remembered seeing Jadzia so serious. "The success of every symbiont relationship rests in part on the ability of the first host to establish a foundation that is both inclusive yet solid. That takes constant self-questioning, and inevitably some doubt about one's own choices. And I've never known anyone better at self-examination than Moll."

Jadzia paused to smile at her, and Moll Enor felt herself respond, relaxing in spite of herself. What Jadzia was saying felt right to her.

"Moll would never purposely endanger herself or her symbiont unless there was some overriding concern," Dax insisted. "If she had turned away from the fossil, knowing as she does how important it is—not just to her or her people, but to everyone in this galaxy—*then* you would have good reason to judge her actions."

"You question this entire hearing?" the voice asked.

"Yes! Being a first host is difficult; we all have the memories to prove it. We also know it's those memories that are most comforting when we're faced with difficult decisions." Jadzia's holo-image stepped closer to Moll's chair. "I envy Enor's future hosts, because they'll inherit a rich and varied lifetime of memories from Moll. And I recommend that you do nothing to interfere with her choices."

The kneading fingers pressed into Moll Enor's back, finding all the sore spots. She groaned in pleasure, twisting on the edge of pain.

"These guys are good," she told Dax. "I'm glad you talked me into this."

Dax murmured agreement as her own masseuse worked on her. Her eyes were closed and she looked almost indecently relaxed and happy. "Just consider it a reward for beating the Symbiosis Commission at their own game."

"You beat them for me." After a moment, Moll said, "Actually, it's poetic justice, because it was your fault in the first place."

"*My* fault? What did I do?"

"You know very well that I went into Starfleet

because of the way you raved about it at the Institute." Their eyes met. "Then when I saw that asteroid, I knew I had to try to save it, because all I could hear was your voice inside my head, insisting it was a once-in-a-lifetime find."

"It is," Dax agreed.

"Remember you told me about that class you took with Professor Galen? I wanted to hear him lecture so badly, but he didn't teach my first two years at the Academy, then he was killed gathering DNA codes that proved his theory."

"The message of peace from our ancient progenitors," Dax remembered. "I think Starfleet finally convinced the Commission you have a serious talent in science."

"I love astrophysics, but I don't think I could take a steady diet of it like you do," Moll Enor demurred.

"Good, I think you should go into command," Dax agreed.

"Command?" Moll blurted out. "I'm terrible with people."

"Nah, you just need to have some confidence in yourself," Dax told her with a grin. "You're a natural leader. Look how you got the other cadets to do exactly what you wanted so you could save that asteroid. Someone who can talk Cadet Mantegna into something would be foolish not to pursue a career in command."

Chapter Six

"HEY, TITUS, UP HERE!" Jayme called out from the upper walkway. "What did you get for the summer?"

Hammon Titus tossed the assignment chip into the air and caught it with one hand. "Errand boy for the Federation Assembly."

"Yeah?" Her voice went up in surprise and doubt. "Really?"

Titus clenched his teeth, still smiling. He couldn't believe it either when he read the chip. All year he'd been stuck at the Academy while everyone else went off on exciting survival courses and temporary assignments onboard science ships or remote space stations. The furthest he'd been was New Berlin City on the Moon last summer while he was running the shuttle supply route. New Berlin City looked a lot like San Francisco without the bridge—not very exotic, if you asked him. He had talked to everyone he could about getting off Earth, including Admiral Leyton, but his requests kept coming back denied.

He slipped into galactic poli sci class, barely beating the bell. As he sat down, he realized everyone was shifting in their seats, talking in hushed, excited tones.

"We have a guest today, cadets," Professor Tho announced. Titus sat up to see better, as Captain Jean Luc Picard entered the room.

The girl in the chair next to him muttered, "No way!" Everyone was on the edge of their seats to see the man who had beaten the Borg at Wolf 359 when thirty-nine other Federation and Klingon starships were destroyed. Picard looked just like his holo-image, especially the way he nodded to them and briefly smiled as he took the lectern.

"Professor Tho asked me if I could speak to you," Picard began, his sonorous voice comfortably filling the room. "You all know of the recent developments between the Federation and Cardassian Empire, resulting in the establishment of the Demilitarized Zone a few months ago. Unfortunately, this necessitates the shifting of some of our colonies, as well as some of those of the Cardassians. The decision to formalize our borders has given rise to political and philosophical debates that will undoubtedly continue for centuries. . . ."

Titus felt his eyes glaze over. Looking around, he realized everyone, including Professor Tho, was entranced by Picard's distinctive rhythmical cadence. There wasn't a sound in the room.

"The *Enterprise*-D shall depart tomorrow for Dorvan V to carry out the evacuation of the last of our colonists. Some of the Federation colonists have protested the treaty and are resisting recolonization, forming a protest group known as the Maquis. In the Academy newspaper this week, there is an insightful editorial on the rights of the Maquis, written by one of your fellow cadets, Harry Kim. Cadet Kim brings up some of the more germane questions we are faced with in this case, specifically, whether the needs of the many outweigh the needs of the few—"

Titus couldn't stand it anymore. "Excuse me, sir!"

The other cadets slowly turned, resenting the interruption.

"Yes, Cadet," Picard acknowledged. "Do you have a question?"

"No, a comment," Titus said, ignoring the stares. "If I may be so blunt, I think you agree with the Maquis that the colonists shouldn't be forced to move from their homes."

Professor Tho was frowning, and whispers rose around him.

"My personal feelings are unimportant," Picard replied quietly. "I am merely performing my duty."

"But isn't it our duty to protest when we feel our orders are wrong?" Titus knew he should just let it drop, but that comment about Harry Kim got under his skin. Kim was one of the last-year cadets that professors were always holding up as an "example." Kim was a nice enough guy, but sometimes they piled it on enough to make Titus choke.

"Our elected officials create policy, not Starfleet captains," Picard gently chided him. "While I may have quite a different opinion as a citizen, it would be arrogant in the extreme to think that I know what is best in such a complicated and far-reaching subject."

Titus nodded, at a loss for what to say.

"Cadet," Picard added, almost with a smile, "you

will soon find that the essence of command is not to lead, but to follow orders."

"Yes, sir," Titus agreed.

He sat back and folded his arms, wondering why he felt so deflated. Maybe it was that hint of amusement in the captain's smile that was so humiliating. But he was convinced he was right. Maybe none of the others could see it, but he knew that Picard didn't agree with this policy. Hell, Titus knew he would fight it if someone told him that his family would have to leave the Antaranan colony.

The guy behind him kicked the seat and hissed, "Nice going!"

Titus clenched his teeth, staring at Picard as he calmly, methodically discussed the volatile political situation and what that meant for the security of the Alpha Quadrant.

Jayme Miranda saw Titus later that day, tilted back in a café chair, his head resting against the brick wall. His jacket was slung over the back and his eyes were closed as he soaked up the afternoon sunshine.

"Hey," she called out, stopping at the low fence around the patio of the outdoor café. "I heard about your argument with Captain Picard."

Sleepily, Titus opened one eye. "You again? Where do you get your information? It wasn't an argument."

"Oh? That's what everyone's saying." She grinned. "Were you kidding me when you said you got Federation Assembly duty this summer?"

"Yup."

Jayme couldn't help but admire how smooth he was, acting like he didn't have a care in the world, and pulling it off, too, when she knew he was dying to get off-world. In a burst of sympathetic goodwill, she told him, "You know, you should volunteer for projects or studies or something. It's sort of an unwritten rule. They like to see that stuff on your record."

Titus raised his head. "I volunteer. Last month I organized the second-level Parrises Squares competition."

"Yeah, and how hard was that?" she shot back. "It's not just a matter of keeping busy. They like to see you challenge yourself."

Now she had his attention, but in typical Titus-fashion, he wouldn't admit she was right. "What are you doing right now?" he asked. "I've got tickets to the Ventaxian chime concert."

One brow went up. "You're asking *me* to the chime concert? Now I know you need to get off-planet."

His expression was wounded. "We've hung out before."

"Not listening to Ventaxian chimes. What happened to Qita?"

Titus shrugged and looked away.

"Oh, I see. Sorry, but I can't help you put another notch on your belt. I'm going to the Maquis debate, so you'll have to ask someone else."

"I thought they already did that."

Jayme nodded. "This is another one. I better hurry, or I'll be late meeting Moll Enor."

"Enor?" He rocked slightly in his chair, laughing. "Don't tell me you're still infatuated with that Trill!"

Jayme flipped her hair over her shoulder. "You don't know anything about loyalty, do you?"

As she walked away, he called after her, "I know plenty about loyalty. I also know when to give up."

"Never say die!" she tossed over her shoulder.

* * *

When Titus got back to his Quad, after going to the chime concert alone, he softly whistled the falling tones to himself as he got ready for bed. His roommate was still out. She was probably at the quantum physics lab studying for finals. This year's Quad project was protectively wrapped and sitting on the table next to the door, unlike last year's fiasco, when they didn't do a final test run until the night before the Board review. But that had been Starsa's fault more than Jayme's.

Jayme Miranda might have her own personal problems—just look at that infantile crush she carried for Enor, while the Trill obviously barely tolerated her attentions. But with at least half a dozen relatives the grade of commander or higher, Jayme certainly knew Starfleet like it was her own family.

Idly, Titus called up the volunteer lists. He quickly keyed past the psych courses. There was no way he was going to let anyone mess around with his head. One of the endurance courses sounded interesting, but he remembered what Jayme had said about challenging himself.

He volunteered to be considered for a few different projects. By the time he checked the computer before going to sleep, he had received notification that he had been deemed "suitable" for Communications Project #104. If he chose to accept this duty, he would have to report to the lab the weekend after finals.

His finger hovered over the cancel square. There were at least four great parties happening that weekend. One was in a friend's habitat bubble in the Antarctic Circle. He was hoping to have a little fun before shipping off to the Federation Assembly where he would be at the beck and call of some ancient legislator for two months.

He pressed the key to volunteer. He didn't care if he missed twelve parties and a trip back in time, he would do anything to get a good field duty assignment.

This volunteer stuff isn't too bad, Titus thought to himself. He leaned back against the soft turf, his hands behind his head, waiting for his partner to get through the light-beam obstacle. He had walked across the wide river without a stumble, but Eto Mahs had fallen five times already.

According to the instructions posted at the crossing, if they fell off, they had to go back and do it again. It was your typical obstacle course as far as Titus could tell. The trick was, they weren't allowed to speak to each other.

Lab technicians had implanted a speech inhibitor in his vocal cords, as well as those of Eto Mahs. Titus was surprised at how many times it had already stopped him from speaking. If he concentrated, he could override the inhibitor, otherwise it kept them from making involuntary statements.

"Yeiiahhh!!" Eto Mahs screamed as he fell, for the sixth time, into the river. He bobbed to the surface, his dark hair dripping with water. *"Eeiihh!"*

Titus grinned to himself. They might be in a holodeck, but that water was cold. Mahs screamed that way every time he fell off the light beam.

The inhibitor allowed them to make inarticulate noises, and they could signal simple directions with their hands. He wondered what the communications specialists could possibly be getting from this. The whole thing seemed absurd, but then again, he was on a private mission of his own to prove he was worthy of a juicy field assignment. Each to his own, he figured.

Meanwhile, he enjoyed the wooded environment, watching the leaves shift overhead in the wind. His colony world didn't have trees, only patches of large types of grass, sort of like terrestrial bamboo. He wouldn't admit it to anyone, but he thought a tree was a miraculous thing. So many odd shapes and designs, each one different yet perfect in itself.

He rolled over to watch Eto Mahs climb out of the river, shivering. Titus raised his hand to his mouth to yell, "Take your clothes off, you nitwit!" but the inhibitor beeped a warning.

Sheepishly, Titus smacked his forehead. The lab techs must be keeping record of every incident when they tried to speak. That could be the purpose of the course. On every obstacle, underneath the instructions, they were told they could quit the course at any time without consequences by simply saying, "End program."

Mahs resolutely stepped onto the narrow light beam one more time, his teeth biting his lower lip. Titus shook his head at the poor guy. He probably hadn't expected an obstacle course on a communications project. Mahs was a third-year Cadet majoring in exobiology, according to the summary at the beginning of the course. His mother was supposedly Japanese and his father was from—what planet was it?—wherever. Titus didn't recall ever seeing him around the Academy, but Mahs had nodded in greeting as if he recognized Titus. They had never spoken a word to each other.

Eto Mahs wobbled, flailing his arms, his wet hair whipping around. *"Yeiiahhh!!"* he screamed again as he fell.

Titus rolled onto his back again, chewing on a piece of grass. What did he care how long it took Mahs to get across? Come Monday, he would be transporting to the Assembly. He could think of worse ways to spend the next two days than relaxing on the hillside enjoying the gentle breeze.

Titus kicked his heels against the stone wall where he sat watching Eto Mahs. Mahs was trying to turn the handle to open the gate obstacle. They could have just as easily jumped over, but the instruction said each of them had to turn a handle to open the gate before they could go through. Titus had turned his handle with one twist of his wrist, while Mahs was practically hanging off his handle. It wouldn't budge.

Titus twisted up one side of his mouth. Eto Mahs was hardly as tall as his shoulder, and was probably the skinniest guy he'd ever seen. But he couldn't understand how anyone could be that weak. The latch did have a tricky notch you had to catch, but Titus had immediately felt it when he turned the handle. How could Mahs not figure it out? But then again, it had taken twelve tries before Mahs got across the river that morning.

As it turned out, the guy did have a great sense of direction. A few times he had been right about which way to go—once after Titus had tramped at least a mile in the other direction, with Mahs tugging at his arm the whole way, trying to make him turn back.

Mahs gasped out, collapsing against the wall, hanging onto the handle for support. Slowly, he slid down until he was huddled on the ground, breathing heavily.

Titus wished he could tell the guy how to open it.

He got down and made motions for Mahs to push in as he turned the handle, but Mahs wearily nodded that he understood what to do. Titus raised his hands, silently admitting that there was nothing else he could contribute, and he returned to his post on the wall.

Impatiently, he glanced around. Were they going to be forced to camp here tonight? It wasn't a bad spot, but there was lake on the other side of the gate that he was dying to get to. A swim before rolling out the bedroll would be perfect. Yet he couldn't cheat and jump the fence. The instructions were very clear that the partners were supposed to remain together.

He stared down at Mahs, wondering if the exobiologist had quit or was getting up the energy for another try. Suddenly Mahs looked up, meeting his eyes, as if he could feel the contempt Titus felt for him.

Startled, Titus looked away. He wondered if Eto Mahs had known all day how pitiful he looked to Titus. He felt kind of bad about it, but also more than a little justified. Why didn't Mahs just say "End Program" and get them both out of here? Titus would still have time to get to the Antarctic Circle before the party ended, and he'd have another whole day before he had to report to the Assembly.

Mahs was still looking up at him resentfully, and Titus let slip a little of his own resentment at being stuck with such a *weakling*.

Mahs flinched as if Titus had shouted the word. Without another glance, he got up and grabbed hold of the handle again.

Titus instantly felt bad about the pain in Mahs' dark eyes. He didn't want to hurt the guy. But watching him struggle with the handle, panting after only a few moments' effort, made him want to roll his eyes and shake his head in exasperation. He heroically restrained himself, even managing to feel a little burst of sympathy toward for him. But that evaporated when Mahs cast another resentful look over his shoulder.

Titus sighed. It looked like it would be a long, dry evening ahead.

Titus made camp all by himself, gathering enough grass to pad both of their bedrolls, when Mahs suddenly turned the handle and the gate swung open.

The inhibitor stopped Titus from exclaiming, "Finally!" He grinned, ready for a long, cool swim.

But Mahs was tugging on his arm, pointing back at the gate. There was an instruction sheet posted on this side, but he must have blown right past it, eyes only for the lake.

"Proceed to the peak to make camp," the instructions said.

Titus turned to look, having memorized the landscape as they slowly traversed the deep valley. They couldn't mean *that* peak in the distance, on the other side of the lake. It was so far away that they would never reach it before sunset.

He realized he was shaking his head when Mahs insistently nodded, pointing to the instructions, then to the peak.

Titus stared at Mahs. Why didn't he just give up?

Mahs narrowed his eyes slightly, jerking his chin at Titus—*Why don't you?*

The challenge hung between them only a few seconds, then Titus slowly grinned at Mahs, making it very clear that *he* would never give up.

* * *

They were trudging up the lower slope of the peak in full darkness when a computer voice announced, "Your time is up. Thank you for participating in Communications Project #104."

The mountainside glimmered, flattening into an obvious projection before disappearing. The familiar orange-gridded walls rose around them.

Titus lifted up one hand wordlessly as the door slid open and two lab techs with padds entered. The instructions said there was no way to "fail" the course, but it wasn't his fault they didn't complete it on time. The inhibitor stifled his initial outburst.

"Cadet Titus," one tech read off the padd. "Follow me."

Titus glanced back down the corridor as Mahs was led in the other direction. Maybe it would be better this way. He could explain in private to the lab tech. He didn't intend to fail this volunteer assignment. That would ruin all of his plans.

But the lab tech didn't give him a chance to explain. The inhibitor was left intact and he was shown into a cubicle with a bed, wash facilities, and a replicator. He gestured, puzzled, but the lab tech just winked and activated the door. It slid shut between them. There was no panel on his side for him to open it.

Titus was about to override his inhibitor to protest—imprisonment wasn't what he signed up for! But before he could speak a holo-emitter activated, creating one of the sign posts, incongruously, next to the door, complete with an instruction card.

"Eat and get some sleep," the instructions said. "You will complete the course tomorrow."

Titus let out a wordless grunt of exasperation. So

this was still part of the project. Well, he could play along with that.

The silence was starting to get to him. It hadn't been so bad the night before, when he was exhausted from their last sprint to get to the peak. He had barely taken time to eat before falling into bed. When he woke, he cleaned up and ate another huge meal, all the while gingerly testing his inhibitor, looking around the cubicle and wondering when they were going to get him out of here.

The same lab tech came to fetch him. He must have been really beat the night before, because he hadn't realized how pretty she was, especially that flip of black hair and those freckles across her nose. Or maybe he'd been shut up too long.

He was led back to a small white room, just like the one where he and Eto Mahs had started the obstacle course. This time a different guy entered along with him—Cadet Vestabo. Titus didn't need to read the instruction post to know Vestabo was a first-year cadet who was considered to be a mathematics whiz. He was also a regular in the Saturday morning laser-tag game that Titus had joined in a few times.

As the door to the holodeck opened, Vestabo was nodding a greeting to Titus, pointing to his throat and smiling at the inhibitor. Titus ran his hand through his hair, letting out a long low whistle as the same countryside appeared, with the peak in the distance.

Not again! he wanted to exclaim.

Maybe they were giving him a second chance. Maybe they realized it wasn't his fault that they hadn't made it to the peak. But why pair him with another scrawny guy? Vestabo wasn't nearly as timid and frail as Eto Mahs, he was just a wiry kid, much like Titus himself when he first came to the Academy. But Titus had bulked up by venting much of his frustration the past year working out with counter weights. Gradually, he had put on an impressive amount of muscle. On a good day, he could even beat Bobbie Ray at Parrises Squares.

His doubts about Vestabo's ability were quickly squashed when they reached the light beam crossing the river. Vestabo read the instructions and, without hesitation, jumped up on the beam and ran across. Titus grinned at him, giving him a thumbs-up when he reached the other side. He felt better for the first time since he realized he was going to have to go through the entire course again.

He stepped up on the light beam and immediately knew something was different. It wasn't solid like before. It wobbled. He frowned as he inched forward, trying to keep his balance. He only got a few feet before he was shifting so wildly that he fell off.

He tried to grab the light beam as he went over, but his hands passed through it as if it was an illusion— which it was.

The stunning cold choked the air from his lungs. He was spitting water and gasping, swimming instinctively against the current. With no time for thought, he was back on the bank shivering, his hands tucked between his legs.

Vestabo's mouth was a perfect *O*, shocked that Titus hadn't made it across. Titus knew the feeling, having stood on that side of the bank himself.

He tried it again, and this time he got nearly to the middle before losing his balance on the trembling light beam. He expected the extreme cold this time, which allowed him to feel what his body had known the first time—there were things in the water!

Hundreds of itching, prickling THINGS.

He was out of the water and shuddering on the bank before he could gasp out loud. His hands convulsed over his body, frantically trying to get rid of the things, but there was nothing there, just a nervous prickling that faded from his nerves.

Vestabo was hunched over, shaking, unable to hide his laughter behind his hands.

That was the last time Vestabo laughed. As Titus tried again and again to get across the flimsy light beam, Vestabo crouched on the other side, chewing the inside of his mouth anxiously. He even stood up to grab Titus's arm when he finally got close to the other side.

Titus kept expecting contempt to rise in the younger boy's eyes, especially after they reached the wall obstacle. The instructions told them to each hold a grip on a transport container to get it over the wall. Vestabo couldn't tell that the vacuum on Titus's grip handle kept breaking, just as he hadn't been able to see that the light beam over the river wasn't solid for Titus.

Time and again Vestabo grunted as he suddenly had the full weight of the container swinging from his grip. It kept thudding back to the ground. Titus remembered how he had been forced to carry it over single-handedly when Eto Mahs hadn't been able to hang on to it. Now he knew why. He cringed to think of how he had stared at Mahs, unable to understand why he couldn't carry a nearly empty transport container.

Vestabo, on the other hand, seemed confused, but once they got over the wall, he shrugged it off and his good-natured smile returned.

It was the same when they reached the transparent

barrier. The instructions told them to go left to find the opening, and Titus remembered traipsing along hip-deep in marsh grass forever while Eto Mahs tugged at his arm, trying to get him to go the other way. As it turned out, the instructions were wrong and the opening was about a klick in the other direction.

Titus knew he probably had the same pained expression as Eto Mahs as he tried to get Vestabo to stop and go right instead of left. It was excruciating, knowing that he knew the right path but he wasn't able to tell the kid. And Vestabo didn't exactly trust him at this point.

Still, Vestabo finally lifted his hands in surrender and returned to the instructions with Titus. He read them again, and pointed in the recommended direction. Titus insistently pointed the other way, and when Vestabo wavered, Titus started jogging toward the spot where he knew the break in the barrier would be.

Vestabo had to run after him. They were supposed to stay together, according to the underlined order on each set of instructions, otherwise the course would automatically end. It turned into to a race, and Titus couldn't bear to look back at Vestabo's concerned expression, obviously worried about his sanity.

Yet when he found the opening and showed him how they could slip through, Vestabo grinned and pounded Titus on the shoulder in congratulations. The kid was so nice about it that he couldn't even get irritated, much as it galled him to have a first-year cadet condescend to him.

By the fourth obstacle—the anti-grav jump, complete with trick pad that let Vestabo sail over while Titus bobbed up and down like a puppet on a string—

Titus was ready to call it quits. He'd had enough of these jokes. He hadn't signed up for this.

Besides, every set of instructions taunted him with the fact that he could simply say "End program" and the torture would be over. He sneered at the wording: "The course will be deemed satisfactorily completed upon the command to End program." The first time around with Eto Mahs, he had hardly paid attention to that disclaimer, believing there had to be some sort of black mark that would result from quitting such an easy obstacle course.

Now, the only thing that kept him bobbing up and down, trying vainly to get over the obstacle, was the image of Eto Mahs with his mouth set in a tight line, his dark eyes burning down at Titus as he leaped up and down, trying to get over. And his grim expression of satisfaction when he finally did make it to the other side.

A low whistle made Titus look up. Vestabo winked and held up an apple he had plucked from the tree. He was sitting on the wall overlooking the gate, in exactly the same spot Titus had taken after he had completed the task of turning the handle. Now it was Titus sweating and grunting over his unmovable handle.

Vestabo gestured with the apple, then tossed it to him. Titus caught it without thinking, then realized it was just what he needed. He sat on the ground, leaning against the gate, and sank his teeth into the plump, green apple. Sweet, tart juiciness spread across his tongue. He hadn't eaten an apple yesterday.

Titus nodded up at Vestabo in thanks. The kid shrugged it off with nothing but sympathy in his expression. Maybe he knew there was some sort of trick going on. Titus hoped so. He hated to think of Vestabo's disillusionment when he had to go through

the course a second time. Titus had figured out that
all the volunteers were made to go through twice.
Little things he hadn't noticed now stood out. The
way Eto Mahs knew exactly where to go to get to each
obstacle, and his anguished expression when they had
first entered the course. Titus knew exactly how he
felt, except he didn't have someone subtly tormenting
him with derision every step of the way.

With that thought, he got back up to tackle the gate.
He didn't care if it killed him, he couldn't give up
when Eto Mahs didn't.

It was full dark and they were trudging up the steep
slope, when the computer voice announced, "Your
time is up. Thank you for participating in Communications Course #105."

The mountainside glimmered, flattening into the
holoprojection before disappearing. Titus blinked
wearily up at the orange-gridded walls. All he could
think was—it's over!

As the door slid open and two lab techs with padds
entered, Titus quickly stuck out his hand for Vestabo
to shake. He even clasped his other hand over the
kid's, looking at him intently, wishing he could warn
him. He hoped Vestabo wouldn't get stuck with
someone like him on the tough round.

This time, Titus was shown directly into a room
where a white-coated scientist was waiting. She
smiled perfunctorily, getting up with a device in hand
and coming around the desk. She pressed the device
to his throat. She was a little taller than he was, very
slender with short reddish-blond hair. She was also
nearly two decades older than him, but he felt an
immediate sense of attraction.

"I'm Professor Joen B'ton," she told him. "There, you can speak now, Cadet Hammon Titus."

"That was a psych project, wasn't it?" he asked, rubbing his throat.

"No, a communications project," she told him, returning to her seat. "But psychology is an integral part of communications, since it concerns a common system of symbols."

"I failed, didn't I?" Titus asked.

Her blue eyes widened slightly. "There is no failure in this project, we simply gather data. The fact that you completed the course two days in a row is excellent. I wanted to thank you—"

"Thank me?" he interrupted, wondering if maybe she had missed Eto Mahs on his way out.

"Yes, you've provided us with some valuable data, Cadet Titus." Professor B'ton held out her hand. "Thank you for volunteering your time."

What could he do? Titus shut his mouth, shook her hand, and got out of there.

But the sour taste in his mouth stayed with him as he packed and left the Academy. Even during the transport to Paris, where he checked into his assigned quarters at the Federation Assembly dormitories, there was a nagging sense of something left incomplete. He unsuccessfully tried to distract himself with the new sights and sounds of European Earth.

Idly checking over his rooms, he actually wished he had a roommate, someone to help fill up the silence. He decided he didn't like absolute quiet anymore, not after forty-eight hours of it. He said, "Computer!" intending to request music.

Instead, he asked, "Do you have an Academy field assignment for Cadet Eto Mahs?"

"Ensign Eto Mahs has graduated and is currently on leave in Rumoi, Hokkaido."

"What will his assignment be when he returns?"

"That information is not available," the computer said sweetly.

"Thanks a lot," Titus muttered.

"Incoming message," the computer responded.

Titus practically leapt for the desk. "On screen!"

The image of Professor Joen B'ton appeared on the screen, her cheeks rounded in a smile. "Cadet Titus, it's good to see you again."

"Uh, you, too, Professor." Titus felt himself go cold inside, despite her pleasant expression. The waiting was over. He had somehow known there was an ax hanging over his head all this time, ready to fall.

"We've had three complete runs, projects 104, 105, and 106," she told him. "That's your two, and Cadet Vestabo completed his final round. Since you are the linking factor for this remarkable series, I wanted to inform you that I have placed a letter of recommendation in your record."

"You did?" he asked, shaking his head. "What about Eto Mahs?"

"Cadet Mahs and Cadet Vestabo will also be acknowledged. But Eto Mahs did not complete his first round because his partner ended the program."

"Oh."

"It's rare we have two completed courses in a row. There's only been a couple of times that we've had three consecutive rounds, which gives us a consistent baseline for the data." Professor B'ton beamed at him, as if she had personally cheered for him the entire way.

"Professor B'ton," Titus told her, unable to smile in return. "I don't deserve your praise. Give letters of recommendation to cadets Eto Mahs and Vestabo, not to me."

Her smile became more sympathetic. "Your participation was an integral part of this success, Cadet. Anything else is a matter for your own conscience."

"I don't deserve it," he repeated, glancing down. He hated to disappoint the professor, but he couldn't lie anymore about what he had done. "Didn't Eto Mahs tell you how awful I was to him?"

"We have the data," Professor B'ton reminded him. "This course was designed to provoke strong feelings, so we could study the common ways humanoids communicate through nonverbal movements and gestures. You'd be surprised how clearly people speak without saying a word."

Titus swallowed, imagining the professor, along with a bunch of young lab techs—including the one with the black hair and merry eyes—reading his movements like he was writing on a wall. He felt himself go red.

"Relax, Cadet," Professor B'ton told him, chuckling slightly at his embarrassment. "You deserve the recommendation. Do a good job at the Assembly, and I'm sure you'll get whatever field assignment you want."

His eyes went wide. Could she read his mind?

"Never underestimate a communications expert." She winked at him, exactly like the young lab tech the day before. "Good-bye, Cadet Titus. I believe you have an *interesting* life ahead of you."

Chapter Seven

Third Year, 2370–71

"MOVE A LITTLE TO YOUR LEFT," Starsa called out.

Louis Zimmerman, Director of Holographic Imaging and Programming at the Jupiter Research Station, inched slightly to his left.

"Now to the right—" Starsa started to say.

"That's good enough," Jayme interrupted, realizing from Starsa's smirk that she was having a good time at the director's expense. She had to put a stop to it before Dr. Zimmerman's dissatisfied expression turned on them.

"Hold . . . three, two, one," Jayme said. "That's it. You can move again."

"I appreciate that," Dr. Zimmerman said dryly, returning to his computer.

Starsa ran the hololoop to make sure they had gotten a good feed. "If you hadn't made yourself the template of the Emergency Medical Hologram, then we wouldn't have to keep bothering you."

"And who would you prefer the EMH to look like?" Zimmerman inquired, concentrating on his screen. "One of *you?*"

Starsa giggled and raised her hand. "Pick me, pick me!"

Zimmerman looked at them closely. "You aren't my regular holotechnicians. Where are they? Well, speak up! Are the cadets the only warm bodies we can muster around here?"

"The others got sick," Starsa said artlessly.

"They have a couple of emergencies down in the power station," Jayme corrected, giving Starsa a hard look.

"I *see,*" he said, as if he doubted their sanity more than anything else.

Jayme kept smiling, trying to push Starsa out of the director's lab. They couldn't tell Dr. Zimmerman that the technicians had eagerly shoved the dozens of routine imaging checks that had to be run every few weeks onto the unsuspecting shoulders of the cadets on field assignment from the Academy. It only took a few days to figure out why—Dr. Zimmerman wasn't the most pleasant man when he was interrupted, and that's what they had to do in order to run imaging checks.

But Starsa was perversely drawn to the imaging devices sitting on the counters of the room, supporting half-completed holographic models.

"What's this?" she asked, sticking her finger through an engineering schematic.

"That's the interior of a matter-fusion assembly." He glanced over and snapped, "Don't touch it!"

"We'll stay out of your way," Jayme assured him, grabbing Starsa to make her come along.

"See that you do," the director drawled, raising his

eyes to the ceiling at the incompetence he had to put up with.

"Please state the nature of the medical emergency," the EMH announced as it materialized.

"Okay, say I've got a double hernia and a severed spine," Jayme suggested. "What would you do?"

The EMH turned, sweeping an arrogant look around the tiny holo-imaging workshop. There was a plasteel wall protecting the neural gel-packs, with only the emitters set up in the shop itself. "Where is the patient?" the EMH asked.

"This is a hypothetical situation," Jayme told him.

The EMH drew himself up, remarkably resembling Director Zimmerman. "I do not deal in hypothetical situations."

"Doctor, you *are* a hypothetical situation," she informed him. At his wounded expression, she added, "Come on, I'm dying of boredom here, running these imaging loops. You might as well test out some of your knowledge."

"Hypothetically speaking?" he asked, edging closer.

"Have a seat," she told him. "I'll finish inputting these feeds, while you tell me what to do with a double hernia and a severed spine."

The EMH hesitated, then glanced around. "I suppose there's no harm in answering a few questions." He settled back with his hands clasped, his tone taking on a lecturing quality. Jayme noted with approval the realistic way the overhead light seemed to shine on his slight balding spot.

"The situation you describe is an interesting one," the EMH began. "The herniated discs must be isolated to ensure they are not causing the spinal distress . . ."

Jayme let it flow over her, smiling at the doctor's dry enthusiasm. She had to admit that Zimmerman was right. He made the perfect template for a medical doctor.

"What's going on?" Starsa asked, interrupting an engrossing discussion of neural surgery.

"I'm running the imaging checks," Jayme said defensively, glancing at the EMH.

"It's after 0100," Starsa pointed out. "I thought you were supposed to do the graviton adjustments—"

"It's that late?" Jayme jumped up. "End EMH program." The EMH had a reproachful expression as he disappeared. "I've got to run."

"You must have been daydreaming about Moll again," Starsa teased.

"That's not true. I just lost track of time." Jayme started out the door. "I better hurry or Ensign Dshed will report me."

Jayme walked along the narrow graviton conduits, tricorder in hand. Each section of the gravity emitter array had to be calibrated every day to compensate for the expanding and contracting ice mantle of Jupiter's moon. Calibrating the system basically consisted of flushing the blocked gravitons caused by the rapid temperature shifts. It was menial labor of the most routine kind. But then again, Jayme was finding that almost all her engineering tasks were mind-numbingly routine.

Except their imaging sessions with Zimmerman. The man always had some curve to throw them, some way to make her feel like he had seen right through her. Well into her third year now, she was becoming used to her professors' disappointment at her lack of engineering skill, but she got the feeling that even geniuses felt stupid around Zimmerman.

She bent down to attach the pressure gauge to the graviton valve. The sensors were two microns off, so she brought the gauge back into line. Jupiter Research Station was one of the oldest functioning stations in the solar system—even the original Mars station had been abandoned centuries ago. All the equipment on Jupiter's moon was like a creaky great-great-grandmother, not ready to retire but moving so slowly and stiffly that she might as well find a nice desk job somewhere warm.

Jayme wished Moll could see the station—she always liked anything that was old. Moll would also love the way Jupiter dominated the sky, as if you could almost fall off the station and down into the swirling clouds of the gas giant. Jayme had taped a message to Moll last week, with Jupiter visible through the window, but she was sure the impact wouldn't be the same. She had suggested that Moll take a hop to Jupiter Station, but she hadn't heard back. Not that she should be surprised. It was fairly typical of the ups and downs of their friendship.

Nobody understood their relationship, and she had almost gotten used to people dismissing her love for Moll as a schoolgirl crush. Nobody saw what happened between them when they were alone, up late at night talking about everything they wouldn't tell another soul. But every time they took another step closer, Moll pulled back again. Jayme wasn't sure why Moll wouldn't commit to a real relationship with her, but that was just one of the mysteries about the Trill. She was different, special. She had always been different, Jayme knew that from the way Moll described her childhood on Trill, all those tests and displays she was forced to go through, showing off her rare eidetic memory for academics and officials.

Jayme would put up with much more than jokes from Starsa and Titus to win Moll's love. Meanwhile, Moll was back at the Academy, beginning her last year, while Jayme was stuck on a two-month field assignment to Jupiter Station, nearly frustrated to death. Starsa could be great fun, but she was no Moll Enor. And a steady diet of mundane engineering jobs was beginning to make her want to scream.

Jayme glanced around. She was in a secured area beneath the station. Why not?

"Aaahhhgghhhhh!" she screamed out loud, hearing her voice echo through the long conduit chamber.

"Hello?" a startled voice called out. "Somebody hurt down there?"

Jayme winced. She had forgotten about the access tubes. Her scream must have echoed up them like wells.

"Somebody screamed down here!" another voice echoed down.

"It's all right!" Jayme called out, turning first one way then the other as people began to yell down the tubes. "I'm *okay!* I just . . . pinched my finger."

The calling stopped, but Jayme caught one comment—"Some cadet!"—before the conduit chamber fell quiet again. Jayme sighed, moving on with her duties. There were valves to be gauged and adjustments to be made.

* * *

". . . and the metatarsal, not to be confused with the metasuma," the EMH was saying as Starsa came into the room, "should be anchored before beginning the procedure. . . ."

Starsa noticed that Jayme was startled when she came into the workshop. The EMH droned on about contusions and subhematoma somethings.

Starsa pointed her thumb at the EMH, "Why is he out? Don't you get enough of Zimmerman making the loops?"

Jayme didn't look at him. "He's okay. He's better than Zimmerman."

"Why, thank you," the EMH said.

Starsa narrowed her eyes at the EMH. "Do you think his smile is still a little too smug?"

Jayme considered the EMH, but he rapidly lost his satisfied look. *"Smug?"* he asked. "I beg your pardon, but I do *not* appear smug."

"Maybe a little," Jayme agreed.

The door opened behind them. "Is there a problem with the EMH?" Director Zimmerman asked.

Starsa thought Jayme looked guilty about something. "No problem," she answered for them both.

"Then why is the EMH activated?" Zimmerman asked, closing the distance between them. "Haven't you completed your imaging checks yet?"

"Yes!" Jayme answered. "That is, I'm just finishing."

Starsa could tell Jayme needed a hand for some reason. "We were just discussing his smile. Do you think it's too smug-looking?"

Jayme kicked her while Zimmerman gravely frowned at the EMH. The holographic doctor wasn't smiling. Actually, he had a rather disdainful expression, like he had smelled something bad.

Zimmerman turned back to them. "I think he looks nearly perfect."

"So do I," Starsa agreed. "Come on, Jayme, we have to get to Lieutenant Barclay's seminar on warp dynamics."

On their way to the warp-core simulator, Jayme didn't thank Starsa for helping her out. In fact, Jayme seemed preoccupied with something. Starsa didn't mind—her friend sometimes got moody. That's just the way she was.

Lieutenant Barclay was waiting for the twelve cadets to assemble who were currently assigned to Jupiter Research Station. For once, Starsa wasn't the last one there, and she had a few moments to tease Barclay by asking questions about the simulation that he set up for them. "Is it a warp breach?" she pressed. "I hope not, because last week's warp breach was a real loser, if you don't mind my saying so."

Barclay smiled uncertainly and stammered, "N-no. This week, it's a . . . well, you'll have to wait until we start the simulation, Cadet."

"Come on," Starsa urged, "give us a hint. Please?"

Barclay kept hedging, but Starsa was surprised that Jayme didn't nudge her to stop, as she usually did. Starsa finally let up when Barclay began going through the duty roster for the simulation, and each cadet took charge of a station. Starsa was on her way to the warp-nacelle monitor when she noticed Jayme, paused next to Lieutenant Barclay, the last cadet to receive her assignment.

"Lieutenant," Jayme said. "I wondered if I could ask you a personal question."

Barclay shifted his eyes, catching sight of Starsa.

She pretended to be busy with the monitor, but she was all ears when he replied, "A personal question? I don't know if that's quite . . . I'm not sure . . ."

"I was just wondering why you chose to go into engineering."

Barclay really looked nervous, as if he wished he had been firm and told her to report to her duty station. But they all got away with murder with Barclay. Starsa liked him better than any of their other field professors.

"Why d-d-do," he started, swallowing to get the word out, "do you ask?"

"I'm just curious," Jayme said quickly. "You seem to enjoy it so much, I wondered when you first knew engineering was for you."

"I've always liked working with machines," Barclay admitted, smiling shyly. "I feel more comfortable with them, I guess."

Jayme was nodding seriously, as if he had given her something to think about. Starsa wasn't sure what that was, but one thing for sure, her old quadmate was certainly acting strange. Then Starsa forgot all about it as the fascinating simulation began. She had just been teasing Barclay when she said the warp core breach had been boring. He came up with the trickiest programs that were incredibly fun to figure out.

The next day, Starsa asked Jayme to stop by her quarters before dinner to see something special she'd been working on.

"There!" Starsa dramatically gestured to the device on her desk. "It's an anti-aging device."

"Starsa . . ." Jayme groaned. "Why are you mess-

169

ing around with mechanical gerontominy? You know all the advances in the past two centuries have been biochemical, not electromagnetic. It's like going back to astrology to understand the stars."

"Humph!" Starsa snorted, turning to beam with pride on her gerontometer, giving it reassuring pats. "At one time people thought the transporter was a looney idea."

"That's true, in a twisted sort of way." Jayme came closer. "Why are you building it?"

"Why not?" she replied. "I got the idea from something Zimmerman said a few weeks ago, so I just started."

"Yea," Jayme agreed wryly, "It's *finishing* a project you have trouble with."

With a pout that acknowledged the hit, Starsa raised her chin. "Where's the fun in engineering if you don't build things?"

Jayme didn't know what to say to that. She didn't want to admit that she'd been thinking the same thing for weeks—where's the fun in engineering? At night, the mess halls were filled with talk of the new warp designs being developed at Utopia Planitia, so that starships could exceed warp five again. But Jayme couldn't see the thrill in the need to eliminate subspace instabilities. The thought of twiddling away on a gerontometer or anything like it made her want to yawn.

In some strange way, Starsa reminded Jayme of her mother. Commander Miranda always had a project or three underway in her quarters. Her great-aunt Marley Miranda's home in France also looked like an engineering lab. Growing up, Jayme had a permanent image of her great-uncle gamely smiling from behind piles of coupling rings and conduit bundles, trying to watch the news on a padd in one vacant corner of the room.

Starsa started to ask, "What's wrong—"

Suddenly the floor lurched under them. Even unbalanced, Starsa dove for her gerontometer and caught it before it could hit the ground.

"What was that?" Jayme asked, afraid of what it *might* be.

Starsa settled her gerontometer back on the desk. "It felt like the graviton array went out of synch for a microsecond."

"Maybe it's another tremor," Jayme suggested, holding her breath.

Another jolt shook the floor. Starsa was ready that time, and she cushioned her precious device safely on the bed. "That's no tremor. That's a system failure—"

The yellow alert began to flash, and the computer announced, "Yellow alert! Emergency personnel to their stations."

Starsa made sure her gerontometer wouldn't be knocked off the bed. "I'm supposed to go to the environmental support substation this week. I think . . . what about you?"

Jayme was already heading out the door. "I've got to get down to the graviton conduit chamber."

"See you later," Starsa called merrily. Jayme wondered how someone could be that oblivious about people and still be such a great mechanical genius. Then she remembered Barclay, who was not very personable himself, but she sincerely hoped he was working on whatever was going wrong down there.

The jolting continued to rock the decks of Jupiter Research Station as Jayme rapidly made her way down to the graviton chamber. Personnel were rushing to their alert stations, purposefully crossing paths. Strictly speaking, Jayme wasn't supposed to be belowdecks, but she grabbed a kit from the rack and followed a work crew down the access ladder, crossing her fingers that they wouldn't notice an extra person.

"This valve hasn't been vented in three days!" Ensign Dshed exclaimed, leaning over to check the gauge.

"This one hasn't either," a technician further down the conduit confirmed.

"The graviton distortion waves are phasing into synch," Barclay informed them, concentrating on his tricorder. "We better get these valves vented fast!"

Jayme grabbed a siphon and ran to check the next valve. It wasn't vented either. In all, more than half a dozen valves in the section hadn't been vented. They were throwing off the synch of the entire array. She hung onto the conduit walkway as the station shuddered, almost knocking her from her perch to the floor a few feet below. She hoped they could get the valves vented before a synchopathic wave ripped the station off the moon.

The next graviton slip was so strong the walkway seemed to fall out from under her. "Ohh!" she exclaimed, landing hard on the conduit walk.

One of the other technicians grabbed her arm, and helped her hang on. He looked at her. "What are you doing down here, Cadet?"

Her stomach leaped into her throat, threatening to strangle her. Her mouth opened wordlessly as the full import of her mistake hit her.

"Never mind," the technician whispered, glancing over his shoulder. "I always wanted to be in on the action, too, when I was a cadet. But you better get out of here before the lieutenant notices."

Jayme nodded, her eyes wide, as she backed away. Then she turned and ran down the conduit, barely grabbing hold of the ladder as another graviton slippage hit the station. For a moment she hung there, staring back at the others, attempting to fix the damage she had done to the conduits, while she had to climb back up where she belonged, unable to help.

"This is gross negligence, Cadet Miranda," Commander Aston of Jupiter Research Station said slowly, considering the report handed in by his first officer. "Do you have anything to say for yourself?"

"No, sir," Jayme said stiffly, staring straight ahead. She couldn't think of another Miranda who had received as many reprimands as she had accumulated in two-and-a-half years at the Academy. She wondered if she was destined to mess up with every commander she served under. If so, it was bound to be a very short career.

"I must say, Cadet Miranda," Aston said severely, "the reputation of your family members led me to expect a much different officer." The commander regarded her thoughtfully, a specimen in a jar.

Jayme winced. "I've been preoccupied lately, sir. It won't happen again."

The commander seated himself. "What's on your mind, cadet?" When Jayme hesitated, Aston urged, "Out with it! I want to know what's keeping you so busy that you neglect your simplest duties."

"I-I'm not sure I'll be happy, sir, as an engineer," Jayme said in a rush, letting out her breath in surprise that she had finally voiced her deepest fear.

"Cadet." The commander stood up and leaned forward, crooking his finger at Jayme. Startled, she leaned forward to hear his low order. "I don't care if you jump for joy all the way from your quarters to your workstation. But you don't let your personal feelings interfere with the safety of my station. Do you understand?"

Jayme snapped back to attention. "Yes, sir!"

The commander consulted his screen. "You'll continue your graviton adjustment duties, but you'll alternate with Cadet Sendonii in the aft conduit chamber. That way you can't make too much of a mess of my array." Jayme squirmed as the commander added, "We've suffered some structural damage, especially to the lower two decks, so you're to report to Lieutenant Barclay for extra maintenance and repair duty in the evenings."

"Yes, sir."

"There will also be a formal reprimand put on your permanent record." The commander's voice softened somewhat, his dark eyes looking on her kindly. "Good luck figuring out your career choice, Cadet. I know how difficult it can be sometimes. I thought I wanted to be a counselor for my first two years at the Academy, but as it turns out, I ended up right where I belong, holding this station together for some of our best researcher engineers."

Jayme looked at Aston with surprise, but before she could thank him, the commander seated himself. "You're dismissed, Cadet."

* * *

Jayme could handle hearing Starsa joke about her blunder—she was used to her former quadmate's completely irreverent attitude about the most serious things. But Jayme hated knowing that everyone else was talking about her incompetence. When she and Starsa went to Zimmerman's lab to run the imaging checks, she had to hear it all over again.

"That was a fine trick you pulled, Cadet." Dr. Zimmerman narrowed his eyes at her. "Come this way. Look at that!" The random pieces of one of his experimental holographic imagers was gathered into clumpy piles. "Ruined! Three weeks of work, destroyed!"

"I'm sorry, sir," Jayme said through clenched teeth. "It wasn't done on purpose."

Zimmerman drew himself up. "I should hope not! Not when there have been so many inconvenienced by your negligence."

"I'm *sorry,*" Jayme repeated. Starsa glanced up, for once noticing the edge in her voice.

"You'll have to be more than sorry," Dr. Zimmerman continued blithely. "You have to look alive to be an engineer—"

"So maybe I should quit," Jayme interrupted. "Sir," she added belatedly.

"Quit? Starfleet?" Zimmerman rolled his eyes. "Now, let's not be dramatic."

"No, I mean quit being an engineer. Obviously I'm not cut out for it."

Starsa was staring at Jayme as if she had just swallowed the holo imaging scanner. "Quit? You can't quit!"

"Quite right," Zimmerman agreed, turning to Jayme. "Don't be absurd. You'll make a perfectly acceptable engineer. *If* you can keep your mind on what you're doing."

"Maybe I don't want to be an engineer," Jayme insisted.

"Why not?" Starsa spoke up, her voice cracking in utter surprise. "I thought you always wanted to be an engineer. Everyone in your family is an engineer!"

"Maybe I'm not." Jayme stubbornly set up the scanner and began her work.

"Well," Zimmerman said doubtfully, "you'll probably feel better in the morning."

"It's not a stomachache," Jayme said in exasperation. "It's not something I can just get over."

"Perhaps you should speak to your advisor about this," Zimmerman suggested, eyeing her in disbelief. "Or a counselor."

"Thank you, sir," Jayme said flatly, concentrating on the imager, trying to get the work done so she could get out of there. The silence was thick with resentment and unspoken criticism.

Once they were back in the corridor, Starsa asked, "Are you serious? You'd really quit engineering?"

"I just said that to get under his skin," Jayme tried to pass it off.

"Really?" Starsa didn't seem convinced. "You're more than halfway through the Academy. Why change now?"

"You're right," Jayme agreed, walking very fast, trying to get away from her, too. "I'd be crazy to switch majors now."

"You want to quit engineering?" Professor Chapman asked.

"Yes, sir," Jayme said, holding her chin level.

"To do what?" Chapman asked incredulously.

"I want to try to get into Starfleet Medical School, sir." Voicing her desire for the first time, especially to her academic advisor, was more difficult than she had imagined.

"Stop acting so formal," Chapman ordered irritably. "How can I have a conversation with you when you're at attention, staring over my head?"

"I'm sorry, sir," Jayme apologized. "It's been a difficult decision."

"I can imagine," Chapman agreed with understatement. "Isn't this a rather sudden change for you? Your secondary schooling was pre-engineering, wasn't it?"

"Yes."

"And you didn't mention you had doubts about your work at our beginning-of-the-third-year review."

"No."

"Are you going to speak in monosyllables this entire converation, Cadet?"

Jayme swallowed, realizing she had to snap out of it. Professor Chapman had always been sympathetic, and the two classes she had taken with him proved he was a brilliant engineer.

"I'm not cut out for this, sir. I love diagnostics, but the routine maintenance work is driving me crazy. You . . . you know about the graviton system malfunction on Jupiter Research Station?"

"I was notified," Chapman admitted. "I'm starting to get used to hearing about your reprimands."

Jayme blushed. "I'm not suited to engineering."

"But you are suited to medical studies? Which you've had no preparation for."

"Sir, I know I want to be a medical doctor. I'm an excellent diagnostician, and I've realized I would much rather work with people than machinery."

"Yes, but a doctor?" Chapman seemed doubtful.

"Yes; I've been working on the EMH here at Jupiter Station, and it's fascinating. I would much rather talk about speculums and seepage rates than rerouting circuitry."

"The EMH? Isn't that Zimmerman's program?" Chapman muttered more to himself than Jayme. "I should have known he was involved in this somehow."

"It's not Director Zimmerman," Jayme assured him. "I've been talking to the EMH holoprogram tied into the medical database. I've known what I really wanted to do for a while, but I couldn't face it until that graviton accident."

"You can't let one mistake upset all your hard work. Your grades aren't as high as they could be, granted, but you're not failing."

Jayme shook her head. "I'm barely a good technician, and that's taken every bit of effort I can muster. I just don't have my heart in it. You have to admit, sir, I'm no B'Elanna Torres."

"Torres left the Academy," Chapman said, his voice hardening with resentment.

Jayme tightened her lips, somehow frightened by the idea of leaving Starfleet. She had been shocked when she had found out Torres had left—the half-Klingon who was ten times the engineer she would ever be. "I hope I don't have to quit the Academy," she said fervently. "I don't know what other life I could have outside of Starfleet."

"Well, it hasn't come to that," Chapman said, somewhat mollified.

"It will if I have to keep studying engineering," Jayme said slowly. "I've been able to fake it up to a point, but now I have to make a real choice. Now I'm endangering people."

"You will have even more responsibility as a medical doctor," Chapman cautioned.

"That sort of pressure I can handle, I know it. You must agree that having a passion for something makes for nine-tenths of the success."

"What about your field assignment at the Jupiter Research Station?" Chapman asked.

"I'll finish here, of course," Jayme quickly said, realizing that was the only right answer.

"Very well then, you may submit an official change of majors, Cadet Miranda. I will approve your choice pending a thorough discussion with a premed advisor, so you know what you're up against." Chapman shuffled through electronic padds piled on his desk. "I'll try to track down an understanding advisor. Give me a few days, will you?"

"Thank you, sir!" Jayme exclaimed, grateful that she wasn't going to be denied her chance to try for medical school. She knew better than anyone if her grades weren't good enough, no amount of wanting it would get her in. It wasn't like she had a slew of relatives who were doctors who could vouch for her.

". . . and clamp the artery at the base of the aorta." The EMH was describing a procedure, his hands twisted to show the angle. "That will allow you to staunch the flow of blood to see the angle of intrusion—"

"Why are you always talking to that holo-doc?" Starsa asked, coming up behind Jayme.

"At least he's not an engineer," Jayme told her. "There's nothing but engineers on this station."

"And you," Starsa said helpfully.

"What am I?" Jayme retorted.

Starsa shrugged, her eyes wide. "Whatever you are, you've got a call coming in."

Jayme turned to the EMH. "Thank you, Doctor. We'll continue tomorrow."

The EMH nodded to her, giving Starsa a reproachful look. "Don't bring your friend next time."

Starsa was looking with interest at the EMH. "Hey, are you the one who brainwashed Jayme into quitting engineering?"

"Cadet Miranda will make a fine medical student," the EMH calmly replied.

"Who are *you* to judge?" Starsa told him. "You're gonna have to learn to stay out of people's minds or you're going to get into lots of trouble."

"*I* am not in trouble," the EMH said smugly. "I am a emergency medical hologram. I perform my duties flawlessly."

"Thank you, Doctor," Jayme hastened to say. "End EMH program."

As Jayme left the lab, Starsa called out, "You know, holograms can be dangerous for your health if you hang around them too much."

Jayme sighed. Her transfer request had been submitted, and now the calls from the relatives were starting to come in.

"But, honey, how can you possibly get into Starfleet Medical School?" her mother asked in concern. She was so busy, as usual, that she was speaking from a station near the warp core of the U.S.S. *Gandhi*.

"Mom, all of my electives have been science courses. I'll have enough credits to be accepted if I take summer courses the next two years and concentrate on biology/premed seminars."

Her mother glanced sideways, probably in the middle of some diagnostic on board the *Gandhi,* the *Ambassador*-class starship she had served on for the past six years. Jayme considered the *Gandhi* to be her second home, but the last time she'd been on board was at the beginning of the summer break. She had only spent a couple of weeks with her mom, as usual rotating among the starships and starbases where her favorite cousins and aunts were posted.

"I don't know, honey, it sounds risky," her mother finally counseled. "You're so close to graduating."

"You're right," Jayme agreed. "But nothing else in my life has been risky, so I think I can handle this."

When Jayme got back to her quarters a few evenings later, with only one week left in her tour of duty on Jupiter Station, there was a message waiting from Moll Enor. Her dark, serious face was so beautiful that Jayme reached out and touched the screen.

"I'm sure you'll accomplish whatever you set out to do," Moll said simply. Then she smiled, and for a moment, it was like they were talking in real-time, Jayme felt so close to Moll. Then the blue Starfleet symbol filled the screen and the transmission was over.

The other message was from her older sister, Raylin, stationed on Deep Space Station 2 in the Allora Prime system. Raylin had already made Lieutenant, and was third in command of engineering on DS2. Jayme remembered how their mother had cried when she found out.

"Jayme!" Raylin exclaimed, her expression horrified. "You don't even like to get a hypospray! Remember how you screamed when I sliced open my thumb with the laser cutter—"

"Don't listen to her, Jayme!" her sister's husband cried out, as Raylin tried to shove him out of the viewscreen. "We *need* a Miranda in blue!"

Raylin pushed him from the view, holding him off as she tried to talk over his babble, trying to put some sense into her little sister.

Jayme started smiling, then giggling, holding her stomach she was laughing so hard. Her brother-in-law was right—it was about time a Miranda represented Starfleet in the blue uniform.

Chapter Eight

NEV REOH SAT GLUMLY waiting in yet another dark and dingy bar on Station 14, in orbit around Beltos IV. This bar was just like the one last week on Station 26, and the one the week before on Station 7—a warren of narrow ledges and tables bolted to the walls around a space of zero-g in the center.

The weightless center was where the Orion animal-women danced. The thrumming beat of the music vibrated from the beam supports of the bar, and tiny laser lights called the exotic green women to shadowed ledges.

What made it worse was that Reoh knew someone like Titus or Jayme or Bobbie Ray Jefferson would revel in this exciting environment, while he kept trying to loosen the collar of his new Starfleet uniform, still uncomfortable after a month on active duty as a grade-three ore examiner for the Beltos IV mining colony.

Every shipment of dicosilium (and the rarer dilithium) that was sold to the Federation had to be checked for purity and radiation-contaminant levels. The Beltos IV mining settlement was near the Rigel system, in the most densely populated area of the Milky Way Galaxy, yet it was under rule of the Pa'a. The Pa'a had thus far refused to become a member of the Federation.

Hence the need for a rotating crew of ensigns with geophysics qualifications. Reoh had dragged his spectro-analyzer through more broken-down freighters and storage compartments than he could count while making his way among the orbiting string of transfer stations around Beltos IV.

Every one of the stations had at least a dozen dancing bars like the one he was in. It made Reoh uncomfortable to know that the Federation couldn't do a thing about the exploitation of the Orion animal-women, except to ensure that no slaves were exported out of the solar system. Here and there, Reoh could see the Starfleet uniforms of the officers who ran the border patrols, ensuring that this pocket of Pa'a corruption was contained. Yet even the Starfleet personnel were drawn to see the Orions—who could resist their magnetic pull?

A green hand clasped the pole near his feet, then another appeared, as the sweetheart-face of an Orion animal-woman emerged from the darkness, pulling herself up to his perch. Her lips parted as she glided through the air, undulating as she came closer. Her dark green eyes were filled with promise as her tongue slipped between her teeth.

Horrified, Reoh forced himself to look away. He wouldn't contribute to the degradation of these poor slaves.

"You want me," she whispered, her hand clasping his perch.

"Uh, no, thank you, Ma'am." Reoh uneasily smiled to let her know it was nothing personal. "I don't think so."

"You are unhappy . . ." she murmured.

"No, really, I'm fine, thank you. I'm waiting for my next appointment to arrive."

"I think you wait for me. . . ."

Reoh tried to look at her, but she was drawing herself up behind him. "No," he told her uneasily, "it's a Pa'a captain."

Her hands slipped over his shoulders, her kneading fingers sending shivers down his spine. Her rumbling purr moved near his ear, then an icy-hot trail flashed up his skin as she licked his neck.

Reoh tried to untangle her green arms from around him. How had she managed to do that so fast?

"I think you have the wrong customer," he told her. He could barely make out the other animal-women— sometimes two or three women—twining themselves around the men resting on the nearby ledges.

"Please . . ." He had to lean closer to hear her breathy little voice, which hardly penetrated the thrumming music. "I will be in trouble if you send me away."

Reoh stopped trying to hold her off, looking her right in the face. "Are you serious? You mean you're punished if a customer doesn't pay for a dance?"

She nodded, busy nestling closer.

"All right, give me your finger," he agreed, holding the tab so she could press her delicate hand against it. He felt bad. He had been sending women away all day, waiting for Captain Jord to let him inspect her cargo of dicosilium. From what he'd learned in the past few weeks, *all* business was done in the dancing bars. "Are the other girls punished for not getting dances?"

"I know only my master," she murmured, seemingly content with curling up next to him on the ledge. But he kept having to capture her wandering fingers, lulled by her gentle stroking of his hand or his chest.

"What's your name?" he asked, pulling back to see the bronze green sheen of her cheeks, the startling whites of her eyes.

"Meesa," she breathed.

"Meesa," he repeated, helplessly trapped by the warm scent of her, the feel of her in his arms.

Reoh shook his head, and pushed her away slightly, trying to get hold of himself. He felt like he had been fighting off Orion animal-women ever since he got to the Beltos system, but this one was more persistent than most. He had been rejecting her advances for nearly an hour before finally giving in. It usually wasn't difficult to hold himself back. Except for momentary lapses of pheromone-induced lust, he mostly felt pity for them, trapped in these hellholes.

"Here," he said, taking her hand and pressing her fingertip to his charge card once more. "There's another dance. Now, I have to be going. No, thank you very much," he assured her, scraping her off as he pushed into the glide lane that carried him through the bar.

He glanced back as he was leaving, but he couldn't see Meesa anymore. He wondered if he had misread Captain Jord's message and gotten the wrong bar. That wouldn't be unlikely in these warrens the Pa'a called space stations.

Reoh consulted his tricorder and hitched the spectro-analyzer more securely on his shoulder. The jostling crowds were mostly natives from Beltos IV, trading their precious minerals or trying to obtain permits from the ruling Pa'a to travel to other planets in the system, or even enter Federation space. Only two gates on each station led to the docking rings—a passenger gate and a cargo gate. Both were close-encrypted by Starfleet personnel, running the front lines of border control. Despite the safeguards, smuggling was a big business among the various arms of the Pa'a.

At the very least, Captain Jord wasn't going any-where until Reoh validated her encryption pass for the cargo. He also had to give her the coordinates where her vessel could penetrate the automated sensor-scan buoys at the edge of the system.

Reoh pressed his thumb to the sensor padd of the passenger gate, uneasily aware of the many envious eyes of loiterers on the levels above and below him, watching the traffic through the immense portal. As he phased through, a silver-tinted Pa'a bustled up and pressed his encryption pass against the sensor padd. The high-ranking Pa'a pushed past Reoh, heading to the upper docking ring where the better vessels were in port.

Reoh's ancient shuttle was parked among an assort-ment of Starfleet ships. Because the stations weren't under Federation rule, Starfleet officers were required to stay on their ships rather than transient quarters. Reoh preferred that anyway. He felt comfortable in his shuttle, the *Dilithium Node,* which had been in service in the Beltos system longer than he had been alive. A modern replicator was jammed awkwardly into one corner and the bunk was barely wide enough for him to lie down, but it was home.

There was a voice-only message from Captain Jord,

informing him that she would be delayed and would be unable to meet him until the next day—at the same dancing bar. Reoh methodically checked to make sure he had found the right one.

He really didn't mind the delay. He had one other inspection to perform in the next couple of days, then his rotation was up and he could return to Starbase 3 for R&R before his next month of duty. He was looking forward to seeing the starbase again. It was one of the biggest in the Federation, servicing a wide variety of systems and species. He had only spent three days on board before shipping out for Beltos IV.

Reoh shook his head at the thought of this assignment. Who would have thought geophysics would be so exotic? He loved rocks, and that was really the only reason he had chosen geophysics. Rocks were safe and enduring. After his spectacular lack of faith in himself as a Vedek and in the Bajoran religion, he had desperately needed to belong to something that was as close to permanent as he could find—the planets themselves.

The Academy was also an enduring place. Stricken with sudden longing, Reoh checked the chronometer for the time at the Academy. It was late, but Jayme usually stayed up until all hours. He sent the signal.

"Hello?" Jayme finally answered, blinking sleepily.

"Did I wake you?" Reoh asked.

"Who is that? Nev Reoh?" Jayme said blearily. "Gad, almost didn't recognize you in that uniform."

Proudly, Reoh straightened his blue-shouldered jacket. "I'm a level three geo-inspector in the Beltos system."

"Glory be," Jayme yawned. "Orion animal-women! Having fun yet?"

"Uh, not really," he admitted. "It's mostly dust and rocks, you know."

"I can understand you're distracted, what with everything that's happening," Jayme agreed.

Reoh felt like he'd missed part of their conversation. "What do you mean?"

"In the Bajoran system. They're battening down the hatches."

"Cardassians?!" Reoh asked, his voice rising in a frightened squawk.

"No, the Dominion." Jayme finally seemed to wake up. "Where have you been the past few weeks?"

"In the Beltos system—"

"Yeah, I guess the rumors wouldn't have reached you yet. Everyone here at the Academy knows, of course."

"What's wrong with Bajor?" Reoh demanded.

"We found out the Dominion are shape-shifters. They're the ones who control the Jem'Hadar, and they're practically invading through the wormhole."

"Invading!"

"Well, not yet. But everyone expects them to." Jayme shifted through some clips on her desk. "I'll send you some of the reports. I'm surprised they haven't called you to DS9. There are so few Bajorans in Starfleet."

"There's not much for a geophysicist to do on a space station by a wormhole," Reoh said numbly, thinking over the implications of Bajor being smack on the front lines of an invasion. His people never seemed to get a break.

Jayme yawned. "You could be some sort of liaison."

"I'm no Sito Jaxa." The thought of his Bajoran friend, a former member of Nova Squadron, still brought him near to tears. Jaxa was believed to have given her life last month by returning to Cardassia as a prisoner of war in order to protect a Federation informant. "I could never be a hero."

"That's nonsense. Heroes are just people who do what needs to be done."

Reoh wasn't sure why Jayme was smiling, but he couldn't ask because she said she had an exobiology exam the next day. Before signing off, she sent a burst transmission of the Academy news service clippings on the recent developments.

Reoh stayed up half the night listening to the reports. He also accessed the Bajoran news on the Federation subspace channel. It didn't look good.

He kept remembering his six months leave in the Bajoran system right after he graduated. He had never been to the homeworld before, so he had taken a complete tour of the colonies and most of the major continents of Bajor, visiting all the great historic sites he had studied during his life.

But it hadn't felt like home. He had talked to other Bajorans who claimed to have had an immediate sense of completeness at being on Bajoran soil and among their own people. A homecoming, they all told him. Maybe it was his disenfranchisement from so much of the Bajoran spiritual life, feeling like he had no right to the comfort of his religion when he had failed his people.

It was worse when he ran into someone he knew from the resettlement colony on Shunt. Ran Sisla was married now and working in one of the fishing villages of Karor. She had been uncomfortable with him, remembering him in his former Vedek's robes when he had acted as the spiritual leader of their tiny community in the north country of Shunt.

Reoh never did get to sleep that night, thinking over his mistakes and wishing he had done things differently. If he had never fooled himself into believing he was called as a Vedek, his life might have gone very differently. He wouldn't have felt such a need to leave Shunt. He could have been on Bajor right now, helping his people.

Then again, nothing was what it appeared to be. In the last weeks of his vacation on Bajor, Vedek Winn had accused Vedek Bareil of being a Cardassian collaborator during the Resistance. Bareil had withdrawn from the election, and Winn was now Kai.

Reoh had written his astonishment to Ro Laran—whom he wouldn't exactly consider a friend, but she was a fellow Bajoran in Starfleet. But his communique had been returned undelivered. Soon after, he received a Starfleet notification that Ro had gone AWOL and was believed to be cooperating with the Maquis, who had recently taken a more militant stand in the Demilitarized Zone. The communique added that any information as to Ro Laran's whereabouts should be forwarded immediately to Starfleet Headquarters, etc. etc.

Meanwhile, he was alone in a very strange solar system, crawling through endless storage containers and checking ore for crystalline impurities.

Nev Reoh tried to wait outside the dancing bar for Captain Jord, but the enforcers insisted he move along or pay the door fee to get in. Once inside, he was able to secure a ledge near the lit entrance. Almost immediately, he had to fend off the advances of Orion animal-women.

Then he saw Meesa slightly above him. A brutish

Rigellian miner was trying to attract her attention with a purple laser light, signaling her to come to him. Reoh quickly motioned for Meesa to join him.

She was at his side in a flash, her expression so grateful and pleased that he suddenly realized how young she was—like a first-year cadet. She snuggled next to him, fitting into the crook of his arm, holding up her finger to be validated on his charge card.

Reoh nervously hoped that he could push the woman away without too much fuss when Captain Jord arrived. It wasn't the most professional situation she could find him in, but what did she expect, asking him to meet her in a place like this?

"How long have you been dancing here, Meesa?" He was grateful that this time she seemed content to cuddle rather than try to seduce him.

She squirmed up to bring her lips closer to his ear. "This many days," she whispered, holding out all of her fingers but one.

"That's all?" he asked, his voice cracking at her sudden closeness.

She nodded, leaning her head back against his shoulder. It was so intimate, yet they were sitting in a crowded room with a couple hundred strangers barely visible through the shifting lights of the bar. In the center, a long-limbed Orion was contorting into unbelievable positions as she spun and rolled in midair.

He cleared his throat. "You come from Beltos IV?"

Meesa nodded, her tiny chin quivering and her eyes filling with tears at the memory.

"I'm sorry!" Reoh exclaimed, fumbling for something to wipe her eyes. "You didn't want to leave?" he asked helplessly.

"I have nothing," she murmured, looking down at her hands.

"That's awful," he said for lack of anything better.

He sat with her for the better part of an hour, hardly speaking. She actually dozed off. He was consumed with pity for the poor woman who was obviously worked round the clock, one of thousands who were burned out in the slave trade.

When it was finally clear that Captain Jord wasn't going to appear, *again,* Reoh pressed Meesa's finger to his card a few more times, telling her, "You can get some sleep now."

Her eyes lingered on him a moment, struck by his gift of time. That made him feel even worse, that she would be so surprised and touched by such a simple thing. He watched to make sure she got through the crowd without being snared by a reveling Pa'a crewmember or vacationing Beltos miner. She disappeared through one of the little slave-holes, leading to the prophets knew where in the bowels of the place.

Shuddering in sympathy, Reoh left the dancing bar.

"Conditions are intolerable!" he pleaded with Commander Keethzarn, the security supervisor of Starbase 3. "You should see what they make these women do!"

Commander Keethzarn was half-Human and half-Vulcan, but at first Reoh had thought he was a Romulan, since he had never seen a pointy-eared humanoid smile. But even with only a few days on Starbase 3, he had heard of Keethzarn's very human-like exploits of fun that were practically legendary. Some of the other security officers said he was aiming to be known as the "happiest Vulcan in the galaxy," and everyone pretty much figured he had the title won, hands down.

"Slow down, Ensign," Keethzarn told him. "I've

seen the dancing bars. And I hate to tell you, kid, but I've seen far worse than that. We're always working on ways to stop the slave trade on Beltos. Soon as we plug up one hole, four other leaks show up."

"Can't the Federation at least make them close the dancing bars on the stations? There's . . . there are Starfleet officers in there."

"The station's regulations are an internal matter, kid."

As one of the oldest cadets at the Academy, Reoh wasn't used to being called "kid." But he figured the commander called all ensigns that.

Keethzarn gave him a sympathetic grin. "Don't let it get to you. We've been working on that cesspool for a century, and already the slave quarter has shrunk to half its size. It's only a matter of time before the Pa'a are squeezed out."

"Time?" Reoh asked, feeling the furrows being permanently etched into his forehead. "Meesa doesn't have time. She's stuck in there now. All of them are."

Keethzarn glanced sideways, motioning for someone to wait. "I tell you what, Ensign. You make a report of the situation there on Station 14 and drop it by my office when you get back to Starbase 3." The Commander grinned, looking like a plump-cheeked elf. "Leave the problem to the higher-ups who know how to deal with it, kid. Or you'll wake up one day old before your time."

Reoh returned to the dancing bar that night with a tricorder covertly tucked in his jacket. He was going to submit the most thorough report Commander Keethzarn had ever seen.

He quickly found Meesa again, as if she had been

waiting for him to come. She showed him to an upper ledge where the music didn't penetrate his bones so deeply, where he could talk to her if he wanted.

There wasn't much to find out about Meesa's scant two decades of life. She had been raised in a creche, working her natural trade since she could remember, dancing even as a tiny girl with a host of other Orion animal-girls, trained in the most seductive maneuvers. She had succeeded in a manner of speaking, and was purchased by "master" after "master," and was finally brought to Station 14 to dance.

It almost broke his heart to hear her simple voice. "Maybe," she whispered, rising up to breathe right into his ear. "Maybe you can be my master now."

He swallowed, patting her arm without saying a word.

Reoh performed his other scheduled investigation for a Pa'a transport the next day. He had also left several messages for Captain Jord, but he hadn't heard from her. So he was on his way into the dancing bar again, tricorder cleverly concealed on his person, when a rough voice accosted him from down the corridor, "Ensign Nev!"

A Pa'a woman in her middle years stood there, with hair shorn so short there was only a faint silver fuzz across her skull. "Is that you?"

"Captain Jord?" he asked, stopping uncertainly at the doorway.

"I'm in a hurry," she said, turning on her heel. "Let's get on with the inspection."

Reoh looked longingly back at the dancing bar, wishing he could have at least said hello to Meesa. He kept worrying about her.

Captain Jord led the way through the freight gate to

one of the upper levels. The *Belle Star* was a transport ship, but Jord was obviously one of the midlevel Pa'a, trusted with the delicate cargo and the enticing run to Federation planets. Pa'a had been known to jump their route before, with the captain and two-man crew turning pirate for a chance of freedom.

Reoh accepted the manifest from Captain Jord, who curtly gestured belowdecks saying, "Come to ops when you're done."

"Here's your encryption pass, Captain Jord." Reoh handed over the approved departure notice.

Jord examined it carefully. "I hope you haven't made me late with this shipment, Ensign Nev. Where were you yesterday?"

Reoh shook his head. "I was waiting at the bar."

"Well, you must have been having a good time because I didn't see you."

Wondering if he should be insulted, Reoh straightened his shoulders. "I was waiting for you at the time you requested."

"Sure, I get it." Jord's smile twisted in a knowing grin. "I have a few slaves in that bar myself."

He looked at her with distaste. "Does Meesa belong to you?"

"I don't know their names." Jord shrugged, checking off the approval marks for each storage bin on her tricorder to confirm the manifest was complete. "I only cash out their dance totals."

Reoh felt like he was choking in the foul air as he clutched his spectro-analyzer to his chest. "You're horrible people, you Pa'a! Enslaving those poor Orion women, using them to make money for yourselves."

"Since *when* does the Federation care, as long as they get their dicosilium?" Jord drawled.

"There are more important things than rocks!" Reoh cried out irrationally.

"Calm down, Starfleet." Captain Jord seemed amused. "We're all slaves in one way or another. The Pa'a expect me to work harder than I can, and I expect my girls to work hard. There's no room for deadwood in Beltos."

"That's so . . . so . . ." he said inarticulately.

"So practical?" Jord asked. "Listen, the only people I ever hear talking about freedom are in Starfleet, and you don't look all that free to me, or what are you doing *here?* Everyone I know is trying to get out of here before the whole thing blows up in our faces. Why are you snooping through other people's ships when you could be anywhere in the galaxy?"

"This is my duty—"

"Good, you do your duty." Captain Jord put her print on one of the encryption passes and handed it back to him to file with the border patrol. "My duty is to stomp on anyone who gets in my way. I don't care if they're a slave or a Starfleet ensign."

He backed up, actually frightened by the malevolence in her flat, silver eyes.

"Now get off my ship," she ordered.

Reoh stumbled as he turned and tried not to walk too fast as he left the room. But his spine crawled with the thought of her looking at his defenseless back. He really thought she could do anything, even shoot him, because he had irritated her.

He went straight to the dancing bar and tracked down Meesa. He had to wait while one obsessed supernumerary insisted she dance number after number for him.

Finally Reoh got Meesa to himself, up on their

private ledge out of the main pathways of activity. She was so pleased to see him, like a kitten starving for simple affection.

Reoh stayed for quite a while, and before he left he gave her a tiny spindle communicator. "That's in case you need to get hold of me. I'll be in range whenever I'm in this system."

She looked down at the spindle, then up at him. "You leave here?"

"Tomorrow."

Her lips pursed together. "When will you come back?"

Slowly he shook his head. "I don't know. Sometime next month, I'm sure."

Her indrawn breath revealed her horror. Reoh felt like he was deserting her. He had started out only trying to help her, but now it felt like he had incurred some sort of obligation.

He showed her how to operate the spindle communicator, and repeated that she was to call him if she was ever in danger. If he wasn't in range, a message would be sent, and he promised to locate her though the transponder in the spindle.

She didn't seem reassured. She followed him all the way to the door of the bar, her eyes pleading with him to stay. But he had no choice but to leave.

Nev Reoh wrote a ten-page report to Commander Keethzarn, ending with another four pages pleading to be allowed to bring Meesa with him to Starbase 3. Reoh worked for hours on the communique, and was fairly pleased with his persuasiveness. He was even prepared to delay his departure another day and lose one of his R&R days on Starbase 3, in order to give the commander time to reply to his request.

Getting ready for bed, the communicator beeped at him. He didn't know what it was at first, then it beeped again. He leaped for his jacket and the companion to Meesa's communicator.

Opening the spindle, he said carefully, "Hello?"

In the silence, he wondered if Meesa's "master" had taken the communicator from her, or if she had lost it somehow. Then her tinny voice came through, "Help me."

"Meesa, is that you?" he asked, straining to hear.

"I'm Meesa," she agreed.

"Are you in the bar?" There was such a long silence that Reoh thought she was gone. "Meesa, where are you? Answer me!"

"Master took me from the bar," she said.

"Where are you now?" Reoh asked, frantic.

"Hmm . . . inside a box."

Reoh realized he wasn't going to get anywhere like this. Meesa was probably fairly street-smart on her own turf, but Orion animal-women were taught to communicate in other ways than with words.

"You hang on to that communicator," he told her. "I'll track you down."

Reoh left through the passenger gate and made his way down to the lower levels, following the transponder signal of Meesa's spindle. These levels housed warehouses and holding cells for import/export merchandise for the planet Beltos. He kept his eyes on his tricorder for lifesigns, aware that he could be walking into a trap. But all he found was room after room filled with stacks of every size of storage container imaginable.

He began to methodically shift through the maze and finally tracked the transponder to a large square container almost as tall as he was. Meesa had said she was in a "box." The transponder pointed at the container even when he climbed over some barrels to circle it.

Rapping on the side, he listened for a response. It felt more solid than it looked. The tricorder indicated it was hermetically self-contained, yet distorted Orion humanoid readings leaked through. Something in the sealant was interfering, but he could tell there was at least one Orion inside, maybe even two.

"Meesa," he said into the communicator.

"Yes?"

"What is your master doing with you?"

"We are going away."

Reoh gripped the communicator harder. That's what he had figured. Meesa's master was planning to smuggle her off-world. They must have figured a way to get the container through the cargo gate without tripping the border sensors. Perhaps this was one of the "leaks" Keethzarn had spoken of.

Reoh was tempted to simply walk away and let the container go through as planned. Meanwhile he could get the transponder to Commander Keethzarn so he could track Meesa and destroy the smuggling chain.

Yet he knew he couldn't do that. It would take almost an entire day to get to Starbase 3 and back, and Meesa could have been shipped out and sent into warp for parts unknown long before they returned. He could ask Keethzarn to send border security to the station, but that would take a few hours. The container could be gone by the time he got back, and the thought of Meesa trapped in the hold of a freighter was enough to make him act immediately.

"Hang on," he said through the spindle. "I'm going to take you to my ship."

An antigrav pallet was nearby, and it only took a few minutes to load the container. Even for a station that never sleeps, there was a lull in the activity in the middle of the third shift. Reoh got the container all the way to the cargo gate without attracting too much attention.

When one Pa'a official passed him, eyeing the large container, Reoh lamely offered, "Putting in a new bunk in my shuttle."

"Double-wide," the Pa'a said with a wink, leaving Reoh completely red and embarrassed, knowing there *was* a woman stashed inside the container.

Reoh overrode the gate sensors to get the container through without sounding an alert. Since it was a Starfleet gate, it wouldn't be noticed until the beginning of the next shift, when the border patrols downloaded the logs. Hopefully by then he would be explaining to Commander Keethzarn, and everything would be all right.

He kept thinking to himself—*it's only one small Orion animal-woman. What's the harm?* Even if he did get a reprimand on his record, or demoted, what was that worth compared to saving another sentient being's life?

Sweat was pouring off him when he finally maneuvered the container through the corridors to the air lock bay in front of the *Dilithium Node*. Positioning the container so the opening faced the air lock, he took some time examining the locking system. No use in getting this far, only to alert Meesa's master that his goods were being tampered with. Reoh knew he was leaving a trail a parsec wide, but he wasn't expecting to get away with this.

"I'm hot," Meesa said plaintively through the communicator.

"I'm opening the door now," he replied.

After inserting a stasis bar into the sensor padd, Reoh cycled open the lock and slid back half the side of the container. "Meesa?" he called, peering in.

A face peeked out, but it wasn't Meesa. A naked green woman, and another, shifted and blinked in the sudden light. Reoh squinted, looking deeper inside. "Meesa?"

"I'm here!" her breathy voice responded.

"Wait there," Reoh told the startled, cringing women. He quickly opened his air lock and grabbed a blanket, trying to shield the bay from the corridor. "Hurry, get inside!" he ordered.

They hesitated for a moment, then several at once surged forward. Reoh stared and tried not to stare as one naked Orion animal-woman after another emerged from the container and scurried into his shuttle. Meesa was one of the last ones, and he wrapped the blanket around her, frantically ushering them into his shuttle.

"Meesa, how long were you in that box?"

"Not so long. Master went to get the ship."

Reoh cycled closed the air lock, figuring that eliminated the option of waiting for border security to show up. Meesa's master could be looking for that container right now, and the Pa'a weren't the type to let him get in their way.

He fought his way to the front and the controls, feeling heady already from the scent of so many Orion women in the tight quarters. There were so many green arms and legs crammed inside the *Dilithium Node* that he wondered how they had all fit into the container. This had suddenly turned from a minor infraction into a full-scale smuggling operation in its own right. He just hoped he got to Commander Keethzarn before anyone else did.

Getting away from Station 14 was no problem. Reoh was supposed to leave that day anyway; he simply moved up his departure time and was cleared by the border computer. The Starfleet officers were on drudge duty, too, and they let him through without a hassle. They probably figured he wanted a few more hours R&R on Starbase 3.

Reoh was really sweating the short communications exchange with the border patrol. There was no way he could explain the Orion animal-women without Commander Keethzarn to back him. He made Meesa sit in the auxiliary control seat to keep an eye on the other women crouched down on the floor, out of the line of sight. He couldn't even look back there—Meesa was bad enough, with her bare shoulders exposed by the blanket. The others were completely naked.

By the time they got two sectors away from the Beltos system, he finally began to breathe easier, figuring he was home free. Maybe he wouldn't be in too much trouble—

Then he received a hail. It was the *Belle Star*, Captain Jord's transport ship.

Puzzled, Reoh opened the channel, voice-only, just to be safe. "Captain Jord?"

"Thank you, Ensign Nev," Jord said, sounding very pleased. "If you will please dock at my aft portal, I will take back my cargo. Now that you've gotten it through the border for me."

"Pardon me?" he croaked.

Meesa was cowering down, looking up at the speakers from which Jord's voice echoed down. "Master?" she asked.

Reoh glanced back at the other women. "Is Captain Jord your master?"

"Why not ask me?" Jord said over the speaker. "I arranged this whole transport, packed the girls up for you and everything."

Reoh gave in to the inevitable and activated the viewscreen. Captain Jord was beaming at him, which was somehow worse than her scowl.

"What makes you think I'll hand these women over to you?" he asked.

"Because it's either that, or we disintegrate the shuttle." Jord bared her teeth. "Behave yourself and you'll be picked up in a few days, your shuttle adrift. Meanwhile I'll be far from here, living the high life on the price I can get for my cargo."

"They're not cargo. They're women—" Reoh protested.

"I'm not going to listen to another speech out of you, Starfleet. You have three seconds to drop shields so I can get a tractor-lock on you, or I'm cutting my losses and getting out of here." She glanced at the chrono. "One, two—"

"Okay! Don't shoot," Reoh protested. Slowly he dropped shields. The shuttle lurched as the tractor took hold.

As the maw of the *Belle Star's* portal loomed closer, he turned reproachfully to Meesa. "Did you know about this?"

The confusion, guilt, and utter innocence in her eyes reassured him that she knew something, but not the complexities of her master's game.

"It's all right," he told her, patting her arm through the blanket.

But he knew it was far from all right. He had just smuggled a load of Orion animal women off Beltos Station 14, and delivered them to a Pa'a renegade. This wasn't going to look good on his record. He might even end up in a penal colony—

Suddenly a siren alert rang through the open channel. Reoh thought at first that something had gone wrong with the docking, then he saw the Starfleet starship hanging over the *Belle Star*.

"Drop your shields and stand down your weapons!" boomed through the speakers. Reoh opened visual, and Commander Keethzarn was on screen. "Captain Jord, release the *Dilithium Node* from your tractor beam."

There was a few moments when nothing happened, and Reoh could imagine Captain Jord rapidly debating her chances of winning in a fight. But the starship looked extremely capable, with a brand new phaser array on the lower saucer section.

His shuttle jolted again as the heavy hand on the tractor released them. Before Reoh could take the helm, they were in the grip of another tractor beam from Keethzarn's ship, being pulled toward the starship.

Reoh went through the air lock first, to face Commander Keethzarn, followed by a seemingly endless line of naked, cringing Orion animal-women.

Keethzarn slapped Reoh on the back and gave him an admiring look. "Bajoran, you don't go half-measures, do you? How many of them are there?"

"Thirteen," Reoh admitted with a gulp. "I think. They don't stop moving. . . ."

Keethzarn let out a low whistle as the girls untangled their green limbs and continued to climb out of the shuttle. The other officers were starting to get a glazed look in their eyes from so many animal-women in the closed space.

"You help escort these women to their quarters, Ensign Nev," Keethzarn ordered. "I'll take care of Captain Jord."

Nev Reoh nervously straightened his collar as he waited outside Keethzarn's ready room. Maybe he needed to get a better autotailor. None of his uniforms ever seemed to fit right.

The door slid open, catching him flat-footed, one finger hooked agonizingly in his collar.

"Good work!" Keethzarn sang out, reaching forward to shake Reoh's hand.

"Uh, sir?" Reoh stammered, his entire body shaken by the large man's grip. "What did I do?"

"You gave us the first good crack into the Orion slave trade on Beltos IV, that's all!" Keethzarn was grinning, his slanted brows rising almost to his hairline. "Captain Jord has plea-bargained and agreed to help us catch the Pa'a high command in their next shipment. It was those thirteen counts of slave smuggling that did it. We haven't been able to get any Pa'a to fold under smaller charges."

"You mean I'm not getting a reprimand?" Reoh asked.

"Reprimand! I couldn't have done it without you, kid."

Reoh hesitated, certain that Hammon Titus would advise him to shut up and thank his lucky stars that he wasn't in deep trouble. But Reoh just couldn't rest not knowing. "Commander, I smuggled all those Orion slaves off the station without telling you."

"You sent me a fourteen-page message last night,"

Keethzarn dryly reminded him. "Full of passion and fury over the plight of these women, pleading for the life of one of them. . . ." The commander keyed through his tricorder. "Meesa, yeah, that one. Requesting to transport her out of the Beltos system despite Starfleet regulations and decades-old trade agreements between the Pa'a and the Federation."

Reoh shifted uneasily. "Yes?"

"Then you left without waiting for my answer." Keethzarn clicked off the tricorder. "Either you gave up on the whole thing, which would mean you're a wacko. Or you smuggled the girl out without permission. Either way, I was forced to investigate." Keethzarn smacked Reoh on the back. "I couldn't have dreamed you'd take so many with you. We saw the Pa'a ship long before we intercepted. All I had to do was wait for Jord to spring her trap and *bang*—gotcha!"

"You're welcome," Reoh said automatically. He felt a little dizzy.

"Brilliant plan! Gave Starfleet deniability in case it didn't work, yet it couldn't miss!" Reoh flinched as Keethzarn gave him a final whack on the shoulder. "After my report goes in, Ensign, the *Enterprise* herself will want a fast thinker like you."

Chapter Nine

"AND IT'S ONLY FOR TWO WEEKS," Jayme finished in a rush. "Just think, you get a trip to Rahm-Izad *and* you can help out an old friend."

Bobbie Ray protested, "I'd stick out like a purple tomshee in the middle of San Francisco. Enor would spot us in a millisecond."

"I don't want to *hide* from Moll," Jayme reminded the Rex. "We'll sort of . . . run into her on the trip. Come on, it's my last chance to spend time with her before she graduates."

"Then go with Enor. What do you need me for?"

Jayme picked up the springball, turning it over in her hands. "She wouldn't agree. She would think it's encouraging me."

Thankfully, Bobbie Ray wasn't the type to question other people's motives. That was the main reason her choice of companions was so limited—all of her other friends would try to talk her out of it. But

Bobbie Ray stuck to the point at hand. "I might go to Bracas V for vacation. Why don't you ask Starsa? She likes running around in the heat."

"Starsa would die. Rahm-Izad has two g's heavier gravity, with lighter air pressure."

"How about Titus?" Bobbie Ray suggested.

"Titus?" Jayme threw the springball against the wall and caught it in midbounce. "By the time he stopped laughing, it would be time to come home. Besides, he's too busy getting ready for his field assignment on the *Enterprise* this summer."

"That's right, that lucky dog. He'll be fighting the Maquis, maybe even going into the Gamma Quadrant. That's what I wish *I* was doing this summer."

"The Rahm-Izad trip is only for two weeks," Jayme urged. "Come on, Jefferson, we almost died together—remember? I stuck by you in the caves. Can't you help me out now?"

"Rahm-Izad, huh?" he asked, thoughtfully examining the sheath on one claw. "Isn't that where all those ruins are?"

"Some of the oldest in the galaxy," Jayme quickly agreed.

"I hate ruins." He looked at her consideringly. "But I don't suppose I have anything better to do."

"Thanks! You won't regret it. Once we hook up with Moll Enor, you can do whatever you want. Sleep all day, if you'd like!" Jayme bounced the springball off the ceiling on her way out.

"Hey, that's my ball!" Bobbie Ray called after her.

Jayme tossed it back. "Just be ready to go the week after finals," she ordered. "And don't tell anyone!"

* * *

Moll Enor knew what Jayme was up to the first moment she saw the young woman accompanied by the Rex, filing off the afternoon airbus after the other tourists. Bobbie Ray looked irritated behind his large sunglasses. He carried a portacooler, and perched on top of his head was a wide-brimmed shade hat. Jayme was busy looking around the courtyard and hostel complex, blinded by the brilliant Rahm-Izad sun.

"Welcome to Rahm-Izad!" a tall Rahm greeted the tourists. The Rahm differed from the Izad only in their dominant attitude and slightly broader noses. "This way to a cool drink and a place to lay your heads. On Rahm-Izad, we are here to serve *you.*"

The other tourists straggled after the Rahm, dazed from the sudden heat after their trip down from the orbital station. Jayme lingered, looking around, but Moll Enor stayed in the shadows.

"You didn't say it would take thirty-two hours to get here," Bobbie Ray complained loud enough that the other tourists turned to look at them.

"Be quiet," Jayme sighed. "I'll get you an Arcturian Fizz somewhere, then maybe you'll stop complaining for two minutes."

Moll knew their meeting was inevitable, so she went to the front of the balcony overlooking the courtyard. "Ah, the happy travelers." The way Jayme's eyes lit up made Moll soften her tone. "You're probably the last two people I would have guessed were interested in the Rahm-Izad ruins."

Bobbie Ray flipped his large, furry hand, his sunglasses sliding down his nose. "Call it a whim."

Jayme tried to ignore him. "I've always been interested in the ancient humanoid cultures. Remember after you found that panspermia fossil? I wrote a history paper on the unity of the cultures on Kurl, Indri VII, and Sothis III."

"I remember," Moll said.

Most of the other tourists had drifted from the courtyard, proceeding to the hostel desk to pick up their room assignments. Jayme started walking sideways, so she could grin up at Moll Enor. "I guess I'll see you later."

Moll shook her head after the incongruous couple. What had possessed Jayme to bring Bobbie Ray? The big orange Rex ambled toward the interior, oblivious to the stares of the alien children with their parents. Moll had already noted the way kids—and nubile young women—were drawn to the fuzzy Rex.

Jayme gave a cheery wave as she went under the portico. Moll sighed again, feeling herself pull back when she really didn't want to. Without a doubt, Jayme was the best friend she'd ever had. Moll just wished she had asked to join her on this trip instead of running after her. But to be fair, she had never given Jayme any reason to suspect that she would have agreed to go on a trip together.

Actually, Moll wished she had thought of it herself. It was about time they confronted this issue between them, and a ramble through the ruins would have been perfect.

Yet now, without a choice in the matter, Moll wanted to get out of the hostel before Jayme cornered her in her room. The chase was on, and as always, Moll Enor was running.

The heavy piers rose into the shadows, with the vaults lit by a few strategic spotlights. Moll Enor wandered among the ruins, consulting her travel padd and craning her neck to see the notable elements of the construction.

Jayme yawned as she trailed after her friend, reconsidering whether this had been such a smart idea. With her eidetic memory, Moll Enor soaked up cultures like water, always wanting to know more. Jayme was ready to return to the beach, where they could have a long, relaxing swim. Yet Moll seemed content to endlessly examine the small sculptures—alien heads and exotic animals, leaves and flowers—that were carved into the huge stone blocks.

Moll went through another one of the narrow slits in the wall, while Jayme sat down to wait in a niche, figuring it was close enough to a bench for all intents and purposes. She sat kicking her heels for a long time, but when Moll still didn't reappear, she decided it wouldn't hurt to prod her friend along a little.

But the slit didn't lead to a side chamber like all the others; it was the entrance to yet another underground maze. Jayme checked down a few turns of the maze, then panicked when she took a wrong passageway and got caught in a dead end. The mazes could take hours to traverse, and the tourists had been warned time and again not to go into one without a tricorder. Moll had their padd-guide, and she was long gone.

Slowly, carefully, Jayme retraced her steps and returned to the entrance. When she was no longer afraid of having to spend hours stuck in the maze, waiting for the Izad caretakers to perform the evening sensor sweep, she groaned and leaned her head against the cool stone. She had been so patient! All she wanted was for Moll to see that she had been loyal, that she cared about the things Moll cared about. She would do whatever it took for Moll to give them a chance, just one, to see if they belonged together.

"Arrgh!" Jayme exclaimed, giving the wall a swift kick.

The stone gave under her foot, and there was a soft *"phwatt!"* as a small chunk of the decorated wall landed in the layers of rock dust on the floor.

Jayme instinctively glanced around, hoping no one had seen it. But the room was empty, as were the next ones. She bent down and picked up the round object, turning it over in her hand. It was a beaked face of some sort, broken off behind the ears. On the wall, there was a ragged spot between two other beak-faces where it used to belong.

She tried to put it back in place but it wouldn't stay. Then voices came from the maze behind her and she stuffed the head into her pouch, backing up as a handful of laughing tourists emerged from the narrow slit.

"You know the way back to the hostel?" a Bolian female asked Jayme.

Jayme couldn't begin to explain, but she could backtrack the path she and Moll had taken. She felt like one of the obliging Izad guides, silently leading a group of chattering tourists through assembly halls where political theory had been argued tens of thousands of years ago.

When Jayme emerged from the ruins, Bobbie Ray was seated at a courtyard table, sipping from a tall bulb of something icy-pink. His blue-and-yellow-striped sunshade was tied to the back of his chair at a rakish angle, protecting his bulk from the harsh sun.

When he saw Jayme trailing disconsolately back to the hostel, he called her over. "Look what I found!"

Bobbie Ray held up a small ceramic figure about thirty centimeters high, painted a ruddy orange. "It's a genuine Kurlan Naiskos. And it only cost *two* slips of latinum."

It only took one look for Jayme to dismiss the statue. "The Kurls made Naiskos. That's on Kurl—a different planet in another solar system, in case you hadn't noticed."

"Oh." Bobbie Ray glanced at his Naiskos. "My mother will like it anyway."

"Have you done anything but shop and drink with the other tourists?" Jayme demanded. "Haven't you even set foot in the ruins?"

"Not yet," Bobbie Ray said, quite pleased with himself.

"Excuse me?" a small voice inquired.

Jayme turned to see an Izad standing slightly out of arm's reach, hands folded in supplication, as usual. There were far more Izad than Rahm—they were the cleaners, servants, cooks, attending to the needs of the tourists and caring for the ruins.

"Yes?" Jayme asked, surprised to be addressed by one.

"You have something that doesn't belong to you?"

"Oh!" Jayme scrambled with her waist bag. "I was going to give this to someone."

The Izad silently held out its hand and accepted the beaked head. Its fingers caressed the head like it knew every chiseled crevice.

Bobbie Ray raised one brow at Jayme. "Stealing the artifacts, Cadet Miranda?"

"Stealing? No!" Jayme appealed to the solemn-faced Izad. "I was going to give it back. I hope I didn't ruin it. It was an accident. . . ."

The Izad glanced at the beaked head, then silently turned and walked away.

"I was going to return it," Jayme told Bobbie Ray before he could say another word. "I couldn't just leave it lying on the floor in there. I had to bring it back to give it to someone, didn't I?"

Bobbie Ray made a show of removing his Naiskos from the table and tucking it safely back in his bag. "Sure, Jayme, sure."

The next day, Moll Enor invited Bobbie Ray to come on the tour of the underwater ruins. Jayme almost choked when he blithely agreed.

Wiping her mouth, she said, "It's under water, Bobbie Ray. *Water,* as in, we're underneath it."

He daintily stuck an enormous piece of meat pie into his mouth. With his mouth full, he said, "I don't care, as long as I'm not *in* the water."

Moll could tell that Jayme took perverse joy in the change in Bobbie Ray's self-satisfied expression once the tour-bubble began to sink underwater. The forcefield held back the green sea, but you could poke your finger through and feel how warm it was. Bobbie Ray shuddered as Jayme slowly shoved her entire hand through.

"It'll break if you keep doing that," he nervously chided her.

"Stay on dry land if you don't want to get wet," she retorted.

The two bickered the entire ride to the underwater grottos, while Moll tried to listen to the narration of the geophysical conditions that led to the flooding of a third of the local ruins. Neither of them noticed anything unusual until Moll protested, "Why didn't we go into the amphitheater?"

She craned her head to look back at one of the most spectacular ruins, which their stasis bubble had simply sailed right past. Some of the other tourists were protesting, too, until they had to be shushed in order to hear the Izad at the controls.

"There is a malfunction?" it said timidly.

Cries rose from the passengers. "Something's wrong?" "A malfunction!" Someone let out a small scream of fright.

"Relax," Jayme ordered Bobbie Ray, trying to remove his hands, which had clenched around her arm on hearing the news.

Meanwhile, Moll Enor got up to go to the front. "What's wrong?" she asked the Izad.

"There is a malfunction?" it patiently repeated. Moll had found that the Izad had a common, subtle tick of allowing their voices to go up at the end of a sentence, making everything they said sound like a question. Moll attributed it to their socially subservient position.

"Where are we going?" she asked.

"We will go to nearest port?" the Izad offered.

"Should you surface?" Moll asked, glancing at the green arch of water held back by the stasis bubble.

The Izad merely shook its head, seemingly unworried about a stasis failure.

Moll returned to her seat, telling the others, "There's nothing to worry about. We're being taken to the nearest port."

The tense whispering in the tour-bubble didn't lighten until they surfaced at the port. Moll was pleased to see Jayme patting Bobbie Ray's leg occasionally, acknowledging his fear at being underwater when a "malfunction" was occurring. They wouldn't be able to get him out of the hostel after this.

But Bobbie Ray got safely out of the bubble without wetting a hair, though he seemed subdued by the scare. Their entire group was a little disconsolate as they trailed after the Izad guide. Moll wondered how they were going to get Bobbie Ray back in a bubble to return, when Jayme edged closer and whispered, "We'll have to find some other way to get him back."

Moll was pleased to have her thought voiced. "There're airbuses everywhere. We should be able to arrange something for him."

Moll Enor blamed herself afterwards for being so concerned about Bobbie Ray that her usually superb attention was distracted from what was going on. But the Izad guide was quite natural about standing aside and gesturing for them to enter one of the massive doors of the coliseum ruin.

Inside, their group merged with a larger, milling group of mixed tourists, all confused and babbling questions over one another. "What's going on?" Moll asked, too late to stop them from entering.

Jayme immediately turned and tried to get back out, but the entryway was blocked by a double forcefield. There were two Izad at the other end, patiently funneling more tourists into the cavernous space. The press of people pushed them deeper inside, and they were unable to stop the influx. Arching overhead and cutting the harsh sun was the sustaining blue light of the forcefield, holding the ruin together.

"It's the Izad!" a Rahm cried out, holding its hands up to stop the angry questions. A scattered group of Rahm had gathered in the center of the enormous coliseum. The Rahm were rapidly trying to join forces against the hundreds of tourists who were discovering they were trapped against their will.

"What do they want?" Jayme called out. "Why did they do this to us?"

But she was drowned out by other voices, louder and closer to the Rahm. One was deferred to by the other Rahm; he stepped onto a fallen block of stone, to say, "I am Oxitar, Senior Manager of the Regional Tourism Board."

Cries greeted his announcement: "What's going on?" "When can we go back to the hostel?" "My friend needs water!"

Others shushed the voices, trying to hear Oxitar. "The Izad won't talk to us, but there have been rumors for cycles that they were unhappy with the way our world is run. We all work hard to make Rahm-Izad a pleasant place for people like yourselves to come, and we will continue to do so—"

"This isn't a commercial!" someone yelled.

Oxitar held up his hands. "I'm sure this will be worked out soon, if you could be patient and let us deal with the Izad." He bent and listened briefly to one of the other Rahm. "You can find water in the rear of this building. Please be courteous to those in need. I will speak to the Izad, and will return to tell you as soon as I have information."

Oxitar jumped down from the block, agile like all the Rahm-Izad despite the age lines on his forehead and ultra-thickening of his nose-bridge. He was surrounded by Rahm as the small group moved through the tourists, sullenly parting to let them through.

"Nice vacation," Bobbie Ray told Jayme. "Stuck in the middle of a local revolution."

Moll didn't like how long Jayme was gone. After the Rahm returned to say the Izad wouldn't communicate with them, Jayme had thought for a long time, her brow furrowed. Every time Moll tried to speak to her, she shook her head. Finally, she had said she was going to try to talk to the Izad.

When Moll offered to go with her, she acted like she would have loved to say yes, but she refused. "They may feel less threatened by one person alone."

"Threatened?" Bobbie Ray had slyly asked. He was lying back on a blanket that padded a large section of the original benching in the coliseum. "They're the ones holding *us* hostage."

Moll lost sight of Jayme—which was a difficult thing to do in those red tights with a black-and-white checked ultrashorts set. Jayme wasn't one to dress down when she was off duty, but she was so flamboyantly personable that people usually forgave the assault on their eyes. At least Moll did.

Jayme appeared, then disappeared for long stretches of time as she went down various entryways, trying to talk to the Izad. When she finally returned, she was grinning like she'd just aced a biochemistry test.

"You want to get out of here?" she asked.

"They're letting us go?" Moll replied, startled at her success.

"Only the three of us, if we agree to help them," Jayme clarified.

"Help them?" Bobbie Ray asked.

At the same time, Moll said, "You were able to get them to trust you?"

Jayme shrugged. "Enough anyway. I told them I've had training as a Starfleet negotiator—"

"What?" Bobbie Ray demanded.

"It's sort of true. I've negotiated family fights plenty of times." She smoothed her hair and resettled the clip. "Anyway, the Izad know they'll have to deal with Starfleet sooner or later because of all these Federation citizens they're holding."

"The Federation won't negotiate in a hostage situation," Bobbie Ray protested, squirming into a more comfortable position on the hard bench. Moll figured he was outraged by Jayme's utter audacity. "The Izad are wrong to keep us prisoners here"

"The Izad have never been given a chance," Jayme insisted.

"And they know that releasing Starfleet personnel—us—will show goodwill."

"What do they want?" Moll asked.

"They don't like how the ruins are being treated," Jayme said bluntly. "All the money is going to support the Rahm elite rather than being spent on maintaining the artifacts. The place is crumbling out from under them. At the very least, they need a weather satellite to keep the temperature swings to a minimum."

"This is about a *weather* satellite?" Bobbie Ray blinked a few times. "You mean I'm napping on a stone because they want sunshine all the time?"

"Drop it," Jayme ordered out of the side of her mouth. Appealing to Moll, she added, "These Izad don't have anybody capable of negotiating with the Rahm or the Federation. Apparently their plan has been boiling for *decades,* until the entire Izad populace simply cracked. I'd hate to see them stomped back down when they're finally standing up for their rights. With your help, maybe we can do something."

Moll nodded. "I want to hear more about their grievances, and I'll need my tricorder to tap the Federation database for precedent—"

"Hello? Excuse me," Bobbie Ray interrupted, finally swinging his legs over the edge and sitting up.

"But aren't you forgetting something? What about the Prime Directive? We aren't supposed to interfere in an internal matter."

Jayme met his eyes. "If I was on a mission, I would do whatever my superiors ordered. It wouldn't be my place to do anything else. But we're not on a mission. I'm here as Jayme Miranda, on my own personal time, and I won't sit by and let an injustice be done."

Moll couldn't have been more impressed. "I'll do whatever I can."

They both looked at Bobbie Ray.

"What are you looking at me for?" he asked.

"You want out of here, don't you?" Jayme asked.

Bobbie Ray got up. "Sure. Show me the way."

Jayme put her hand on his shoulder, ushering him toward the entryway where she had appeared. "They've had injuries. Some of the Rahm fought back when the Tourism Board hall was stormed."

"You've had one semester of premed," Bobbie Ray protested. "You think you're going to act like a doctor?"

"No, you are. I'm going to be busy as a negotiator."

Bobbie Ray stopped dead. "You can't be serious."

"They need another pair of hands," Jayme retorted. "I volunteered *you*. It's the least you can do, Jefferson."

He smoothed his whiskers irritably. "Are you sure the Academy won't get upset?"

"Positive," Jayme assured him. "They'll be mad if you *don't* help."

Bobbie Ray grumbled, but he actually had a good time assisting in the hospital. The Izad were so grateful for any crumb they were tossed, since they were accustomed to having to do all the work.

Besides, there was an elaborate gymnasium attached to the hospital for physical therapy—an integral part of the recuperation for agile Rahm-Izad physiology. So Bobbie Ray spent several hours a day in the gym, swinging and clambering among the unusual arrangements of bars and swings. In the early evening he would grab a nap on the roof, waking up feeling refreshed for the spectacular meals that the Izad continued to prepare.

It took a few days before he realized there were three Izad cleaning his room every morning, trapped in the habit of catering to hoards of tourists. For the first time in memory, the Rahm-Izad ruins were closed, but the Izad continued to work as hard as if there were thousands of people to pamper.

The *Enterprise* herself was in orbit, leading the negotiations. Cadet Enor and Cadet Miranda had managed to place themselves in a very enviable position, but Bobbie Ray still shuddered at the risk they were taking. If the Izad got irrational and decided to get rid of a few tourists to prove their point, Jayme and Moll would end up on the losing side. But they had maintained the balance, and were getting full credit for representing the Izad in these negotiations.

He followed their progress on the Federation news service, piped in live to his deluxe suite, appropriated from the now empty quarters around the hospital. The other tourists were still quarantined in huge groups in various key ruins. Even the Rahm wouldn't risk destroying the ruins by turning off the forcefields supporting them. They had never considered the fact that the forcefields could also prevent anyone from transporting out people who were trapped inside.

Bobbie Ray had to admire the Izad's tactical advantage. Who would have thought they were capable of such a neat coup? He chuckled to himself, stretching under the sunset. This was his favorite part of the Rahm-Izad day, sunny but not scorching.

"Better enjoy yourself while you can," Jayme said behind him.

He lazily rolled over to watch Jayme and Enor come up the stairs to the roof, arm in arm. Something had happened in the past week. They seemed to have come to an understanding. Far be it from him to pry, but when two humanoids started spending every second together, their faces so close they were practically rubbing noses, you had to figure things were getting intimate.

"What's the rush?" Bobbie Ray asked. "Are you planning another revolution?"

"No, but this one is over," Jayme told him, relaxed and satisfied as he had rarely seen her. "The Izad are releasing the hostages."

"So it's over?" he asked, feeling oddly let down. He had liked the empty sidewalks and squares, like the ruins should be, as if they were suspended out of time. "I thought revolutions took a long time."

"Not well-organized ones," Moll told him.

"We still have some serious points to negotiate," Jayme admitted. "But the bulk of the work is completed. The Izad will gain their rightful voice in ruling their own world. The ruins were Izad, you know, long before the Rahm came here. But they can live together if they cooperate."

"So it will be a few more days?" Bobbie Ray asked.

"At least," Moll Enor agreed.

"Good." Bobbie Ray settled back, the towel over

his eyes. But he did peek once or twice, watching Moll and Jayme standing by the balustrade, leaning against each other, as the sun went down.

"Congratulations," Moll murmured to Jayme. "It's because of you the Izad had a chance."

"Not true," Jayme denied. "They were ready for this move. We both helped, is all."

Bobbie Ray groaned loud enough for them both to turn with irritated expressions. Then he grinned, wrinkling his nose. "It's about time," he told them enigmatically. Then he rolled over, covering his eyes again.

The next day, Bobbie Ray did go with Jayme to the Capitol building to witness the new combined government take over the reigns of power. Now that the agreements had been made, Jayme and Moll were pulling out of the spotlight. Moll wasn't even going to be present—she had been called up to the *Enterprise* to complete some of the last details. Bobbie Ray could tell Jayme was dying of envy and would have preferred that job to this merely ceremonious one.

"I've never been on the *Enterprise*," Jayme said for what must have been the eighth time. All of their negotiations had taken place in the Capitol building, at the Izad's request.

The inarticulate ceremony droned on below, witnessed by dozens of sulky Rahm surrounded by hundreds of the Izad clerks who did the real work. But Bobbie Ray and Jayme were far enough away from the hurried exchange of keys—to the forcefields or the computer files, Bobbie Ray wasn't exactly sure—that he could ask, "What happened with you two?"

"Oh, so you noticed?" Jayme smiled to herself as she smoothed her bright pink shirt.

"Everyone has noticed," he assured her.

Jayme waved him off, knowing he was exaggerating. Instead, she nudged him to look out the nearest window. They were up high enough to see down into the street where a sudden flow of cranky tourists were running through the streets or hanging on to airbuses, intent on getting their belongings and getting out before the Izad changed their minds.

Bobbie Ray thought their panic was comical, but then he had been dealing with the mild-mannered Izad for over a week. "Have I told you how much I enjoyed vacationing in a revolution?"

Jayme snorted, trying not to laugh at a stout colonist from the terraformed planet of Browder IV. He was running after an airbus, trying to get a foothold on the running board. "At least he can't complain that the Izad haven't fed us well," she whispered. "Did you hear about the buffet they set up in the coliseum last night?"

Bobbie Ray was too curious to let the matter of Moll Enor slide. He had been there when Jayme began to get misty-eyed every time Enor spoke, and he had seen Jayme unfailingly nurture their relationship no matter how many obstacles Enor put in their path.

"So, what *did* happen with you two? Don't tell me it's just a wartime romance . . . the spur of danger, and all that?"

He watched her carefully, but her expression remained serene, smiling down at the chaos in the streets. "No, I think what happened is she finally had a chance to see me for who I really am, a chance to see that she could rely on me. I think we both realized we're a good team."

"So it's serious between you two?"

"Serious as they come," Jayme agreed.

"Titus will *die* when he hears about this," Bobbie

Ray laughed. Now he couldn't wait to get back to the Academy to spread the word that Jayme—the woman who never took no for an answer—had finally bagged her quarry.

Jayme didn't see Moll at all the final day of the Izad Revolution, as it was being called. Moll called late, from on board the ship, and told Jayme that she was calling from guest quarters, where she was planning to stay overnight. Jayme wished it would be reasonable to ask to beam up, too, but she was in her nightie and practically in bed already.

"I met an old friend of yours," Moll added.

Jayme was feeling slightly left out of all this talk of what Commander Data had said or how Captain Picard had talked to Moll over lunch for almost half an hour about the Rahm-Izad ruins. Jayme would give her right arm to meet these quasi-mythical people she'd heard about for years. But they had agreed that "Ensign Enor" was the better choice to interface with Starfleet, while the more personable Jayme dealt with the Izad.

"You mean Nev Reoh?" Jayme asked, remembering their old quadmate had gotten duty last winter on the *Enterprise.*

"No, I did see him, but I meant someone else."

Jayme thought for a moment. "Who else do I know on the *Enterprise?*"

"Guinan, the bartender."

Jayme had to laugh. "That's right! The night I was tracking Elma. I bet I didn't make much of an impression on her."

"Actually, I think she figured you out immediately." Moll Enor ducked her head to smile, shy as always. "She congratulated me on knowing a good thing when I ran into it."

"Thanks," Jayme said, feeling mollified and more than a little flattered. Moll Enor was talking about *her* in Ten-Forward.

"Do you want to come up to the ship tomorrow morning?" Moll asked casually.

"Do I!" Jayme gave her a look. "You *know* I do."

"Tomorrow then, 0800, be at the beam-down point." Moll Enor hesitated, looking closely at Jayme's face. "I have a surprise for you."

Moll could tell Jayme was bursting with joy to finally be on the *Enterprise.* One of her great-great aunts had served on the *Enterprise*-B, the *Excelsior*-class starship, and a third cousin had served on the *Enterprise*-C briefly, just before the ship disappeared under the command of Captain Rachel Garrett. But Jayme had told her that no Miranda had had a permanent post on board the Starfleet flagship since then. Moll had felt guilty being on the *Enterprise,* knowing how much it would mean to Jayme—who really deserved all of the credit for the negotiations.

"Titus is so lucky, getting a field assignment on the *Enterprise,*" Jayme said soon after she beamed up. "Too bad he isn't here yet. And we have to stop by and say hi to Nev Reoh."

"He's down in the geophysics lab," Moll agreed. She gestured toward Jayme's bodysuit—an acid-green swirled through with white streaks. When she moved, it made Moll's eyes cross. "Nice outfit."

Jayme shrugged, glancing at Moll's plain black coverall. "You know me—I don't want anyone to forget me."

"Don't worry. I'll introduce you to everyone."

Moll Enor gave Jayme the grand tour, introducing her to the officers they encountered along the way, and making a special trip to sick bay to let the premed student meet Dr. Beverly Crusher.

Jayme shook the doctor's hand so hard that Crusher winced as she pulled it away. But she smiled, and said, "Don't worry about starting late, Jayme. Tyler Brannigan was number one in my graduating class from Starfleet Medical, and he decided he wanted to go into medicine in his *last* year at the Academy. He said he had to cram three years of premed into a solid year and a half of study."

"That's what I'm doing now," Jayme admitted.

"Welcome to the world of medicine," Crusher told her. "You'll never get another good night's sleep."

Jayme was radiant by the time Moll took her to deck sixteen, through a door into one of the spacious crew quarters. Since they were on the bottom of the saucer section, the long wall slanted inward, providing a startling view of the brown and red planet of Rahm-Izad.

"Ohh . . ." Jayme breathed in admiration. "Is this where you stayed last night?" Without waiting for an answer, she wandered into the adjoining room and bounced down on the bed. "Does everyone get such a big place to live, or is this just the guest suite?"

"These are my quarters," Moll Enor told her.

It took a moment for her meaning to sink in. "You were offered a post on the *Enterprise?*"

"Yes, Captain Picard told me last night."

Jayme made an inarticulate sound, rushing over to hug her. But her voice broke as she said, "Nobody deserves it more than you."

Moll kissed her and hugged her back. They were

both thinking of having to part, but leave it to Jayme to put that aside, knowing how important this was to her.

"When do you go?" Jayme asked.

"We leave tonight." At Jayme's silence, she hurried on, a catch in her own voice, "There's no need for me to go back to the Academy. I can have my things sent on." When Jayme was still silent, she added, "We both knew I would be leaving on assignment once I graduated."

"Yes, but, the *Enterprise* . . ." Jayme said. "You'll be at all ends of the Alpha Quadrant."

Moll Enor cleared her throat. "I trust you to track me down no matter where I go."

They both grinned at that, then they hugged each other again. Moll felt so reassured by that simple contact, by knowing how much Jayme truly loved her. She hadn't realized how long she had relied on her best friend to always be there for her. Now they were partners.

"Maybe some day I'll get a post on the *Enterprise,* too," Jayme said valiantly, wiping her eyes. "But I have years of school ahead."

"We both have a lot of hard work to do." Moll pulled back, giving Jayme a shake. "But this isn't the end for us. We're just beginning. You remember that."

Chapter Ten

Summer, 2371

MOLL ENOR SERVED ONE SHIFT every other day at the third aft station on the bridge, known as mission ops. All the new ensigns who were on the command track served their required years at mission ops or assisting the operations manager.

Ensign Enor slid into the seat, smiling as she relieved Ensign Dontorn, serving his second year on board the *Enterprise*. Mission Ops duty was mostly a matter of watching the computer activity of specific research projects, taking care of unforeseen situations that didn't fall within the parameters of the preprogrammed decision-making software.

Seated at ops was Lieutenant Meg'han instead of Commander Data. Moll never needed to refer primary mission conflicts to ops when Data was on duty. He would see the need before she was capable of registering what was happening, and it was eerie the way the primary routing would change under her fingers, with the lower-priority tasks falling neatly into a line for her to deal with at a more human speed.

The other ensigns often talked about how superfluous they felt under Data's command, knowing that he didn't need their assistance. But Moll privately considered it a comfort to know things were under control no matter what she did. Assisting ops was also somewhat better than her occasional posting at the environmental systems station, which was usually left staffed.

"Sir!" Lieutenant Meg'han announced. "I'm receiving a distress call. It's from the Federation Observatory at the Amargosa solar system."

Lieutenant Commander Kriss ordered, "Red alert! Inform Captain Picard, Lieutenant. Helm, set a course for the Amargosa Observatory, warp five."

Moll Enor hoped it wasn't a false alarm. All of the senior officers were in the holodeck, celebrating Lieutenant Commander Worf's new rank.

But she didn't expect them to return to the bridge wearing intricate costumes of blue, red, and white. Moll didn't realize she was staring at Worf's bellshaped hat until the officer removed it and gave her a reproving shake of his head.

"Just do it!" Captain Picard ordered Commander Riker. Everyone on the bridge instinctively jumped at the unusual sound of Jean Luc Picard losing his temper.

Moll Enor felt as if she had been slapped back to duty, and she instantly looked to see what disaster had occurred during her moment of inattention. But Data took ops, and Lieutenant Meg'han came back to mission ops, bumping Moll to the only panel left on the bridge—environmental systems station. It was either that or leave the bridge, and since they were in emergency-response mode, she took the station and began monitoring life-support activity.

Since environmental systems didn't really need her attention, she listened as data was relayed from the sensors, indicating that the Amargosa solar observatory had been attacked. There was no response from the crew—a compliment of nineteen scientists.

When they reached the observatory and there was still no communication from the scientists, most of the senior staff joined the away team to the station.

Moll Enor moved back over to missions ops, and there she had a bird's-eye view of the action. Mission ops was responsible for monitoring the telemetry and tricorder data from away teams as it was relayed to the proper departments. She watched the inflow of data, wincing at the readings of the dead humanoids who were part of the observatory team. In all, there were twenty dead, and one injured Federation scientist, Dr. Tolian Soran.

She recognized the patterns of two of the medical readings because of a chart she once saw in Jayme's medical tapes. Her remarkable memory was the only reason she knew, moments before the word came in from the away team, that they had found two dead Romulans.

Nev Reoh worked late in the geophysics lab on the unusual readings, helping pinpoint what the Romulans were after. It was trilithium, an archaic substance used as an explosive. Trilithium resin was made by exposing dilithium to matter/antimatter reactions, but it was highly unstable and therefore difficult to identify. But the geophysics lab did identify it, and after Lieutenant B'll ran their analysis up to command, the entire lab decided to go to Ten-Forward to celebrate their intensive, successful effort.

They had just entered the lounge when someone nearby whispered, "There's Captain Picard."

Reoh strained to see the captain among the room full of off-duty personnel. Then he caught sight of the dignified figure in red having an oddly tense exchange with a white-haired man. Someone else identified him as the sole surviving scientist from the observatory. After a few seconds, Captain Picard left as quickly as he had come. Soon after, the scientist left in the other direction.

Nev Reoh rarely entered Ten-Forward. A couple of times he had met Moll Enor here, but the Trill didn't seem comfortable in the crowded, merry atmosphere. Reoh didn't know many other people, so he usually ventured out to the crew lounges near his quarters—to the ones on the interior of the ship.

The main reason he avoided Ten-Forward was the enormous window. It currently offered a panoramic view of the observatory and the Amargosa sun, which was bigger than the size of his hand held out at arm's length. Reoh put his back to the sight and concentrated on enjoying himself with his friends.

Reoh had been on board about six months, but he still felt like it was a mistake, his being here. He wasn't exactly comfortable knowing he was always on a ship, flying through space. It seemed very dangerous to him, and he had finally given in to his feelings and requested interior quarters without windows. It wasn't an uncommon experience, Counselor Troi had assured him, for people to take a while to get their space legs. Reoh hadn't mentioned it to anyone for months, but he still felt very uneasy.

It was all right for the first two rounds, then more people joined them and he had to shift chairs. Suddenly he was facing the window, practically right next to it. He could hardly pay attention to the conversation anymore, keeping a wary eye on *space*.

It didn't really bother him when he was on a journey, getting from one point to another. But why would anyone choose to live on a ship? Even in Starfleet, while most people equated duty with living on board a starship, he had come to associate it with the Academy and starbase duty. Even a space station didn't seem as *risky* to him as space travel.

Nev Reoh had a ringside seat when a spark left the solar observatory and flew directly toward the sun. He rubbed his eyes, thinking he was seeing things. But the sun flared dark orange as a rippling, burning pattern coursed over the surface.

Suddenly a blue white, blinding burst of light emanated from the star. Even as it receded, Reoh saw spots in front of his eyes from the quantum implosion.

Officers immediately began pushing their way out of Ten-Forward as red alert sounded. Nev Reoh couldn't have moved if he'd wanted to. But the duty of a geophysicist during alert situations was to remain in a secured area until notified that he was needed for an emergency team.

"What's happening?" someone nearby asked with a nervous edge to his voice.

"B'll, the senior geophysicist, answered, "It looks like all nuclear fusion is breaking down. The star will collapse within a few minutes."

"Look, a shock wave," someone called, pointing to the elliptical halo of light that was ripping through subspace, creating a visible distortion.

"It's coming right at us," Reoh said, pushing back as far as he could from the window until the table blocked him from going further. It had to be at least a level-ten shock front.

"We've got a few minutes until it reaches us," the senior geophysicist muttered.

"Why isn't the ship moving? It should . . ." Reoh began to gasp.

An inarticulate exclamation from a Gagarin IV scientist cut him off.

"Ah . . . ah . . ." Reoh choked, also pointing back at the window.

A Klingon bird-of-prey fully materialized from its cloak off the port bow of the *Enterprise,* positioned right next to the Amargosa solar observatory. It glimmered a sickening green, like nothing else Reoh had seen on their travels.

Voices rose from those closest to the window, and for a few moments, Reoh felt as if he was trapped in a bad holonovel. Surely this many things couldn't go wrong at once—

He lurched as the warp engines engaged, overriding inertial dampers for a millisecond. Reoh hung on, helplessly watching through the window as the *Enterprise* swung around to run from the shock wave while the Klingon ship took off at a different angle.

As the ship reached warp speed and the stars began to turn into light streaks, the subspace distortion hit the Amargosa solar observatory. The impact blew it apart, sending electric discharge in every direction. Nev Reoh could hardly breathe as the *Enterprise* banked and raced away just on the edge of the shock wave.

Titus's duty roster the next day said the *Enterprise* had re-entered what was left of the Amargosa system, and that he was to continue his normal duties. The official explanation was that Tolian Soran, a Federation scientist, had blown up the Amargosa star.

Titus rummaged around and gathered some ship's gossip: that Soran had been on the El-Aurian ship, the *Lakul,* that had been destroyed by an energy ribbon in 2293. Soran—along with forty-seven other El-Aurians, including Guinan—had been saved by the *Enterprise*-B. That was the mission that had killed James T. Kirk.

Titus would have given a lot to have duty on the bridge, like Moll Enor. Instead, he was crawling through umbilical resupply connect ports, performing a routine check of the joint leakage of the cryogenic oxygen lines in the gaseous atmospheric support systems.

When he had a second, he called Enor from a wall unit. But she was in the guidance and navigation center today, compiling telemetry reports on how the implosion of the Amargosa sun had affected the area.

"Even if I was on the bridge, I wouldn't be able to tell you anything," Enor insisted.

"I want to know why some mad scientist would destroy a star?" Titus insisted. "Why did those Klingons show up and beam him away? What have they got to gain from all this? And why did *Romulans* attack the observation station looking for trilithium? It doesn't make any sense."

"It's not supposed to make sense to us," Enor patiently reminded him. "We're supposed to do our jobs and provide the data for the senior officers to answer those questions."

"But nobody's asking the big questions. They just want to know how much stress was put on this joint or how much leakage is coming from that conduit. It's useless!"

"You leave the big questions to the captain," Enor told him.

Titus grudgingly signed off, still convinced that there were things Enor, a full-blown ensign, could find out that a cadet on field assignment wouldn't be told. But some progress must have been made, because a ship-wide announcement came across the comm that they were departing the disaster area and were en route to the Veridian system.

Titus crawled up another long conduit, figuring that by the end of the day he would be back in the saucer section again, having worked his way up the entire stem of the engineering section. He took another break and accessed routine information on the Veridian system. Veridian IV had a preindustrial humanoid society, population about 230 million. Veridian III was also a class-M planet, but it was uninhabited. Titus couldn't see a thing that would prompt Captain Picard to decide to go there.

He could tell by the heightened activity exactly when they entered the Veridian system. He took another break, and this time he was caught leaning over the wall comm, watching as they went into orbit around Veridian III. Ensign Karol made it clear that

Titus had better finish checking the conduit before the end of his shift or there would be questions asked. Titus had been considering sneaking off to Ten-Forward to watch the action—it was one of his favorite places on the ship. Or to the observation ports, if the lounge was too full.

But Titus was glad he heeded Ensign Karol's advice and finished the conduit. In the docking latch, he could tell from the way the conduits passed through that the huge latch wasn't properly seated. It was known to happen if the grab plates failed to seat within the passive aperture of the saucer section.

He checked and found the latching system had a failure rate of 1.5 latch pairs per ten separations. The other half of the pair was fine, so the situation did not warrant an emergency alert to the bridge. Titus was almost disappointed.

It was the most exciting thing he had done in four weeks. He carefully checked the quick-disconnect umbilicals through the docking latch to make sure there was an unbroken flow of gases, liquids, waveguide energy, and data channels. Everything was well within normal parameters, so he simply logged the aberration and crossed his fingers that he would be allowed to join the crew tomorrow to help reseat the latch.

He was down on his knees, trying to peer under the edge of the trapizoidal latch to see if he could detect a physical problem. But it was nearly eight meters across, and the distortion from the structural integrity field interfered with his view.

The ship jolted to one side, throwing him headfirst into the side of the latch. He was rubbing his scalp and groaning when red alert sounded.

He was already on the ground, so he wasn't badly hurt when the next shock ripped through the ship. It left him crumpled against the wall of the Jeffries tube this time. From the number of rapid concussions that followed, he concluded they were being attacked. Romulans or Klingons, he wasn't sure which. He decided that Captain Picard did know what he was doing if he had managed to track down either one.

A heating conduit ruptured, sending a plume of steam shooting down the center of the Jeffries tube. Titus rode out the battle, hardly able to see his hand in front of his face. He decided it felt much worse than he had been led to believe from simulations. Or maybe the shields had failed, in which case they were in big trouble. From the concussions, it felt like the hull was caving in.

He gritted his teeth against the next impact, counting nine so far, when the tenth never came. When he finally untensed and began to unwrap himself from around the joint of the docking latch, the computer announced, "Warp-core breach in progress. Evacuate the battle section. All personnel proceed to the saucer section."

Ensign Karol came bounding up the Jeffries tube. "Stay here to help everyone through! I'll get to the next access tube. We've got—"

"Warp-core breach in four minutes thirty seconds," the computer interrupted.

Titus helped funnel people through his tube, urging them to crawl as fast as they could past the blinding rupture in the atmospheric conduit. The computer relentlessly counted down every fifteen seconds.

"Warp-core breach in two minutes."

"Enor!" Titus called out as the Trill climbed through the hatch.

"We're clearing the last ones through," she told him.

"Why aren't they using the corridors?" he asked, pulling back to let the other officers go by, protecting their eyes against the steam. "This isn't safe."

"We're leaving the easier routes to the children and civilians—"

The computer interrupted, "Warp-core breach in one minute thirty seconds."

"That's it," said a lieutenant, the last officer to pass through the hatch.

Titus lingered, knowing that the hatch would self-seal when the docking latch retracted. But he couldn't understand why the magnetic interlock hadn't been activated. He wondered if it had been ruptured in the battle, along with the coolant leak. Or it could be pinched open by the jammed latch.

"Why won't the magnetic interlock switch on?" he asked, frantic.

The lieutenant glanced back before disappearing down the Jeffries tube. "There's no systems alert. It will activate."

He was gone before Titus could report that the docking latch wasn't properly seated.

"Usually there's a crew member on the other side to manually assist!" Titus insisted to Enor, the only one left behind with him.

"It'll open," Enor told him, but she was frowning as she looked at the lock.

"No, it's stuck." Titus jumped through the hatch, grabbing up the gravlock unit on his way in.

* * *

Moll Enor tried to stop Titus, but she didn't move fast enough. Who would have thought he would go back?

A blue forcefield burst across the hatch. Moll leaped after Titus, running into the field, smashing her fingers against her body. The enormous latch lifted with a bone-chilling grating. An inch of separation turned into two. Then her eyes met Titus's, on the other side of the forcefield.

She tried to shove her hand through the field, wanting to somehow physically pull Titus through the widening gap between them. He stood up straighter, still holding his hands out to her as the saucer section pulled away.

Moll Enor hung in space, frantically tapping her comm badge and crying, "Go back, go back! He's still on the battle bridge. Go back—"

At first it was only a body length of separation, then a room away, then so far she could no longer see him.

The saucer section was still comparatively close when the Battle bridge exploded in the distinctive pattern of a warp-core breach. The saucer seemed to move too slowly, turning slightly, when the burst of sparks and the blue white shock wave hit them. Moll was flung against the ceiling of the Jeffries tube. She couldn't see for her tears, dazed by the impact and the last sight of Titus, with the knowledge in his eyes that he was dead.

Moll Enor couldn't remember how she got back to her quarters, past the crewmembers braced in the corridors. Her door was only around the corner, but an eternity away. The ship was shaking strangely, a deep rumbling through the hull, like it was running over rocks.

She just couldn't believe that Titus had died in the explosion. There was a lifepod near the Jeffries tube—if he had gotten to it somehow . . . She did remember seeing a white spark of light leaping from the side of the battle section, or had that been the first indication of the warp-core breach?

She crouched next to the door, watching as Veridian III loomed through her inward-slanting windows. Fire seared off the leading edge of the saucer section, turning the room lurid with its light.

The saucer module wobbled side to side as it banked, entering the midcourse correction of phase one of the theoretical best-case atmospheric entry. Her shocked brain was busy trying to convince herself that Titus couldn't be dead—he must have made it to a lifepod somehow—while her impeccable memory followed the textbook landing procedure. It had only been performed in computer models because Starfleet had deemed it too costly to subject a *Galaxy*-class spaceframe to a full-up atmosphere entry test.

But now the *Enterprise* was going down, testing theory in action. Moll ran over the preferred landing fields: beach sand, deep water, smooth ice or grassy plains on class-M bodies—

As the saucer section banked the other direction, Moll stared out at a jagged green mountain with ice on top. They skimmed just over the top. She could see the ice sheets, and exactly where the tree line started.

The helm was trying to level the descent, then *wham!* One side of the saucer section hit the ridge, then the other side hit. Right in front of Moll's horrified eyes, her windows slammed into the ground.

The rumbling and smashing went on forever as a spray of rocks and dirt and green matter blanketed the structural integrity field. With a final slam, Moll was thrown forward, striking her head against the bulkhead. Even as they slowed to a halt, everything went black.

Chapter Eleven

JAYME WAS LATE for her humanoid anatomy class because she'd been up all night, unsuccessfully trying to track down Moll. She hurried through the commons, even though she knew she wouldn't hear a word of the lecture. But she was fairly sure Moll was all right. She had finally gotten hold of the Trill Symbiosis Commission and found out they hadn't been notified about Moll Enor—and they were the ones who would hear first if a symbiont was killed.

There was still that nagging doubt in the back of her mind because she hadn't gotten a message yet from Moll, but she could almost hear her disapproval that Jayme had missed a class on account of that. After two years of solid *B*'s in engineering and her struggles to get B+ or higher in the premed courses, she would still be lucky to make it into medical school. And the commendation she received after the Izad Revolution was her only ace in the hole to counter the rather unimpressive stack of reprimands she had received.

Jayme was reassuring herself about Moll when the image of Admiral Brand appeared on the public screens, halting her in midstride. She joined the swarm of cadets who crowded in close as Brand glanced down for a moment before making her announcement.

"As all of you know, during the battle and emergency saucer separation of the *Enterprise,* one of the crewmembers was killed." Jayme drew her breath, seeing her own fear reflected in the anxious faces of her fellow cadets.

Admiral Brand's expression was often considered to be severe, with her white, upswept hair and striking dark brows, but today she looked older than Jayme had ever remembered. "I'm sorry to inform you that it was one of our own cadets, Hammon Titus, who perished while performing his duty on board the *Enterprise."*

A young woman nearby gasped out loud, clutching her hands to her mouth and staring at the screen. A friend took her arm, offering support, as Brand continued.

"Hammon Titus will receive posthumous field promotion to ensign, and his life and accomplishments will be celebrated in a memorial service soon after the *Enterprise* crewmembers have returned to Starfleet Headquarters." Her lips tightened. "We never like to hear when a fellow officer has been forced to give their life in the line of duty, especially an officer as young and talented as Ensign Titus." Brand had to pause for a moment. "We all would have liked to see the career Hammon Titus was destined to make for himself, but we shall have to be content with the time he spent as part of our family in Starfleet."

Jayme was so stunned she couldn't move. She had never considered that it could be Hammon Titus! All she had worried about was Moll, figuring Nev Reoh would never get near trouble and Titus could always get out of it. Titus dead . . . she couldn't believe it!

Bobbie Ray went with Jayme to the beam-down point at Starfleet Headquarters to wait for Moll Enor and Nev Reoh to return to Earth. Bobbie Ray had returned to the Academy early when he found out that it was Titus who had been killed. He didn't really think about it, actually. He beamed over to the Academy before he realized he hadn't said good-bye to his mother. She wasn't exactly pleased that he wouldn't be coming back for a few days, and he got the idea she wanted to "mother" him, which would have made him hang by his claws from the ceiling in less than an hour.

Jayme wouldn't wait for Enor to come to the Academy; she insisted on going to Starfleet at the ungodly hour Enor was scheduled to return, having already been debriefed en route.

Bobbie Ray pretended to grumble about being routed out of bed, but it really didn't take much to get him to the beam-down point exactly on time. And as they waited for the transporter to materialize, he was hit with a pang of remorse when only Moll Enor and Nev Reoh appeared. He was glad to see them, but it was suddenly very real, when Titus didn't appear with the others, that he would never see Titus again.

Moll Enor saw it in his eyes, and she patted his arm with a furrowed brow. With only one glance, he could tell she was taking it very hard. Jayme was hugging

Enor like she never wanted to let go, laughing and crying at the same time.

"You were with him, weren't you?" Bobbie Ray asked her, even as Jayme was trying to tell Moll Enor how happy she was to have her back.

Enor looked at Bobbie Ray. "We were at the hatch and he thought the docking latch was jammed. He just leaped through and the forcefield snapped on before I could follow. And then . . ."

Jayme was wiping her eyes, her face crumpled as she thought about Titus, but she comforted Enor. Bobbie Ray turned away, telling the transporter operator, "I want to go back to the Academy."

"C-can I come with you?" Nev Reoh asked.

Bobbie Ray put one arm around the Bajoran's shoulders, giving the smaller man a solid shake. "You know I wouldn't leave without you."

They left Jayme and Enor at Starfleet Headquarters so Enor could get her orders. As they materialized back at the Academy, Reoh said, "I've transferred back to the Academy. I'll teach in the geophysics department. I've had enough of starships for a while—"

"*Aaahhh!*" Starsa screamed she ran into the room and saw the two of them together. She didn't stop until she ran straight into Nev Reoh, throwing her arms around him and kissing first one cheek, then the other, over and over again. "I'm so glad you're alive!"

Everyone in the transporter room began to chuckle, then laugh at the awkward expression on the former Vedek's face. Even Bobbie Ray began to smile, thinking Nev Reoh deserved to have such an exuberant welcome. He should have done it himself, but he couldn't stop thinking about Titus.

* * *

Moll liked the way Jayme kept holding her hand or stroking her arm, as if she had to reassure herself that she was really there. Moll felt bad about how long it had taken for her to get a message through to Jayme, but she had been unconscious for nearly twenty-four hours after the crash.

Now, as she hurried to get her orders—sick leave until she was recovered from her concussion, then two weeks R&R before she had to report to Starbase 153 to join an astrophysics team on Dytallix B.

"That's not far," Jayme said when she saw the orders. "Only a few hours away. How long will you be there?"

"Months," Moll Enor assured her. "Maybe a year! There's a neutrino migration taking place in the outer hydrogen-reaction zone to the inner helium core of the star. It's instantaneous as far as galactic events go—and incredibly complex."

"You're going to love that," Jayme said. "And I'll love it that we'll get to see each other all the time. I was afraid I'd lost you when we just found each other."

"You mean, just after I gave in and finally admitted that I loved you," Moll said, only half teasing.

Jayme ducked her head. "I know it wasn't until the Izad Revolution, when you saw that I could accomplish something, that you started to love me."

"That's not true!" Moll stopped her so she could look her right in the eyes. "Engineer, doctor, you know that doesn't matter. I loved you long before the coup."

Jayme furrowed her brow, shaking her head uncertainly. "You never said that before."

"No." She walked over to the railing overlooking

248

Paris, twisting the disc with her orders. "It was Titus who convinced me that I was pushing your love away."

"Titus!" Jayme exclaimed. "He did nothing but torment me. He kept saying I was 'infatuated' or 'in puppy-love.'"

"Well, before my . . . *our* trip to Rahm-Izad, we somehow got to talking." Moll's smile was sad. "He brought *you* up, of course. He said that anyone who continued to love me for almost three years was worth giving a chance."

"He said that?" Jayme's mouth stayed open.

Moll nodded. "Actually, he said you were either completely 'off-your-crock' for being so persistent— or I was encouraging you. He was right. I did love you, I always have, and I've been telling you that in so many ways—except openly. I was unfair to you, but I've hardly known what I think since I got this symbiont."

Jayme was still shaking her head. "You knew you loved me before Rahm-Izad? Then why did you wait until after the coup to tell me?"

Moll Enor pursed her lips, knowing she was the image of her old, standoffish self. "You know why! You were chasing after me so hard that all I could do was run!"

Jayme looked sheepish, but she suddenly started blinking and Moll remembered, too—Titus. Moll felt her throat tighten again, as it always did, as it haunted her—Titus. Her only consolation was that his life wouldn't be forgotten, not for a long, long time.

Jayme put her arms around Moll and leaned her forehead against hers. "I wish I could thank him."

"So do I," Moll agreed with a sigh.

* * *

Captain Picard faced the cadets in the grand assembly hall at the Academy. "We are gathered here together to remember our comrades who have fallen in the line of duty. Ensign Hammon Titus selflessly performed his duty on board the *Enterprise,* and for that he gave his life."

Nev Reoh swallowed, bending his head. He was standing to one side of the stage, summoned there by an aide to Admiral Brand, who asked him if he would mind saying a few words about Titus. Reoh agreed, of course, but he really didn't think much about it. There were dozens who would rise to speak about the spirited cadet who had been so full of life.

Reoh kept forgetting Titus wouldn't stride into the room with a quip and a laughing jibe to send in his direction. Reoh had liked Titus because the cadet worked hard to make sure everyone liked him, especially those he teased the most. Look at Jayme—she was torn apart by his death, yet anyone at the Academy would have said the two squabbled like they couldn't stand each other. Like they were brother and sister . . .

"Ensign Titus is in good company." Picard's measured tones were somehow soothing, a somber yet fitting closure for too short a life. "Captain James T. Kirk also gave his life to save the entire Veridian system, ensuring that 230 million people are alive and well today. They don't know whom to thank for their survival, but we can remember the deeds of Captain Kirk and Ensign Titus, and we can look to their example. As . . . Jim told me, we must never stop trying to make a difference."

On that ringing note, Reoh held his head higher, remembering how Titus wanted nothing more than to be the best Starfleet officer he could be.

"Now," Picard added, "I would like to turn this over to one who is more spiritual than I, one who knew Ensign Titus and was a member of his first quad. He also went through the battle and crash of the *Enterprise.*" Picard somehow picked Reoh out of the crowd. "Ensign Nev Reoh."

Reoh's throat closed shut. More spiritual! He was supposed to speak after Captain Picard! *No!*

But the eyes of the cadets were urging him toward the stage. As he slowly made his way forward, he realized that many of the cadets knew him, more than he would have imagined. And he recognized the two people in the front row from their similarity to Titus, family members who had probably come for the memorial. How could he speak—he couldn't even think!

Somehow he made it to the stage, where Captain Picard shook his hand, resting his other on Reoh's shoulder. Reoh looked into his captain's eyes, remembering in a rush the first day he had met Picard, reporting to duty on the *Enterprise.* It had felt as if, with one keen glance, Picard had taken his measure as a man.

Now he felt reassured by Picard's sympathy, and by his murmured assurance, "Speak your heart."

Reoh returned the pressure of his hand, straightening up. "Serving you was an honor, sir."

Picard smiled, accepting Reoh's acknowledgment.

Then he was facing the grand assembly hall, row after row of silent cadets, jammed in so tight that they were sitting in the aisles and standing along the sides and in the doorways. He knew his image appeared on every screen in the Academy, and everyone was watching because everyone knew Titus.

"We all miss Titus," he said, his voice breaking a

little. "The fact that I am standing up here today is a testament to his ability to draw people to him, to add everyone who came within his reach to his vast network of friends and allies. As far as I could tell, he only had one requirement for friendship. That you always do your best, and try your hardest to overcome your own limitations and those of others."

Nev Reoh ducked his head for a moment, hearing perfect silence. "He once told me that he joined Starfleet because we were given the freedom to work for our rights, and unlike most people he knew, he didn't believe those rights should be given to him or anyone. He was always more than willing to work for what he believed in, and to tell others they should work for what they believed in. Some people were irritated by his bluntness, his honesty—I don't know, I always treasured that about him because I always knew exactly where I stood with him." Reoh realized he was choking up. "We still need Titus, but now we'll have to carry on his work for him, instead of with him."

Chapter Twelve

Final Year, 2371-72

A SHADOW PASSED over the window of Nev Reoh's tiny associate professor's office in the geophysics building. The structure had sloped sides, and the antigrav boarders couldn't seem to resist using the updraft to skim their boards high into the air.

Nev Reoh cringed as yet another one went by. His office was on the fourth floor, higher than most antigrav boards were designed to go. He could hear the whine as the gears tried to resist the updraft. And the laughter of the boarders, floating near the first floor, taunting their friends to more daring heights.

It was the weekend, so most of the professors were gone. Reoh was only working because he didn't have much else to do but grade papers, so he put his heart into it. He was turning away to call security to chase the cadets from the dangerous geophysics building, when his eye caught sight of Starsa's long, burnished-gold hair flying through the air.

Starsa skimmed her antigrav board away, then turned, pausing for a moment, her teeth biting into her lip as she judged the building.

Reoh called out, *"No!"* but she couldn't hear him. She probably couldn't even see him through the tinted glass.

His hands gripped the windowsill as she began her run. Balancing beautifully, her board ran straight toward the windows, turning at the last moment as she swooped up the side of the building. Somewhere near the fifth floor, the gyros cut out, flipping the top edge of the board away from the wall.

Starsa tried to turn it into a loop, but she was so high that it was actually a dive. Her foot slipped out of the notch and the grav board twisted out from under her. She fell past the board, catching it with one hand as the safeties quickly sank them toward the ground.

Starsa let out a yell, trying to grab hold of the board with both hands to let it carry her down. Nev Reoh was pressed against the window, and he could see the white skin of her fingers as they slipped off one by one.

"Aahh!" she screamed as she fell the last two stories.

Reoh would have leaped out the window after her if he could. He pressed up against the plasteel, trying to see if she was dead. But her continued screams echoed against the wall of the geophysics building, assuring him that she was alive.

By the time he got to the ground floor, medics had beamed to the site. Reoh had to shove through a loose group of off-duty cadets to see Starsa. She was white, even her lips, and her eyes were glazed from the contents of the hypospray that had just been administered to her neck. He could understand why. Her bare leg was tattered and twisted in an odd angle in two places.

Starsa didn't like the clear brace the doctors had insisted she wear on her leg for a couple of weeks. They explained that her physiology required extra care to ensure that the bone healed properly. Meanwhile, she couldn't bend her knee, and the thing threw off her balance when she tried to do a loop-the-loop on her antigrav board.

"Starsa!" someone screamed at her, making her lose her balance. "Stop that!"

She hopped off her board, with the brace making her hobble a few feet forward before she came to a complete stop. "What?"

Reoh came running towards her, clutching a bundle of padds in one arm. "What are you doing?" He looked around at the others. "How could you let her ride her board with a cast on?"

The other cadets shrugged and mumbled, fading away in the face of an angry professor. Reoh acted like he had forgotten he was an authority figure now. "You know you aren't supposed to grav board for another ten days. At least not until that leg is healed."

"I'm fine," she told him, not at all impressed with his new rank. "You spoiled the fun."

"What's gotten into you lately, Starsa? You never used to be *this* reckless—"

Starsa flipped her board over and jumped on, banking it in the air. "Everyone should learn to relax a little, Nev. That includes you."

Without a farewell, she swerved and skimmed off,

over the tops of some Triskel bushes imported from Ventax II. She knew Reoh was just concerned about her. He had spent hours accompanying her through the medical regeneration, and she had been grateful for the company.

But to Starsa, it felt like she was back in her first year in the Academy instead of finishing her last. Back then, everyone was acting all repressed and gloomy over the flying accident in the Saturn fields that had killed Joshua Albert. Now, the year she would graduate, aside from the grief over Titus's death and the disappearance of the crew on *Voyager,* there were the growing fears about the rise of the Dominion. It was like a shadow cast over Starfleet itself, making everyone frightened.

Starsa banked and returned to the small square she had just sailed through. The signal for a general announcement was on the air. She jumped off and ran a few steps, next to the cadets gathered in front of the screen. Usually Admiral Brand or one of the Academy officials appeared, but this time Admiral Leyton was in the midst of announcing:

". . . a joint strike force, consisting of the Romulan Tal Shiar and the Cardassian Obsidian Order, was ambushed near the Founders' homeworld in the Omarion Nebula." Leyton took a deep breath, the lines in his forehead deepening. "The Federation did not participate in this secret strike force against the Dominion, and Starfleet sent no ships until the *Defiant* was called to the Gamma Quadrant to rescue the two sole survivors. The destruction of both the Cardassian and Romulan elite forces will surely be a factor in galactic politics in the coming months."

Admiral Leyton's blue eyes stared out of the screen

as if he wanted to say more, but he simply shifted and the screen returned to the blue Starfleet symbol.

"Well, *there* goes all the fun," Starsa blurted out.

"Be quiet, Starsa!" one of the other cadets ordered. "This is serious."

A few of the younger cadets were looking at her, so she shrugged and gave them a wry smile. They didn't smile back, obviously too intimidated by the hushed voices of the other senior cadets.

"Lighten up," Starsa muttered, jumping back on her grav board, feeling unusually irritated with the world.

Jayme returned from a relaxing vacation with Moll during the midwinter break to find several communiques from Nev Reoh, asking her to contact him. She went straight to his office in the geophysics building.

"Hey," she said, first thing, "you should get hold of Enor if you want to send anything back to your family on Bajor. She's going to replace an assistant on the Federation science team at DS9 for a few weeks, monitoring the wormhole."

Reoh shook his head. "I don't have any family on Bajor."

"I didn't know that," Jayme said. "You went back for six months that one time, didn't you?"

"It's required. Part of being Bajoran means you have to see the holy sites." He shrugged. "It also made it real to me, to know for certain that we had gotten our world back."

Jayme remembered how happy he had been last semester when the Bajorans signed a peace treaty with the Cardassians. "Now they've got the Jem 'Hadar breathing down their necks, not to mention all those Klingon birds-of-prey flying through their system. I guess that's what Admiral Leyton meant when he said the failed strike force would change galactic politics."

Nev Reoh nodded, looking down at his hands.

"So what did you want?" Jayme asked.

"Nothing so important," Reoh told her, downplaying everything, as usual.

"I have to study, Reoh. What is it?"

"You know that virus that sometimes switches a paragraph from your old personal logs with someone else's?"

"Yeah, that's happened since my first year, every few months or so. More often lately. Some glitch, they say, in the Academy computer system."

"I think I found out what it really is," he told her.

"Oh? Then maybe you should tell programming—"

"It's Starsa."

Jayme's mouth twisted. "No . . ."

"Yes. I didn't think about it until this odd sentence appeared in one of my old logs. Then I realized that my logs didn't start skipping until my third year. The same year I was in the same quad as Starsa."

"That's not enough reason to blame her! I know she's a lunatic sometimes, but that would take . . ."

"A lot of effort, to have kept it up for almost four years." Reoh called up the skipped paragraph he had found. "Read this."

Jayme bent closer and read:

"I can't believe nobody's figured it out yet. I always have to ask people if their logs have skipped before they start to talk about it."

She straightened up, furrowing her brow. It's true, nobody looked much in their old logs, even the most recent ones. And Jayme always seemed to hear about it from Starsa first.

"She wouldn't dare!" Jayme breathed in disbelief.

"I checked," Reoh agreed, "and of the three-hundred-and-forty-seven cadets who have reported this skip virus, all of them were either in one of Starsa's classes or on a project she worked on."

"She's been gathering people for years!" Jayme exclaimed. "That little slime devil!"

Reoh was shaking his head. "I don't understand why she would expose her own personal logs to the virus."

Jayme was reading the sentence again, laughing at how much it *sounded* like Starsa. "The risk of being caught is part of the fun. Besides, she wants to read someone else's paragraph as much as we all do. Don't you run to your logs to check when you hear it's happened?"

"She has to stop," Reoh said, ignoring the question.

"Fine, you talk to her."

"Starsa doesn't listen to me. She wouldn't even stop when I told her not to ride her grav board with her cast on."

"Everyone tried to tell her that," Jayme reminded him. "She never listens."

"I'll have to inform Admiral Brand," he said slowly. "It wouldn't be good for Starsa to get away with something like this. Do you think she needs counseling?"

"Hey, we *all* need counseling for one thing or another."

"I'm worried about her," he insisted.

Jayme tried not to laugh. "Then talk to her. Do what you have to do. But if it happens again, *I'll* tell everyone it was Starsa who did it."

Reoh walked her to the door. "I'll take care of it."

"Ohh . . . you sounded very professorial there."
Reoh blushed, but it reminded Jayme of something
else. "I almost forgot, have you heard anything about
this Red Squad?"

"I heard when Johnny Madden made the Squad,"
he admitted. "I checked, but it's not an official
Academy designation."

"Maybe not, but they're sent on special trips and
field training as a group. You have to be recommended by a high-ranking officer in Starfleet, so it
might be something new they formed for us cadets."

"Have you been asked?"

"No!" Jayme shrugged, figuring she should ask
some of her relatives. "I think it's elitist."

"I'll see if I can find out more," Nev Reoh promised.

Jayme had to smile. "Thanks. With you on the job,
I feel I have nothing to fear."

Reoh tried to talk to Starsa on the grand square, but
she only wanted to know how he had discovered the
log skips were caused by her. She also wanted to know
what Jayme had said, and she kept laughing.

Reoh became impatient, and finally he snapped at
her, "Do you want to die, like Titus?"

Starsa blinked at him, then her eyes filled with
tears. She sat down on the bench, her head in her
hands.

"I'm sorry, Starsa," Reoh told her helplessly.

"He's dead!" she said, looking up with a tear-
stained face. "It's worse now, you know? At first it
seemed like I'd see him any day. He'd appear behind
me and pull my ponytail or call me a pest. But now I
know he's never coming back."

Reoh sat down next to her. "Is Titus the first person you've ever known who died?"

Starsa nodded, wiping her eyes.

"It's not something you ever get used to," he told her. "That's why I worry about you so much. You do these dangerous things for no reason. It could have been your head you broke instead of your leg when you fell off your grav board. And you could get into real trouble if you keep doing things like sending a virus through the computer system."

Starsa didn't look up, her brow furrowed. "It's just a joke."

"I don't understand you, Starsa. You've never let your pursuit of fun override your good sense. How many times in the past few months have you made the logs skip? Three times? It's like you wanted to get caught."

Starsa stood up with a huge sigh. "If you're just going to counsel me, I might as well go confess to Admiral Brand and get my official counseling over with."

Reoh tried to stop her. "Don't go, Starsa. Talk to me about this—"

"Gotta run." She grinned, that old sly look in her eyes. "You never know what trouble I could find between here and Brand's office."

He couldn't keep her from jumping on her grav board and taking off. She skimmed around two cadets, then did a somersault over the fountain, making his heart leap into his throat. Then, with a wave, she was gone.

He sat back down, his heart pounding. Starsa had never been cruel before. Thoughtless, yes, but no one could ever call her unkind.

"That girl has a problem," someone said from behind the bench.

Reoh turned to see Boothby, the oldest gardener at the Academy. "Hi, Boothby. Haven't seen you lately."

"Been tending a hillside of blueberries behind the recycling center," he said, very satisfied with himself. "I see you're taking up cadet counseling on the side."

Reoh shifted, remembering how he used to come to Boothby when he needed advice. "It's part of my job. Do you want to know something? I've been chosen to be the cadet advisor for an incoming student—a Ferengi. He's the first Ferengi to apply to Starfleet, but he used to live on DS9, so they thought a Bajoran would be a familiar face for him."

"What is this place coming to?" Boothby said in mock-wonder. "But I know nothing will top our first Klingon cadet."

"What about a Borg cadet?" Reoh offered. "Or a shape-shifter?"

"We can only hope it comes to that," Boothby agreed seriously. He cleared his throat. "About that girl; she's in big trouble."

"Oh, Brand will give her a reprimand and some community service. I'm afraid she'll enjoy the attention more than anything."

Boothby shook his head. "No, she's in trouble. She needs help."

"Help? What kind of help?"

"Medical help, if you ask me," Boothby said.

"You think she's sick?" Reoh knew better than to question Boothby. "I thought she'd been acting oddly, but nobody would believe me."

Boothby shouldered his spade. "See what you can do about getting her to a doctor."

"Of course!" He started toward the medical building. "I'll tell them to call her in right now!"

Starsa didn't like doctors. She had never been sick in her life until she left her homeworld and went to the Academy. Then it had taken nine long months for her to acclimate, and she had hardly been able to run up a flight of stairs without killing herself. She hated her medical monitor so much that, when they told her she no longer needed it, instead of turning the device back in she had thrown it off the top of Quad Tower Two.

So, at first, she resisted being called in by the doctors to be prodded and analyzed again. But when they started giving her hormone and biocellular treatments, she began to realize how ill she really was.

"Hi," Reoh said, edging his wrinkled nose past the door. "Can I come in?"

"I was wondering when you'd visit," Starsa told him. "I have to thank you for getting me into medical."

Reoh grinned shyly. She was struck by how it lit up his face. "You were pretty angry at first."

"I didn't realize how bad I was. I was wound so tight I was hardly sleeping. These hormones," she said, shaking her head. "You had to go through this when you were twelve years old? That's so young."

Reoh swallowed as if she had asked an awkward question, but she was used to that. "Bajoran puberty lasts several years and isn't as . . . dramatic as yours."

"I'll be glad to get it over with." She looked down at her chest. "I'm developing, aren't I?"

Reoh turned beet-red. "Uh, I think I've got to go."

Starsa laughed as he ran out of the room, but later she felt awful for making him uncomfortable. She started to cry about it and couldn't stop. Eventually a nurse noticed and gave her another hormone shot. Starsa fell asleep feeling lost and alone.

"Our doctors believe Starsa should be returned to her homeworld for treatment," Admiral Brand explained to Nev Reoh. "Her body is reacting abnormally for her species, and they believe it is due to the environment."

"It will take several weeks for her to get home," Reoh said, already thinking about how to accomplish whatever was necessary as fast as possible. "Will she be all right until then?"

"With treatments and environmental adjustments to her quarters, Starsa should arrive fine. But the doctors say it will be emotionally as well as physically difficult for her. They recommend that someone accompany her." Admiral Brand smiled slightly. "Starsa asked if you could go with her."

"Me?" Reoh asked, feeling very much the odd choice.

"She says you are one of her first friends here on Earth. You are also the one who alerted us to her problem. We could arrange to have your classes taken by the other professors, if you would agree to go." Brand spread her hands on her desk. "It would take you at least six weeks, maybe longer."

Reoh already knew it would take longer, because he would have to stay to make sure Starsa was recovering. "I'll do it. When do we leave?"

* * *

Red alert klaxons sounded for the third time since they had neared Klingon territory and the supply lines passing through numerous inhabited sectors, including Bajor. Clearly, Klingon fingers were stretched toward Cardassia since the recent invasion.

As Reoh ran to Starsa's rooms, he wondered what the alert was about this time. Last time it had been two jumpy Cardassian escort ships and an arms freighter passing through to refortify one of the border planets. The time before that, it had been a pleasure yacht that the Maquis had outfitted with a fairly hefty phaser capacity.

The U.S.S. *Cochrane* was only an *Oberth*-class starship, one of the smallest Starfleet science vessels, but she had ably defended herself and given chase to the yacht. Yet other duties called, and their captain had been forced to transmit the Maquis ship's last coordinates to Starfleet Headquarters.

The *Oberth* had been ordered to transport dignitaries from the far reaches of the Federation back to Earth to discuss the Dominion and the new danger they posed to the Alpha Quadrant. Even before they left the Academy, Reoh had heard that Starfleet Command was concerned that shape-shifters could have infiltrated the Federation High Command.

Then, hardly an hour ago, President Jaresh-Inyo made an announcement about the bomb blast that had disrupted a major conference between the Romulan and Federation governments at Antwerp on Earth. It was the worst crime to occur on Earth in a century—twenty-seven people were killed. President Jaresh-Inyo had declared a planetwide day of mourning, but Reoh could read more than grief in the eyes of the Starfleet admirals, including Admiral Leyton, standing to one side of the president in his office.

Reoh was knocked off his feet as the *Cochrane* was hit by a phaser shock wave. His stomach clenched as body-memories of the battle at Verdian III came back in a vivid rush. He could almost feel the disrupter blasts, over and over again. Then the panic of the saucer separation. And the crash, when he had screamed like he had never done before, certain he was going to die—

"There you are!" Starsa exclaimed, leaning out of her quarters, eyes wide with fright. "What's happening? Who's shooting at us?"

The deck jolted again. "That feels like a phaser hit. The shields are trying to absorb the shock." Reoh pushed Starsa back inside her quarters, heading toward the couch. "Better sit down and hang on."

"Will the shields hold?" she asked. "Who is it?"

Reoh was already activating the screen to see outside the ship. "It's Klingon. No, there's two of them."

Starsa was gasping in shock. Reoh had never seen her so frightened before. She had always been the soul of courage, without a thought of failure or defeat.

The *Cochrane* was hit again, and they were thrown back against the couch as the valiant ship maneuvered.

Starsa clutched his arm. "Are we going to die?" she whispered.

"Eventually," Reoh had to admit. "Maybe not right now."

It might have been callous, but it did make Starsa stop and think instead of sending her into hysterics. Reoh knew part of her problem was the unstable hormone fluctuations, but her emotional reaction was very real.

She hunched down in the couch, wrapping her arms around her legs, her ruddy hair spreading against the back cushion. "I never thought about it before," she admitted, her voice husky, as if everything inside of her was twisted tightly closed. "Everyone is going to die. I'm going to die. You are." She flinched as the shields took another hit. "I haven't seen my family in so long."

Reoh took her hand, realizing how inevitable that fear was. "I lost most of my family early. Maybe that's why I can't ever forget about death. I think it's why I failed as a Vedek. What is faith next to that? Nothing you can say or do can avert it."

"So what do you do?" Starsa asked, hanging onto his hand for dear life.

"I try to do the same thing *you* always did. Just go on. In spite of everything." He squeezed her hand. "Only now, I hope you give us a break and don't tempt fate so much."

She blew out her breath, shaking her head at the very thought of some of the things she had done in the recent months. It was only when she leaned her head against his shoulder that he realized how close they had gotten in the past weeks. He had always had a special, protective feeling for Starsa. Yet how easy it was to reassure her, how naturally he put an arm around her shoulders.

He didn't move until long after the jolting stopped and she fell asleep on his shoulder.

Starsa felt better the moment they beamed down to Hohonoran on Oppalassa. Treatments began at once, and she was required to stay in the medical center while her hormone levels were adjusted and her transition into maturity could proceed at a more steady pace.

After a few days, she hacked into the medical computers and accessed her file. It was remarkably easy after the challenge of Starfleet computers. She read that her doctors were surprised by the onset of her puberty, having believed she would be able to complete the course at the Academy and return to Oppalassa before her transition. Starsa didn't care, even though she was young to mature for her kind. It seemed right to her—she'd been through a lot in the past four years. She should be an adult.

Starsa read everything in her file, then closed it back up like she'd never been there. She wasn't even tempted to mess with the medical computer, but she had to laugh at her log-skipping virus that had lasted for almost four years. Because of her illness, her practical joke hadn't even been discussed at the Academy. She wondered if it would fade into the past or be dealt with when she returned. Perhaps they figured it was bad enough punishment to have to repeat this semester's work during the summer.

She had hardly closed her tricorder when Reoh appeared. He smiled, then stepped over some animal trinkets on the floor. "Oops, almost stepped on your frog."

"Everyone keeps bringing them to me," she explained, gathering up the small animal androids that her people loved to give as gifts. Mostly she was getting Earth animals, and everyone seemed so pleased they could offer her a "remembrance of Starfleet." She didn't have the heart to tell anyone that frogs and mice didn't exactly fill the hallways at the Academy. She held up a giant-sized tick before tossing it to him. "Don't ask what that one is."

Nev Reoh seemed uncomfortable. "The *Cochrane* is returning through this system day after tomorrow. They called to let me know, in case I was ready to return. You're doing fine now, so I thought—"

"You're leaving without me?" she asked, forgetting about the trinkets that were milling around in the basket at the foot of her bed. "You *can't* leave without me!"

"You want me to stay? But you have your family here—"

"It will only take a few more weeks of treatments," she assured him. "Maybe less. Can't we go back together? It's such a long trip. . . ."

Slowly, Reoh said, "I would have to ask Admiral Brand for an extension of my leave."

Starsa put the lid on her trinkets to keep their noise muffled. "It would save Starfleet from having to send two ships for us."

"That's true," Reoh agreed, but he was busy looking at the tick, its legs methodically moving even though it was upside-down.

"And I think I can get you a private room," she told him, watching him closely. "I've felt bad about squeezing you in with everyone."

"I don't mind sharing with your cousins," Reoh denied. "They're very nice boys."

"And it doesn't rain here all the time," she assured him. "It should clear up in a few days. And I'll be able to go home while I finish the therapy. There's lots of things we can do then. Go to the simu-races, and the sky-dive. Or if you're feeling stuck in the city, there's a big parkland between Hohonoran and Swin, only an hour away. You feel like you're in Yosemite in Earth . . . almost."

"It's not that I'm bored," Reoh tried to explain. "But you've got everyone you need here with you—"

As if on cue, Starsa's sister and her spouse appeared in the doorway, calling out greetings. Starsa hugged her sister, but she was trying to see Reoh, who was strategically trying to slip away. "Call the superintendent," she urged him, over her sister's shoulder. "Find out, okay? It would mean a lot to me."

Reoh nodded uncertainly, holding up the tick before placing it on his empty chair. "I'll do it right now."

"Don't rush off," her sister protested. "I've been wanting to meet Starsa's *caraposa*. Sit down and join us."

Starsa felt the heat rush to her face as Reoh stammered and excused himself, saying, "I'm sorry. I have to send an important communiqué."

Starsa mumbled good-bye, but she didn't know where to look. No wonder he wanted to get away! Why hadn't she realized what her family was doing? They had picked up on her feelings for Reoh and assumed that he returned her admiration simply because he was such a truly good and kind man. She was a fool! After so long at the Academy, she hadn't counted on the subliminal sensitivity the Oppalassa had for one another, developed from being forced to live on top of one another for centuries. When she realized she loved Reoh, she took it for granted, so they did, too.

Her sister touched her hand. "What's wrong, Starsa?"

"He might have to leave," she told her, knowing it was useless to lie about her feelings.

"I hope not. You'd miss him terribly."

Starsa nodded, unable to say a word. The question was—would Reoh miss her?

It took a few days, but Reoh finally received a message back from Admiral Brand's assistant, assuring him that he could stay on Oppalassa for an additional few weeks. Reoh got the distinct feeling that his request was the least of their worries.

He was watching Starsa's other sister, Maree, trying to get food into her two boys. They were nearly as big as Reoh, but acted like ten-year-olds, poking at each other instead of eating. Reoh sat in the only other chair in the room, trying to stay out of the way. He preferred this room to the bedroom because it had a window overlooking the living towers of Hohonoran, marching down the steep hillside.

"Hello, everyone!" Starsa sang out, as she came through the door.

"Starsa!" the boys called out, scrambling up to hug her. She laughed and tipped her basket of trinkets over, letting the rodents and bugs crawl on the tiled floor.

"What are you doing home so soon?" her sister asked.

"They kicked me out. Mom stopped by and fetched me." Starsa pointed upward. "She took my stuff up to their rooms. I guess I sleep there, but I thought the boys would like the trinkets."

She left them shouting over the intricate constructs, coming towards Reoh. "Hi."

"I'm glad they released you," he said, not sure what to say. Her body had changed in only a few weeks. It was a subtle difference, but a vital one. She even moved differently, more smoothly, like everything now fit together properly.

"I made them send me home," she told him in a confidential voice. He could smell her skin, she was so close. "I want to have some fun with you."

Reoh swallowed, not sure how he could tell her his doubts. The way her sister smiled over at them made it clear. Starsa's entire family was acting like they were pledged to each other. He wasn't sure how they had formed that mistaken impression, but he could find no polite way to correct them.

"Let's go on the balcony," Starsa suggested over the squeals of her nephews.

Outside they heard the din of the city noises, and the low percussion sound of a pneumatic drill, digging the support posts for yet another tower just uphill. But the balcony offered a liberating view of the city, nearly 180 degrees of shimmering forcefields that encased the towers. Reoh moved carefully, barely able to see the rainbow edge of the forcefield at the edge of their balcony. He couldn't get used to not having a railing.

Starsa went right to the edge, of course. He smiled, glad to see a bit of her fearlessness had returned. He would hate to have her forever bowed down by the loss of her innocence.

She checked to be sure her sister couldn't hear. "I heard about the failure of the power grid on Earth. And the declaration of martial law. They think there's an invasion force coming, don't they?"

"They're preparing for it," he agreed, not expecting this.

Looking over the city, she asked, "Are you leaving on the *Cochrane?*"

Reoh hesitated. "I probably should, Starsa."

"Why?"

He was glad she was still looking away from him.

She was notoriously blunt, but this could stretch even her limits. "Because of what your family thinks. You know, that *caraposa* stuff."

"Oh." She wasn't acting as shocked as he thought she would. "That bothers you?"

"Uh, I thought it would bother *you.*"

She shyly smiled. "I don't mind it. It's just my busybody family."

"Really?" Now he didn't know what to think.

"I know this wasn't your idea, Reoh. It was thrust on you. You only meant to be sweet, bringing me home and taking such good care of me along the way. They don't understand that's just the way it is in Starfleet. We take care of each other."

"Yes, we do." He kept thinking Starsa didn't understand what was happening, which was not an unreasonable assumption when it came to her. Yet she basically said she didn't care if her family called him her "boyfriend."

As if that wasn't enough, Starsa grinned at him. "Don't you want to stay with me?"

Nev Reoh felt the tightness in his stomach ease. He never wanted to leave Starsa behind. He wouldn't be comfortable unless he could personally make sure she got back to the Academy safely. But Starsa was offering him more—or at least it seemed that way. If he stayed, he'd have a few more weeks here and the trip back home to find out how she really felt about him.

"If you're sure," he said, waiting for her nod. "Then I'll stay."

"Good!" She beamed at him, then faced the city again, as if those brief words had settled everything to her satisfaction. "But what if the Dominion invades Earth? What will we do then?"

Reoh turned to face her homeworld. He had a lot to see in the next few weeks. He wanted to find out everything there was to know about Oppalassa.

"Don't worry," he told her. "There's hundreds and hundreds of starbases, and hundreds of starships. Even if the Dominion attacks Earth, we'll always have Starfleet."

Epilogue

"WHERE'S MY TRICORDER?" Starsa called out.

"Check the black bag," Reoh replied from the other room. "I can't figure out this Cardassian replicator . . . and the vent is stuck closed in the bedroom."

"Just be glad we got a posting together," Starsa told him, going in to put her arms around him.

"Not many people want to be on DS9 right now," he reminded her.

They stood arm in arm, looking out the eye-shaped window in their bedroom as the wormhole opened up. They both held their breath until a Starfleet runabout appeared.

"Probably Lieutenant Dax," Reoh said, "with those samples. I should go help her—"

"I'm going to call my family after I check in with O'Brien," Starsa interrupted. "They're less than a week away. Maybe some of them can come visit?"

Susan Wright

Reoh laughed on his way out of their quarters, remembering how he had been thrown headfirst into Starsa's family months ago when they were first getting together. "Sure, why not? Have them all come."

Ensign Jayme Miranda kicked open the door to her room—finally, after four years of quads, it was private! She did a little hop-skip as she entered, tossing the stack of transport containers containing her growing medical disk library on her bed.

She flung open the curtains, and breathed deep of the mild Paris weather of late summer. The comm beeped before she could fall on the bed and relax.

"Hello!" she called out.

"Hi, Jayme," Moll said even before her image had fully appeared. "Welcome to your new place."

"Moll! You look great." Jayme sat up on her knees, pleased that her first call had come from Moll.

"I just got back from dinner. You'll never guess with who."

"Did you already get back to DS9?" Jayme guessed the answer, as Moll knew she would. "How are Reoh and Starsa? What a couple, eh?"

"They're happy. It makes me wish I could see you," she added wistfully.

"Ten weeks," Jayme told her, "Midterm break, unless you get sent back to Earth before then."

"I'll see you soon," Enor agreed. "I can't tell you how proud I am. The first Miranda to ever be accepted to Starfleet Medical."

"Watch out, galaxy!" Jayme agreed. "Here I come."

Bobbie Ray Jefferson walked along the line of young humanoids, sniffing slightly as he eyed each

276

one. "I've never seen such a . . . puny lot of new cadets." He didn't mention the fact that this was the first lineup of cadets he had *ever* seen. It was his first year teaching Self-defense 101. But these cadets *did* look much smaller than those he remembered from his first year, though that had been four years ago.

Bobbie Ray sneered at each one as he swaggered by. "You do what I tell you, and by this time next year, nobody in ten solar systems will be able to touch you. You want that, don't you? *Don't* you?!"

"Yes, sir!" they shouted as one.

Such bright and eager faces, the best and the brightest from all the Federation planets. Bobbie Ray showed his teeth in a grin. This was going to be interesting.

Read on for an excerpt from
Vulcan's Forge. . . .

STAR TREK®
THE NEXT GENERATION™
THE
CONTINUING
MISSION

A TENTH ANNIVERSARY TRIBUTE

♦The definitive commemorative album for
one of Star Trek's most beloved shows.

♦Featuring more than 750 photos
and illustrations.

JUDITH AND GARFIELD REEVES-STEVENS
INTRODUCTION BY RICK BERMAN
AFTERWORD BY ROBERT JUSTMAN

Available in Hardcover
From Pocket Books

POCKET
BOOKS

1413-01

STAR TREK®
VULCAN'S FORGE
by
Josepha Sherman and Susan Shwartz

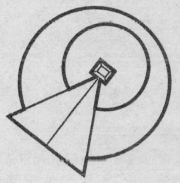

Please turn the page for an excerpt from
Vulcan's Forge . . .

Intrepid II and Obsidian,
Day 4, Fifth Week, Month of the Raging *Durak,*
Year 2296

Lieutenant Duchamps, staring at the sight of Obsidian growing ever larger in the viewscreen, pursed his lips in a silent whistle. "Would you look at that. . . ."

Captain Spock, who had been studying the viewscreen as well, glanced quickly at the helmsman. "Lieutenant?"

Duchamps, predictably, went back into too-formal mode at this sudden attention. "The surface of Obsidian, sir. I was thinking how well-named it is, sir. All those sheets of that black volcanic glass glittering in the sun. Sir."

"That black volcanic glass is, indeed, what constitutes the substance known as obsidian," Spock observed, though only someone extremely familiar with Vulcans—James Kirk, for instance—could have read any dry humor into his matter-of-fact voice. Getting to his feet, Spock added to Uhura, "I am leaving for the transporter room, Commander. You have the conn."

"Yes, sir."

He waited to see her seated in the command chair, knowing how important this new role was to her, then acknowledged Uhura's right to be there with the smallest of nods. She solemnly nodded back, aware that he had just offered her silent congratulations. But Uhura being Uhura, she added in quick mischief, "Now, don't forget to write!"

After so many years among humans, Spock knew perfectly well that this was meant as a good-natured, tongue-in-cheek farewell, but he obligingly retorted, "I see no reason why I should utilize so inappropriate a means of communication," and was secretly gratified to see Uhura's grin.

He was less gratified at the gasps of shock from the rest of the bridge crew. Did they not see the witticism as such? Or were they shocked that Uhura could dare be so familiar? Spock firmly blocked a twinge of very illogical nostalgia; illogical, he told himself, because the past was exactly that.

McCoy was waiting for him, for once silent on the subject of "having my molecules scattered all over Creation." With the doctor were several members of Security and a few specialists, such as the friendly, sensible Lieutenant Clayton, an agronomist, and the efficient young Lieutenant Diver, a geologist so new to Starfleet that her insignia still looked like they'd just come out of the box. Various other engineering and medical personnel would be following later. The heaviest of the doctor's supplies had already been beamed down with other equipment, but he stubbornly clung to the medical satchel—his "little black bag," as McCoy so anachronistically called it—slung over his shoulder.

"I decided to go," he told Spock unnecessarily. "That outrageously high rate of skin cancer and lethal mutations makes it a fascinating place."

That seemingly pure-science air, Spock mused, fooled no one. No doctor worthy of the title could turn away from so many hurting people.

"Besides," McCoy added acerbically, "someone's got to make sure you all wear your sunhats."

"Indeed. Energize," Spock commanded, and . . .

. . . was elsewhere, from the unpleasantly cool, relatively dim ship—cool and dim to Vulcan senses, at any rate—to the dazzlingly bright light and welcoming heat of Obsidian. The veils instantly slid down over Spock's eyes, then up again as his desert-born vision adapted, while the humans hastily adjusted their sun visors. He glanced about at this new world, seeing a flat, gravelly surface, tan-brown-gray stretching to the horizon of jagged, clearly volcanic peaks. A hot wind teased grit and sand into miniature spirals, and the sun glinted off shards of the black volcanic glass that had given this world its Federation name.

"Picturesque," someone commented wryly, but Spock ignored that. Humans, he knew, used sarcasm to cover uneasiness. Or perhaps it was discomfort; perhaps they felt the higher level of ionization in the air as he did, prickling at their skin.

No matter. One accepted what could not be changed. They had, at David Rabin's request, beamed down to these coordinates a distance away from the city: "The locals are uneasy enough as it is without a sudden 'invasion' in their midst."

Logical. And there was the Federation detail he had been told to expect, at its head a sturdy, familiar figure: David Rabin. He stepped forward, clad in a standard Federation hot-weather outfit save for his decidedly non-standard-issue headgear of some loose, flowing material caught by a circle of corded rope. Sensible, Spock thought, to adapt what was clearly an effective local solution to the problem of sun-stroke.

"Rabin of Arabia," McCoy muttered, but Spock let that pass. Captain Rabin, grinning widely, was offering him the split-fingered Vulcan Greeting of the Raised Hand and saying, "Live long and prosper."

There could be no response but one. Spock returned the salutation and replied simply, "Shalom."

This time McCoy had nothing to say.

It was only a short drive to the outpost. "Solar-powered vehicles, of course," Rabin noted. "No shortage of solar power on this world! The locals don't really mind our getting around like this as long as we don't bring any vehicles into Kalara or frighten the *chuchaki*—those camel-oid critters over there."

Spock forbore to criticize the taxonomy.

Kalara, he mused, looked very much the standard desert city to be found on many low-tech, and some high-tech, worlds. Mud brick really was the most practical organic building material, and thick walls and high windows provided quite efficient passive air cooling. Kalara was, of course, an oasis town; he didn't need to see the oasis to extrapolate that conclusion. No desert city came into being without a steady, reliable source of water and, therefore, a steady, reliable source of food. Spock noted the tips of some feathery green branches peeking over the high walls and nodded. Good planning for both economic and safety reasons to have some of that reliable water source be within the walls. Add to that the vast underground network of irrigation canals and wells, and these people were clearly doing a clever job of exploiting their meager resources.

Or would be, were it not for that treacherous sun.

And, judging from what Rabin had already warned, for that all too common problem in times of crisis: fanaticism.

It is illogical, he thought, for any one person or persons to claim to know a One True Path to enlightenment. And I must, he added honestly, include my own distant ancestors in that thought.

And, he reluctantly added, some Vulcans not so far removed in time.

"What's *that?*" McCoy exclaimed suddenly. "Hebrew graffiti?"

"Deuteronomy," Rabin replied succinctly, adding, "We're home, everybody."

They left the vehicles and entered the Federation outpost, and in the process made a jarring jump from timelessness to gleaming modernity. Spock paused only an instant at the shock of what to him was a wall of unwelcome coolness; around him, the humans were all breathing sighs of relief. McCoy put down his shoulder pack with a grunt. "Hot as Vulcan out there."

"Just about," Rabin agreed cheerfully, pulling off his native headgear. "And if you think this is bad, wait till Obsidian's summer. This sun, good old unstable Loki, will kill you quite efficiently.

"Please, everyone, relax for a bit. Drink something even if you don't feel thirsty. It's ridiculously easy to dehydrate here, especially when none of you are desert acclimated. Or rather," he added before Spock could comment, "when even the desert-born among you haven't been *in* any deserts for a while. While you're resting, I'll fill you in on what's been happening here."

Quickly and efficiently, Rabin set out the various problems—the failed hydroponics program, the beetles, the mysterious fires and spoiled supply dumps. When he was finished, Spock noted, "One, two or even three incidents might be considered no more than unpleasant coincidence. But taken as a whole, this series of incidents can logically only add up to deliberate sabotage."

"Which is what I was thinking," Rabin agreed. " 'One's accident, two's coincidence, three's enemy action,' or however the quote goes. The trouble is: Who *is* the enemy? Or rather, which one?"

Spock raised an eyebrow ever so slightly. "These are, if the records are indeed correct, a desert people with a relatively low level of technology."

"They are that. And before you ask, no, there's absolutely no trace of Romulan or any other off-world involvement."

"Then we need ask: Who of this world would have sufficient organization and initiative to work such an elaborate scheme of destruction?"

The human sighed. "Who, indeed? We've got a good many local dissidents; we both know how many nonconformists a desert can breed. But none of the local brand of agitators could ever band together long enough to mount a definite threat. They hate each other as much or maybe even more than they hate us."

"And in the desert?"

"Ah, Spock, old buddy, just how much manpower do you think I have? Much as I'd love to up and search all that vastness—"

"It would mean leaving the outpost unguarded. I understand."

"Besides," Rabin added thoughtfully, "I can't believe that any of the desert people, even the 'wild nomads,' as the folks in Kalara call the deep-desert tribes, would do anything to destroy precious resources, even those from off-world. They might destroy *us,* but not food or water."

"Logic," Spock retorted, "requires that someone is working this harm. Whether you find the subject pleasant or not, *someone* is 'poisoning the wells.'"

"Excuse me, sir," Lieutenant Clayton said, "but wouldn't it be relatively simple for the *Intrepid* to do a scan of the entire planet?"

"It could—"

"But that," Rabin cut in, "wouldn't work. The trouble is those 'wild nomads' are a pain in the . . . well, they're a nuisance to find by scanning because they tend to hide out against solar flares. And where they hide is in hollows shielded by rock that's difficult or downright impossible for scanners to penetrate. We have no idea how many nomads are out there, nor do the city folk. Oh, and if that wasn't enough," he added wryly, "the high level of ionization in the atmosphere, thank you very much Loki, provides a high amount of static to signal."

Spock moved to the banks of equipment set up to measure ionization, quickly scanning the data. "The levels do fluctuate within the percentages of possibility. A successful scan is unlikely but not improbable during the lower ranges of the scale. We will attempt one. I have a science officer who will regard this as a personal challenge." As do I, he added silently. A Vulcan could, after all, assemble the data far more swiftly than a human who— No. McCoy had quite wisely warned him against "micromanaging." He was not what he had been, Spock reminded himself severely. And only an emotional being longed for what had been and was no more.

Look for STAR TREK Fiction from Pocket Books

Star Trek: The Next Generation®

Star Trek: Deep Space Nine®

The Search • Diane Carey
Warped • K. W. Jeter
The Way of the Warrior • Diane Carey
Star Trek: Klingon • Dean W. Smith & Kristine K. Rusch
Trials and Tribble-ations • Diane Carey

Star Trek®: Voyager™

Flashback • Diane Carey
Mosaic • Jeri Taylor

#1 *Caretaker* • L. A. Graf
#2 *The Escape* • Dean W. Smith & Kristine K. Rusch
#3 *Ragnarok* • Nathan Archer
#4 *Violations* • Susan Wright
#5 *Incident at Arbuk* • John Greggory Betancourt
#6 *The Murdered Sun* • Christie Golden
#7 *Ghost of a Chance* • Mark A. Garland & Charles G. McGraw
#8 *Cybersong* • S. N. Lewitt
#9 *Invasion #4: The Final Fury* • Dafydd ab Hugh
#10 *Bless the Beasts* • Karen Haber
#11 *The Garden* • Melissa Scott
#12 *Chrysalis* • David Niall Wilson
#13 *The Black Shore* • Greg Cox
#14 *Marooned* • Christie Golden
#15 *Echoes* • Dean Wesley Smith & Kristin Kathryn Rusch

Star Trek®: New Frontier

#1 *House of Cards* • Peter David
#2 *Into the Void* • Peter David
#3 *The Two-Front War* • Peter David
#4 *End Game* • Peter David

Star Trek®: Day of Honor

Book One: Ancient Blood • Diane Carey
Book Two: Armageddon Sky • L. A. Graf
Book Three: Her Klingon Soul • Michael Jan Friedman
Book Four: Treaty's Law • Dean W. Smith & Kristin K. Rusch